A MAN'S HUNGER, A WOMAN'S NEED, THE DEVIL'S APPETITE

Agatha had heard rumors about the Hell-Fire Clubs that decadent English noblemen had formed to explore the depths of debauchery and lust. Now, as she peered through the windows of an abandoned church, she saw those rumors were true.

Men in dark robes embraced scantily clad women in occult rites while standing before them—wearing a white robe and with one hand caressing a laughing young wanton more than willing to surrender her body—was a man whose handsome features Agatha could not mistake.

It was her husband, Richard—the tender man who had taught her what love was . . . and who now before her eyes seemed to be exploring the darkest of passions. . . .

THE DEVIL'S HEART

KATHLEEN MAXWELL

A SIGNET BOOK
NEW AMERICAN LIBRARY
TIMES MIRROR

NAL BOOKS ARE AVAILABLE AT QUANTITY DISCOUNTS WHEN USED TO PROMOTE PRODUCTS OR SERVICES. FOR INFORMATION PLEASE WRITE TO PREMIUM MARKETING DIVISION, THE NEW AMERICAN LIBRARY, INC., 1633 BROADWAY, NEW YORK, NEW YORK 10019.

SIGNET TRADEMARK REG. U.S. PAT. OFF. AND FOREIGN COUNTRIES
REGISTERED TRADEMARK—MARCA REGISTRADA
HECHO EN CHICAGO, U.S.A.

SIGNET, SIGNET CLASSIC, MENTOR, PLUME, MERIDIAN and NAL BOOKS are published by The New American Library, Inc., 1633 Broadway, New York, New York 10019

First Printing, September, 1983

1 2 3 4 5 6 7 8 9

PRINTED IN THE UNITED STATES OF AMERICA

With love,
for
Lester H. Ptacek,
a father most uncommon

PART I:

THE ENGAGEMENT

ONE

St. Valentine's Feast, 1709

THE SUN WAS AN ORANGE orb glowering in a sullen sky, while on the ground the snow slowly melted with the first true warmth of the season. On the road along which Agatha Grey, only child of Squire Alfred Grey, traveled on foot the snow had seeped into the dirt, creating a mire of mud and half-melted ice. By an earth bank, now free of its winter encumberance, she paused to admire a dab of color set against the still bleak February landscape.

A single crocus had pushed its delicate blue petals up through the heavy mantle of white. She smiled, her spirits lifting instantly. She touched the fragile flower with gloved fingers, considered picking it to take home, but quickly pushed that thought away. Better some other traveler should find this early sign of spring and be as cheered as she had been for a moment.

And, too, her father would not be pleased. He laughed when she cut the roses in the garden to arrange them in china bowls throughout the house. sneering at what he termed her childish ways.

Her father.

Her spirits, buoyed a moment before by the discovery of the flower, now sank leadenly as an image of her parent loomed in her mind.

Anxiously, as if abruptly made aware of the passage of time, she peered upward. The sun was lower on the horizon than she'd thought. Late afternoon, and she had promised she would be back long before it was dark. She would have to hurry to arrive home on time. And she did not think she would make it.

He would be livid. He would be lying in wait for her in his study, and when the front door opened, and Temple, a look of affectionate concern on his face, admitted her and had taken her cloak and hat, she would turn and find him not more than a few steps away from her, his arms crossed, his foot tapping impatiently, and an ugly sneer twisting his lips. He would demand to know where she had been—although she had told him in the morning before she'd left—and even as she drew in a breath to answer him, he would commence shouting, blus tering that she was a most undependable and unworthy chit, that she loved him not at all, that she cared only for his wealth, that she was wild and reckless and spared thoughts only for herself, and that he was surely the most put-upon papa in all of England, that he'd marry her off soon and *that* would teach her, by God!

And she would listen to the strident words she

had heard so many times before. Her eyes downcast, she would wait for him to calm down, because there was nothing else she could do. In the past she had tried tears and defiant words, and none had succeeded. Best to wait out the storm. Finally he would sputter to a stop, glare at her, and in the abrupt silence she would beg to be excused. Gruffly he would grant her request and she would flee to her room to lie on her bed, dry-eyed, for all the tears had been squeezed out when she was a mere child, and she would stare, unseeing, at the ceiling.

Time after time . . . so many occasions . . . she had heard his tirade. It rarely varied; always he was angry, always he had to humiliate her before the servants, and 'twas even better for him if his friends were present.

Sighing deeply and dreading her return, but knowing she had no choice, she pulled her cloak tighter around her as a cold gust of wind swept down the road. Clouds, long and dirty-white, inched across the face of the sun, obscuring the light, and all that had been bright a moment before now dulled.

She could not lay the blame at Vicar Lewis's feet, for she had been the one to overstay her welcome. That morning she'd left Grey's Manor to take baskets of food to the poor in the district, and in early afternoon had at last stopped at the vicarage for a cup of tea with the Reverend Lewis, who had tendered an invitation last Sunday after services. The hours had flown as they discussed the Duke of Marlborough's latest victories on the Continent and how he had just ended the Oudenarde campaign the previous month. Time had slyly slipped by until she had suddenly heard the soft chiming of the German shelf clock and realized, horrified, that she was long overdue at home. Thanking him for his kindness and asking his forgiveness for rudeness in staying so long, she had curtsied, left the small vicarage, and begun her long trek back to Grey's Manor.

And to make matters even worse, she'd taken precious time to stop and admire a silly flower!

She shook her head in exasperation and pushed on through the melting snow and mud. She gripped her basket tighter in her hands as she slipped on a patch of ice, almost falling. She managed to get her balance, and continued. She could not walk quickly through the mire, and with each passing moment more light fled the sky. She glanced around at the countryside. Off to the right she saw a distant cottage, its windows barricaded against the winter's harshness. A white plume of smoke curled lazily out of the chimney, and she envied the cottage's inhabitants their coziness. The surrounding fields lay mantled yet by snow, and she could see no one else moving about. Just a few miles beyond, dense forests edged the coast, and to the south were the fens.

She would be so very late, and her muddy appearance would only serve to heighten her father's anger, of that she could be quite certain.

Still, she had enjoyed her day's absence from the house—and her father. She had had a pleasant time conversing with the vicar, a middle-aged man who found his advanced education going to lack in the village and who had discovered in

Agatha a like mind given to much reading and contemplation.

Contemplation—she would have much time for that now, no doubt. He would probably forbid her to leave the house for weeks.

Ah, well, did not pleasure bring punishment—as he had taught her over the years?

Determined not to let him completely spoil her day, she thought again of the small flower and pressed ahead.

Grey's Manor was a massive two-story Tudor house in the shape of an L. Heavy dark beams contrasted sharply with the whitewashed walls, and the windows, set deeply, were of heavy leaded glass. From the road a wide gravel carriage sweep wound through an expansive park with tall graceful trees, past a pond in which ducks and geese and swans swam freely during the clement months, past massive double front doors, to end at the stable, a long building some distance from the house. Behind the mansion rose a tall stone wall enclosing an extensive garden lovingly planted by Agatha's mother in the first days of her marriage. It had fallen into neglect after her death, but had once more assumed its full glory under the patient and attentive hands of Agatha and Willy, the housekeeper's son. Beyond the house lay deep woods, and past those the carefully tended fields of the squire's tenant farmers.

The manor predated the Tudors, but the Grey family's support of the politically wrong side in Good King Harry's days had produced immediate imprisonment of the Grey ancestor and a night-time torching of the house. Although all the members escaped unharmed, most of their treasures had been destroyed, and a lesson in political expediency learned the hard way. Still when Peter Grey had been released from prison some long months later and had gathered together his scattered family, the King, bluffly forgiving of such a distinguished peerage, had loaned him money to build anew and the family had since proven to be the most loyal of subjects.

By the time she arrived at the immense gates of the mansion, all light had fled the sky. The house loomed black against a charcoal sky, and several windows on the first floor glowed yellow with candlelight. A wind, damp and chilling, had sprung up, setting her teeth to chatter despite the thickness of her mantle, and she hurried along the long walk to the house.

As she reached the steps to the front doors, the doors swung inward to reveal Temple, a look of concern on his face. A tall unbent man, many years past the prime of his life, he was attired somberly in dark unadorned breeches and coat. He wore a powdered wig, quite plain in style.

Their eyes met briefly. He closed the doors, shutting out a cold blast of wind. Mud dripped from her boots onto the tiled floor on the entry hall. Somewhat chagrined, she stared at the mess and meekly handed her cloak and hat to the servant, then braced herself for what was to follow

She turned around.

Her father wasn't there.

Temple's face relaxed. "The squire is otherwise engaged, Miss Agatha."

A heavy weight seemed to lift from her shoulders, and her good humor revived.

"Is he here, Temple?"

"Yes, miss, but a number of gentlemen are closeted with him in his study, and he asked not to be disturbed. Mrs. Howard and I delivered a tray of food to him not above an hour ago, and he has not called upon us again."

"Then he does not yet know I am here."

"He does not."

Relief, then.

"He did leave instructions, though, that upon your arrival you were to go abovestairs at once and change into something fine."

She narrowed her eyes, a tendril of suspicion forming. "Why should he request that, Temple?"

"Perhaps," the tall man offered, "he intends to present you to the company."

"Perhaps," she said slowly. She thanked Temple, left the entry hall, and paused at the foot of the stairs, her hand resting on the bannister. Across the hall the study door was closed. From behind it she heard the deep rumble of male voices. Occasionally someone laughed, and once she heard her father's voice lifted in song.

The only time her parent could be found in a merry mood was when he was in his cups—and it did seem rather early in the day for even the squire to be in an inebriated state. Still . . . this seemed to be developing into a most unusual day. What could she expect of the evening?

As she climbed the stairs and headed down the hallway to her room, she wondered what he was about.

For he surely was up to no good.

He was a creature of habit, and 'twas mightily odd he had invited all these men to visit, and had not been out in the entryway to greet her. She should have been comforted, but strangely she was not.

Frowning, she opened the door to her bedchamber and paused to stare at the warm room. Most of its furnishings and decorations were salvaged possessions of her mother's that the squire had intended to burn when his wife of four years had died in a second childbirth. The child, a son with a mop of dark tousled curls, had died, too, and the squire had retired to his study for a solid sennight. There he had sat, drinking, and cursing the gods for the death of his heir, until finally he had emerged, on the day of the double funeral, red-eyed and slovenly. Temple and Mrs. Howard had managed to shave and dress him so he might attend and be no disgrace to the memory of Lady Grey.

When he had come back, silent, his eyes hardened, he had gone at once to his late wife's rooms and begun tearing down the wall hangings, the paintings, smashing the delicate glass vases, all the while cursing her at the top of his lungs. Temple had persuaded him to leave, had taken him to the study and fetched a bottle of French wine, followed it with Spanish wine, and soon the squire had been stretched out on the floor, snoring loudly. Temple had then gone upstairs to help Mrs. Howard clean their late mistress's chamber. They had hidden her belongings, thinking that the small girlchild in the nursery might some day wish to surround herself with her mother's possessions, and they had been correct. When she reached the age of fourteen, she'd had the story from Temple, and he had led her upstairs to a part of the attic unused since the day they stripped Lady Grey's rooms. She had spent long hours going through everything carefully, studying each item, finally selecting those things she wanted and bringing them to her rooms.

Later, when the squire had seen them, she had thought, looking at his face growing increasingly redder by the moment, that he would be taken by a fit of apoplexy. But somehow he had managed to bring himself under control, and after uttering a profound oath, he'd wheeled from the room and had never once more set foot in his daughter's bedchamber.

That well suited Agatha, for her rooms soon became a haven, a retreat from her parent's anger and ridicule. No matter how angry he was, how violent, he would never again cross the threshold.

Now she stepped into the room. She paused in front of a tall teakwood chest decorated with jade, mother-of-pearl, and lapis lazuli. Gently she rubbed her fingers across the brass fittings. Above it hung a fifteenth-century French tapestry, depicting a hunt through the Bordeaux countryside.

How he could have harmed all this loveliness she did not know. No, she did know. It was because he was a brute. He had tried to destroy all signs of her mother, not out of grief for his wife, but out of grief for his lost son. He had cared not a fig for her mother's death, had mourned only for the lost heir. He was a brute and a boor, and bullied his servants, his daughter, even his acquaintances. His awesome temper was well known and when, a year later, he had sought to marry again, he found to his disgust that no other young woman in the district would have him. Thereafter he could speak no good of womankind, and at its lowest level he placed his late wife.

She shook herself, as if she could shake free of her heavy thoughts, and crossed to the dressing room. Instantly, Nettie, her maid, appeared and curtsied. As she pulled her mistress's soiled half-boots off, Nettie glanced up shyly at her, concern on her freckled face.

" 'E's got somethin' goin' on, fer sure."

"Indeed, Nettie, I gather as much." Her frown deepened into a scowl. "I fear nothing good will come of it."

"Well . . ."

"Now, admit, Nettie, what good would my father be up to?"

Nettie's pinched face turned thoughtful as her mistress stood and shrugged out of her clothing. "Ye be right, miss. It's up to bad he is."

A long sigh escaped her lips. "Oh, I do not know what he can be planning." She sank into the midst of her petticoats, her elbows planted on her knees, chin in hands, and stared morosely at a rip in one of her stockings.

"Come now, miss, ye've got to be hearty. It might not be so bad, eh?" She helped Agatha to her feet.

What Nettie did not say, Agatha thought, was that it might be very much worse than what they anticipated. For some reason, tonight she felt quite fainthearted.

"'Tis another scheme to get me married," she said at last. "It has to be. Why, he hasn't brought home a single suitor in above two months!"

"Aye, that do sound right," Nettie cautiously allowed. She had no love for the squire—her brother having been whipped as a youth by Sir Alfred—but she was wont to say little against him for fear her words would reach his ears and she, too, would feel the sting of the lash.

Agatha stared into the depths of the walnut armoire and selected a mauve bodice and skirt. Both were redolent of the sweet tangy odor of oranges—a result of one of the pomanders of oranges and cloves she made to hang in all the wardrobes. Another habit of hers which he detested, she recalled. There were few, after all, of which he did approve.

She buttoned the bodice, then stepped into the full skirt. She adjusted the cream-colored point de gaze lace edging the elbow-length sleeves while Nettie fastened the hooks on the skirt. From a row of shoes she chose a pair of white silk slippers with gold lace edged with gold gimp down the front and back of the heels. She slipped them on her feet.

"Jewels tonight?"

"Pearls, I think. Something simple."

Her fingers traced the line of simple black embroidery on the skirt as she considered her parent's jovial mood and what it would mean for her.

'Twas a suitor downstairs, she little doubted it now. Her stomach knotted at the thought. She had been lucky in the past to elude the men whom her father had selected for her, but "the odds were agin the filly," as Thomas out in the stable would say.

The odds . . . She did not think she would finish this heat in victory.

This ritual of his presentation of suitors had begun just after her sixteenth birthday, some six years earlier. On that first night her father had appeared at dinner with a young man whom he'd invited to join them. The two men had talked and laughed and consumed more than five chickens, three geese, and two legs of mutton between them. It was only after the dinner plates had been removed that the squire had remembered to draw his daughter into the conversation, though she had been well aware of his gaze resting on her from time to time. After dinner she excused herself and rose to leave so the men might go to the study to smoke and drink, but to her distinct surprise—and complete suspicion—the squire had called her back and asked her join them. The three had retired to his study, and she had had further opportunity to talk with the stranger, one Lord Bratten.

She had not been impressed by him. He was empty-headed, impressed with his handsome profile and well-turned leg, given to admiring himself in a tiny pocket mirror dangling from a chain at his waistcoat, and it was obvious he saw her as a chance to come into a large fortune, his inheritance most likely having been squandered on cards and gambling and loose women—indeed the chief diversions generally occupying much of her father's free time. 'Twas either at one of the card games or the races that the squire had made the acquaintance of this foolish fellow, she assumed. Sometime after midnight Bratten had excused himself and left, and the squire had rounded on her and announced she would be wedding the fellow.

She had stated in a quiet tone that she most certainly would not marry that Jack-o'-dandy, left the room, her back rigid, and thereafter for the next three days had steadfastly refused to budge from her room—not even for meals. Her father had ordered the servants not to deliver trays to her door, but Temple had managed to sneak food to her, and at the end of the three days the squire had relented and said he'd dismiss the fellow. So it had continued each year, sometimes twice and thrice in a twelvemonth, and always she managed to sidestep each of the squire's matrimonial plots.

Yet each time it grew progressively more difficult.

Her good friend Lucy Wilmot had once asked why she did not jump at this chance to be out of her father's tyrannical grasps.

"I wish," she had vowed, "the groom to be of my own choice. I fear the man he selects will simply be a cut of his own cloth."

Lucy, her brown eyes brimming with tears, had declared in a most dramatic tone that Agatha's only other alternative was to run away, and Agatha had laughed at the suggestion. "You goose, where shall I run? And once I have arrived wherever I should be going, what then should I do? I have no money that is not given to me, no relatives to whom I might go, and all my father's neighbors are terrified of him and would not dare to harbor me."

Lucy, realizing the truth of the matter, had burst into tears and had to be comforted by her friend.

The cool touch of the pearls at her throat brought her back to the present, and she stepped to the mirror and studied herself.

Nettie had brushed her mistress's brown curls until their golden highlights gleamed; the maid had also placed two small pearl pins into the dark mass; and the pearl choker set off her long neck to good advantage. She did not think she was unattractive, and in fact, had been called pretty by many of her acquaintances, but she dismissed their praises as prejudiced. Her blue eyes, almost the shade of her mother's lapis lazuli brooch, were set wide in a small triangular face with a pointed chin that gave her a foxlike look at times. Her lashes curled, long and black and luxuriously thick, and were the envy of Lucy. Her nose was straight, and she thought it neither too small nor too large, but just right. Her skin was a creamy shade, again envied by Lucy, who suffered most dreadfully from a dark skin which she thought most unladylike.

Yes, she had to admit she did look rather nice. In a modest way. Nothing outstandingly beautiful, to be sure, but then beauty would be wasted here at Grey's Manor—wasted, and despised.

"You look fit as a ripe plum," Nettie said admiringly, stepping back to survey her handiwork.

"Indeed," Agatha murmured, "I am afraid I look too fine." She sighed. "Still, there is nothing I can do, short of rubbing my cheeks with fireplace soot and blacking an eye."

The girl stared, appalled, at her mistress, and Agatha laughed at her horrified expression.

"Do not worry, Nettie, I plan nothing so extreme."

"I should hope not, miss!"

Agatha dabbed a bit of oil of roses at the base of her throat and on her wrists, and smiled at the servant. The mixture was her own—the roses from the garden below her window.

"Come, Nettie, 'tis time for me to go downstairs."

Nettie nodded and skipped across the room to open the door. Agatha swept out and slowly descended, hoping to put off as long as possible this terrible moment. But at last she stood outside the squire's study door. Nettie peeped at her from between the rowls of the bannister and gave her an encouraging grin. Even from where she stood she could see the fear in the maid's eyes.

The reflected fear settled, cold and hard, in the pit of her stomach. She took a deep breath. She wanted to leave, to not have to go into the study, but she couldn't. She had to do it.

Again she heard the deep laughter, the end of a ribald joke, and a high-pitched male giggle. A chill crept down her spine.

Yet she was no coward. She would go in. She *would* face her father—and whatever it was he'd planned.

She straightened, threw back her shoulders, pushed aside a curl that had fallen over one eye, and knocked. Knocked again when she thought no one had answered, and then after a moment's pause, she opened the door.

TWO

THE AIR WAS THICK WITH swirling layers of blue-grey smoke, and the voices, now that she was in the too-warm room, sounded loud and harsh. Nearby, a man attired in canary yellow and speaking in mincing tones, finished telling a joke that brought a blush to Agatha's cheeks. There was much clanking of drinking glasses, and subsequent belching. She coughed, peered through the haze for her father, and found him near the French windows that opened onto the flagstone terrace. At present the squire was engaged in conversation with a young man who appeared to be about her age.

She glanced about, studying the other men, and counted at least fifteen in the spacious study. A handful were of her father's age, but most appeared to be under the age of thirty, and all were welldressed. Obviously other gentry, though she recognized only a few from the surrounding estates. It would appear that her father had found new companions, and that did little to allay her suspicion. In fact, the observation served only to heighten her sense of dread.

At that moment the squire chose to look in her direction. "Ah, Agatha, my dear!" His voice boomed out above the others, and she could scarcely ignore him. He was beckoning wildly with one large hand for her to come join him.

She picked up her skirts, carefully threading through the crowd, aware of the many men glancing her way. The expressions on their faces pleased her not at all. Determinedly, she kept her head down until she saw a pair of highly polished boots come into her limited range of vision. Quite before she knew what was happening she had bumped into someone and managed to knock his ebony cane from his hand.

"Oof!" he said in a most inelegant fashion.

She stooped to retrieve the cane, decorated with black silk bows, then stricken by her clumsiness, rose and handed it to him.

"I beg your——" Her voice faltered to a stop. An ugly puckered scar cut across his forehead, almost as if a saber had slashed him at some time. The scar's whiteness contrasted starkly against his tanned skin. Otherwise he was a handsome man, possessed of dark brooding eyes, high cheekbones that gave his face the look of a bird of prey, a high-bridged aristocratic nose, the powerful build of a gentleman much given to walking and riding. Clad somberly in breeches and coat of good black cloth and a plainly styled cravat, the man bore no sign of a dandy except the ribbons upon the cane. Quite unlike the other men she'd observed in the room.

Once more the scar on his forehead drew her attention. He was aware of the direction of her gaze and his lips, initially curved in a smile, pressed flatly into a thin bloodless line. He seized the cane, their fingers brushed for an instant, and she jerked her hand away.

"Thank you." His voice was deep, and resonant and totally impersonal.

She realized how rude it was for her to stare at his disfigurement, and dropped her eyes demurely, albeit too late for ladylike politeness. "I beg your pardon, sir. I was not looking where I stepped."

"You should watch at all times, Miss Grey, for you will certainly encounter more serious trouble if you do not."

Puzzled by what he had said, she made her excuses and brushed past him.

"What kept you?" her father demanded as she approached. She started to answer, but he wasn't interested. "Never mind. Don't signify, damme." He turned to his companion, a handsome youth, if somewhat soft-featured, wearing russet velvet breeches, a matching coat and satin waistcoat heavily embroidered with gold lace, and a white lawn cravat tied in the Steinkirk style, one end pulled through a buttonhole. His hair was not his own, she noted, and diamonds glittered on the buckles of his shoes as well as on his hands. At present he was occupied with sliding a tortoiseshell snuffbox into a pocket. "Here's my daughter now, Lord Alford."

"Charmed," the man said, raking his pale blue eyes over her. His voice carried the slightest hint of a lisp, and he sounded as if he spent most of his time being petulant.

"Agatha, this is my good friend Rupert Norton, Lord Alford."

She dropped a curtsy, and held out her hand perfunctorily. Norton clasped it in his moist fingers, and pressed a kiss, much against her wishes, upon it before she quickly freed it.

"Fine filly, ain't she?"

Alford smirked. She did not like the expression.

"I'll allow you two children to get better acquainted," the squire said in a genial voice, and left before Agatha could stop him.

"How are you this evening, my dear?" Lord Alford asked. He leaned closer to her, his breath thick with wine, and she wished she'd selected a different bodice, one not cut so low, one displaying less of the swelling of her breasts.

He licked his lips, belched, and raised a quizzing glass on a gold riband to regard her.

She stepped back a little. "Well, Lord Alford," she asked, feeling uncomfortable under his intense gaze and not knowing what else to say, "are you newly arrived in our district?"

"Yes, m'dear, 'fraid I am. Never been here, 'smatter of fact. Tolerable little place, 'though I prefer the bustle of London, to be sure. Nice to visit the backwater spots every now and then, I'm sure." He winked.

Desperately she cast about for her parent, but could not see him. Oh why had he abandoned her with this insufferable prig? What spiteful scheme did her father now devise?

Several of the men around her boldly stared at her; she looked away from their frank appraisals. A man uttered something under his breath, and his two companions laughed. She could feel her cheeks color.

Alford, no doubt aware she had just been made the butt of some crude jest, seemed unwilling to rescue her. Her hands at her side tightened.

Again she looked around for her father, saw him talking to an older man, then walking toward the far end of the room, which was submerged in shadows.

When she turned back to Alford the tortoise-shell snuffbox had once more appeared in his hand and he flicked open the top with the edge of a fingernail. He offered it to her, and she firmly shook her head. On the inside of the lid she could see a miniature painting—a nude woman, reclining upon a divan being menaced by three roughly dressed men with farm tools in their hands.

She frowned at the obscenity. She well knew from her readings that this was not at all uncommon, but to find it in her house—her father's house, she corrected herself—made her distinctly uncomfortable.

Alford, oblivious to her discomfort, settled a pinch of snuff upon the pale underside of his wrist, inhaled, sneezed, and gently patted his nose with his handkerchief. He blew his nose noisily and then returned both handkerchief and snuffbox to his pocket.

He smiled at her, and she could tell that in his

excessive vanity he thought she had already lost her heart to him. How wrong he was. He reached for her hand and she pulled back.

"Sir, you forget yourself."

"No, I don't."

His smile had become a leer. He advanced toward her. She retreated, stopped as her back bumped into the solid French window. A bulky chest blocked one side, and to the other stood a knot of men, arguing heatedly about horseflesh, and through whom she could scarcely barge in an effort to escape.

She was trapped. She couldn't get away from him. And he knew it. His leer broadened.

Across the room she caught a glimpse of movement, and saw the man with the scar upon his brow heading in their direction.

Just as Alford was reaching out to her, his fingers directed toward the warm depths of her bodice, the man reached them. Alford stepped back, an ugly expression on his face as the man nodded politely to him.

"Miss Grey," the man said, "I do not believe I fully thanked you for retrieving my cane earlier."

"Indeed, sir," she said, turning away from Alford with an inward sigh of relief, "I could hardly do otherwise, after nearly knocking you off your feet."

" 'Twould take far more than one little gel to knock Ol' Scratch down," Alford said in a tight voice. He was obviously not happy that the somberly attired gentleman had joined them.

Agatha watched as the color faded from the man's face at the mention of the nickname.

"Ol' Scratch." Alford laughed, a loud and irritating sound. "Looks like the very Devil, don't you think, m'dear?" He had raised his quizzing glass to stare at her bosom once more, and his lips were wet from the constant passing back and forth of his tongue.

"Indeed, I do not, Lord Alford," she responded at once.

The second man stared in surprise, her answer apparently not what he had expected to hear.

"Ah, but he is, you know," Alford said, "why——"

"Do you know, sir, that I do not have your name," Agatha said, interrupting. She could not bear to hear Alford prattle on.

"Forgive me, Miss Grey, for I do know yours." He bowed over her hand, a courtly gesture from him, she thought. "I am Richard St. Leger, Viscount of Drummond, at your service."

Before she could respond, a familiar voice boomed out at her side, startling her for she had not heard him approach.

"Flirting with all the men, are you, my fine filly?" the squire chuckled. "Those days are soon to be ended."

Alford joined her father in laughing and her sense of foreboding returned. Drummond did not laugh, but only watched her.

"What?" she began.

Squire Grey laughed again, grabbed her by the hand, and dragged the protesting girl to the front of the room to his desk. There he bellowed for the assembly to be quiet. At length the conversation stopped and all eyes were directed at them.

"Now, you may learn why I've called you here this evening." He grinned, the expression making him look most unpleasant. He jerked Agatha closer to his side. "This is my daughter, for those who don't know her face—and a very pretty one it is, if I may say so."

Some of the men responded by chuckling or clapping, and Agatha flushed, mortified by this unseemly attention. Chuckling, he pinched her cheek, and she half turned away, as much as his grip would allow. Although her eyes were lowered in her shame, she could see that Drummond still stood by the doors to the terrace, that he watched them, strangely impassive.

"The reason!" called out one burly young man toward the front.

"Ah, yes, the reason." Squire Grey beamed at her, revealing teeth stained yellow by tobacco. "Tonight I wish to announce the engagement of my daughter, Agatha, to Rupert Norton, Lord Alford!"

There were instant shouts of "Well done!" and the men thronged around the desk to pound her father, and Alford, upon the back.

Agatha only stared in horror at her father. Surely she could not have heard him correctly. Surely he could not have said he was announcing her engagement to this buffoon. One glance at the squire's face dispelled all reason and reinforced her fears. She *had* heard correctly.

"But, Father——"

"Save it, girl."

"Papa," she tried once more.

"A kiss," said Norton, approaching her. "A prenuptial bussing." He slipped an arm around her waist before she could protest, and she could not wiggle away because her father's fingers had tightened on her arm. Then Alford's face was drawing close, his lips pressed greedily against hers, sucking at them, and his tongue, rough and unexpected, darted out and tried to ram its way into her mouth. Horrified, she clamped her teeth down, succeeding in nipping him, then turned away. Waves of nausea washed over her.

Norton only laughed, and dropped his hand from her waist to her buttock where it lingered.

She flinched, and in a moment her agony was over. The men stepped away, and she was left alone behind the desk.

A movement in the shadows caught her eye. Drummond. Across the room, she could see the pity in his eyes, and she looked away, shame flooding over her once more. When she glanced back at the windows, he was gone.

She stared at her father, seated now at the opposite end of the study, surrounded by his sycophants. Trembling, with her hand on the edge of the desk to support herself, she sank into the chair and stared, unseeing, at the neat stack of paper there.

How could he be so cruel? So harsh? So unfeeling? She could not marry Alford! She couldn't wed—couldn't touch—a man whom she despised, a man whose very touch made her skin crawl. No. 'Twas a fantastic mistake, and she would speak to her father, would wheedle him, would cozen him—would *talk him out* of this nonsensical idea.

First she must get herself under control. She breathed deeply and slowly, and slowly the sickness in the pit of her stomach receded, and equally slowly the heat in her cheeks cooled.

When she thought her knees would not buckle, she stood. She knew she must appear the very picture of composure, but if someone were to stare closely they would be able to see the desperation in her lovely eyes.

Steady now, she crossed the room and waited patiently while her father finished a story. The men around him laughed, raised their glasses in a toast, drained them.

She beckoned, and caught his attention.

"What?"

"Father, I must speak with you."

He looked up, scowling. "Very well." He heaved himself to his feet. "Got to go see what ails the chit." He shook his head sagely and winked at his friends. "These delicately nurtured females, y'know."

They laughed, and she moved away, her father following.

"Now, Agatha, this is far enough." The joviality of his voice had faded and been replaced with a brusque tone. "What is this nonsense you must talk about? Is it some silly female notion?"

"No, Father, 'tis not." She stopped, twisted her hands together, gathered her courage, and said, "You must end this farce at once—call off the engagement immediately."

He lifted a heavy white eyebrow. "Do you demand this?"

She hesitated. "Yes, I do."

"Well, missy, *I* demand *this*—that you marry Lord Alford. I've been generous enough in the past when you cozened your way out of one alliance after another. Now, I won't have it any longer. My generosity is finished."

"Generosity!" she exclaimed, truly surprised. "I would hardly describe it as generosity, but rather as sensibility to your daughter's feelings."

He smiled, and she did not like the expression. "Thought you knew by now, Agatha, I don't give a tinker's damn about my daughter's feelings. Thought I'd made that clear over the years."

She could only stare, unable to find words, not able to really understand that all of this, this *nightmare* was truly happening to her.

"You're getting too old by half—going on to be long in the tooth now—and it's time you began bearin' brats. I've got to have an heir for Grey's Manor. I ain't gettin' any younger myself."

"I don't love him!" she protested bluntly.

A glowering expression settled on his face and the squire grabbed her by the shoulders and shook her so roughly she could scarcely stand upright. With difficulty she bit back a whimper.

"I thought," he said, his voice low and menacing, "I'd made myself clear, girl. I do not care for your feelings in this matter. As for love—ha!" He looked as if he were about to spit. "Love, well, that ain't all it's puffed up to be, my girl, and the sooner you learn that lesson the better. And believe me, as a married woman you'll soon learn other diversions more interesting by half." He flung her away. She stumbled, managed to grab the edge of a table and keep upright. "Now that's the last of it. I don't want to hear any more from you 'pon this subject."

"But——"

He whirled on her, and glared. She subsided. Finished with her, the squire returned to his friends, all of whom had been watching with the utmost interest. Laughter rose up around her, and though she did not know what the men were laughing at, she suspected she was the butt of their amusement.

One of the men drawled something, ribald laughter was the response, and she felt the shame rising in her once more. Desperately she searched about for the sympathetic face of the Viscount of Drummond, but saw him laughing with her father and Thomas Padgett, a neighbor who was almost a twin in appearance and temperament to her father. She paled at her discovery. No, she would find no support from him. She wondered bitterly at his earlier sympathy.

Not sympathy, but rather understanding and cruel amusement. He was no different than all the others. Just as indifferent to her, just as boorish. Why she had expected kindness or sympathy from him, she did not know. Fool, she told herself, fool. The word echoed through her mind.

Feeling oddly drained and somewhat unsteady on her feet, she headed toward the door of the study. If anyone witnessed her exit, she did not know, nor did she care.

In the hall she passed Temple approaching with a tray of various delicacies prepared by Cook. He called out to her, but she did not answer. Instead, her hand resting on the bannister, she climbed heavily up to the second floor. It took longer than usual, or so it seemed, to reach her bedchamber, and once there she fell, face-up, on the bed, not caring if she crushed her mauve skirt.

Nettie had been in earlier to lay a fire, and now the room was lit by the golden flames. From her position she could not see it, but rather watched the flickering everchanging shadows on the ceiling.

Her wrist and arm ached from her father's rough grasp, and she knew she would be bruised by morning.

But 'twas not only her arm that ached. Inside her a lump had settled in the region of her chest, behind her ribs, almost level with her heart, and she could scarce breathe because of it.

She was engaged to be married to that . . . that pompous leering caricature of a man. She shuddered, remembering his wet lips glistening in the candlelight, the stale odor of his breath, his fondling fingers. She was engaged to marry a man her father had selected, engaged to marry a man whose very sight she despised, and she knew there was no way she could weasel out of this, not as she had in the past. She could not cry off, for her father would not allow it.

She was doomed, trapped.

Oh, but she had certainly outfoxed herself now. Clever Agatha, she thought bitterly, who had rejected suitor after suitor whom her father had brought, men who on a moment's reflection did not seem by half as hideous as the creature to whom she now found herself affianced.

His wife. She would be his wife. Subject to his whims, his pleasures . . . his desire.

A deep sickness swept over her, and she sat up abruptly, one hand pressed to her lips. Hot angry bile filled her mouth, then was gone.

She jumped to her feet and ran to the ewer and basin. She splashed water on her face, reveling in the coldness of the liquid. She washed her face and her hands and neck, and scrubbed at every spot her father and Lord Alford had touched. She felt so dirty. Soon the point de gaz lace lay limply against her arms, soaked from the water. Her bodice, too, was stained, but she didn't care. She glanced at herself in the mirror over the washstand, and was appalled at what she saw.

What a change had come over the smiling woman she had been a scant few hours ago. Gone was the color in her cheeks, the vibrancy of her eyes. All was flat, dead, wasted. Even her hair seemed to have lost its curl, and one pearl pin threatened to slide out. Angrily she jerked it out, biting back a cry as it pulled her hair. She hurled the pin against the far wall. It broke, the pearl rolling back under her bed.

She stared at her hand, appalled at what she had done. Slowly she sank to the floor, her skirt blossoming about her, until she was bent over, her face in her hands, her forehead only inches from the wooden floor.

"Oh, what am I to do?" she whispered aloud, and only the crackling of the fire answered her. She wished she could cry, but even that release was denied her. Crumpled on the floor, she did not move until Nettie found her.

THREE

THE VISCOUNT OF DRUMMOND WATCHED through narrowed eyes as Agatha quietly made her way across the study to the hallway. The men surrounding the squire were now singing, their voices loud and enthusiastic, few knowing the correct lyrics, fewer caring. None but he appeared to notice her retreat

He watched her hesitate at the door; she glanced back over her shoulder and for a moment it seemed she looked at him, but she dropped her gaze and swept out.

"Fine filly, ain't she, my lord?" shouted a voice behind him.

He turned to see Lord Alford approaching him, a wine glass in each hand. He raised the left glass to his lips, swallowed, then repeated the procedure with the right one. He grinned stupidly, nodding toward the door which had just closed behind Agatha.

"She is, indeed," Drummond replied in a lazy tone. "You are to be congratulated upon your impending marriage, Lord Alford."

"Ain't I, though," Alford said, an unpleasant expression on his face. He chuckled to himself, set the two glasses down on a nearby table, and fussed for a few minutes with his snuffbox. He sneezed, then grinned as Lord Ruthen, a friend supplied with an equally dissolute nature, joined them. He stuck out his hand to Drummond, who pointedly ignored it.

"I salute you on your good taste," Drummond continued.

If there were irony underlying the viscount's words, Alford missed it. "My good taste, eh? More like my brains, you know. I ain't dumb. I won't pass a sizable fortune by. Not me." He shook his head, guzzled more wine. "She's spirited, though. It don't show much, but it's there."

The squire's voice lifted in a powerful guffaw. One of his hunting dogs, brown and lean, had appeared and the squire was presently busy tossing tidbits to the dog, who would beg, sitting on its haunches, then snap at the food. His companions laughed uproariously when the squire threw the contents of his glass on the poor animal. The hound shook its head, then licked at the liquid dripping from its muzzle.

Ruthen grinned, while Alford snickered. Drummond, watching the squire's performance, said nothing, his face remaining impassive.

"Damned fine girl," Ruthen observed to no one in particular. His voice was slurred, his stance unsteady. " 'Course one don't expect the squire to have anything less than first water, eh. He's got damned fine horseflesh, damned fine dogs, and damned fine girls. Er, girl." His hold on the glass in his hand grew progressively looser, and Drummond wondered how long it would be before the glass fell—and how much longer afterward before the glass would be followed by the man. Much to the viscount's surprise, Ruthen managed to stay planted, if not precisely firmly, on his feet.

Alford nodded in what the viscount deemed a particularly inane manner, then smiled, an expression bearing more resemblance to a smirk. "Very spirited, but there's never been a filly yet I couldn't tame." He winked broadly. "Eh, Nobby?"

"Thas right, old friend. Spirit. Got to break it." Ruthen belched loudly, tossed down more wine. " 'Tis the best way—the *only* way, by God—and after that they're the most docile of mounts."

The two friends laughed heartily at Ruthen's jest. Drummond's smile reached only the level of his lips. His eyes still remained dark and somber.

"Take 'em under rein," Alford continued. "That's what I do, and never give 'em their head again. Tucked and under, y'know, and they'll soon learn who their masters are. Don't you agree, my lord?" His eyes eagerly sought approval from Drummond.

The smile on Drummond's face thinned. "A most unique style for handling horseflesh—or women."

"It's been damned effective," Alford said by way of defense. "Always managed to keep my gels that way."

"Indeed."

" 'Course, *you* needn't worry 'bout such a matter,"

Alford said, his tone more reckless now. He grabbed Ruthen's glass from him and drained it, then thrust it back at Ruthen.

Drummond raised an eyebrow inquisitively.

Ruthen glanced nervously at the quiet nobleman.

"That scar of yours'll scare off any gel you might ask. Eh, Nobby?" The barely perceptible movement of Ruthen's head could have been a nod of agreement or it might have been a slight shake, intended to warn Alford to be wary where he treaded. In either case, Alford paid little heed. "Imagine the fright a filly'd get on her wedding night." He leaned forward, leering, and winked conspiratorially at the two men. "Why, she'd be more than willin' to do anything you asked, my lord, as long as she didn't have to look at you. Why, if you were to indulge a bit in the Greek habit, she'd probably——"

"That is quite enough," Drummond said.

Ruthen glanced at his friend, waiting.

Alford, sensing the viscount meant what he had said, snapped his mouth shut. "I only meant——" He stopped at another warning glance from Drummond.

There was a moment of uneasy silence, then Alford said, "How did you get that scar, my lord?" He peered at its white length.

Ruthen gaped at his friend. "Rupert!"

Drummond smiled, a none-too-pleasant expression. "I fell from my horse."

"Looks like you fell on a sword."

"A rosebush," he said, still smiling.

Alford laughed as if that were the funniest thing he'd heard in his life. He slapped his knee, burst into renewed laughter again, and finally resorted to wiping his eyes with the back of his hand. He gasped, chuckled, then breathed deeply. "Well, if that don't beat all. A rosebush, of all things."

Ruthen eyed the viscount and was little reassured by the man's expression. " 'B-Bout your b-bride-to-be," he put in quickly, hoping to divert his friend's attention from Drummond's deformity.

Alford scowled at the interruption "What about her?"

"She does seem docile enough. I-I mean she's got some spirit—the old man hasn't succeeded in totally cowing her—but I don't think you'll have any problem with her at all, Rupert."

"Nor I. I don't think she'll be givin' me any problem. No, none at all. She don't have control of the money, but the old man could easily kick off after the marriage, and the money would come to us. I'll get her belly full as soon as possible, and that'll make things cozy for me."

"A child every year after that," Ruthen recommended, "that'll keep her docile enough." He leered up at Drummond. "Is that not so, my lord? 'Tis a practice guaranteed to break any spirited filly."

"So I have heard. I have little doubt your method would soon wear away all rebellion the chit might have."

Rupert Norton chuckled. "If I'm lucky enough, mayhap one of the brats will take her with it when it dies, and that'll leave me in charge of that grand fortune." His chuckle deepened.

"She is rather well-heeled, isn't she," Drummond observed thoughtfully. "Or rather, the squire is."

"It's his now, but it all comes down to the same

thing—one of these days it'll be hers. Then mine." The snuffbox appeared. He offered it to Drummond, who shook his head. Ruthen dipped a stained finger in.

"Yes, you did make an excellent choice." Drummond clapped Alford upon the back, saluted him with two fingers uplifted, sketched a bow, and strolled off.

"He's an odd fish, to be sure," Ruthen said uneasily. "He might say something to the old man. Mayhap even to the girl."

Alford shrugged casually. "Don't worry 'bout old Drummond. He's odd, but he won't say a peep. He's a gentleman, like us, ain't he? We stick together, don't we?"

Ruthen nodded somewhat dubiously. He wiped his fingers with his handkerchief, tucked it in his pocket. "I suppose so," he allowed.

" 'Course so. Besides now, if you were that gel, would you believe what a man what looked like Ol' Scratch said?"

"I don't suppose so."

" 'Course not. He'd scare the very wits from her. Come now, Nobby, let's get more to drink. I don't intend to go home until I'm fair coddy-banged."

Having made his excuses to his host, who could barely stand up at that point, the Viscount of Drummond called for his cloak and horse. Temple obliged him quickly and before long he was outside, preparing to begin the long ride back to Falcon's Hall.

The yawning boy who brought around his grey gave him a lift up, and once in the saddle, Drummond gathered the reins and nudged the horse toward the drive. He tossed a coin to the boy, whose face lost its sleepy look. He grinned and waved.

As his mount slowly walked through the gravel, he could hear an occasional lyric of drunken song gusted toward him by the wind. When he reached the curve of the carriage sweep that would lead him out of sight of the mansion, he glanced backward at the house. The windows of the entire first floor burned brightly, and he knew it would be many more hours before the servants would be dismissed to go snatch a few welcome hours of sleep. Abovestairs no lights burned, and he wondered where the poor girl had gone. Off to bed to cry her eyes out, no doubt.

She had been basely humiliated by her father tonight, in the company of his crude friends. There'd been no excuse for the squire's behavior, but then from the stories Drummond had heard of Grey, the squire invited no excuses. He had been surprised when he received the invitation from Sir Alfred, for he didn't often socialize with the man, but when he had seen the other guests he realized what the man was about. Grey had invited men from all the surrounding districts–not simply close neighbors—so that when he had announced his daughter's betrothal, he had been surrounded by impartial witnesses. There was no way the poor girl could wiggle out of this.

Her face, pale in the darkness, seemed to float in front of his eyes. He rubbed a gauntlet across them. She seemed well-behaved and polite. More than a little pretty, too, with those deep blue eyes.

eyes that had beseeched him across the room, eyes that he had been forced to ignore.

What had she done to merit this humiliation by her father? The squire's loathing for women was all too well known, and it seemed Agatha's only crime had been in being born a daughter and not a son.

And now she would be shackled with that Alford. His lip curled as he thought of the young lordling. A puppy whose bite was poison, Drummond thought. A disgusting toad that should be stuck with a toad-eater. Ruthen he dismissed. The man did not have wits enough to think for himself, he was the perfect sycophant. It was Alford who possessed a modicum of intelligence combined with a wicked cunning, a most uneasy combination.

The wind whipped back his cloak, breaking the train of his thoughts, and he yawned, secured the cloak. He reached the gates, and rode out onto the road, where he nudged his horse into a steady trot, giving the Greys no more thought.

It was a black night. The moon was nearly full, but was obscured by dark clouds tumbling and roiling across its yellow face. The wind had arisen and the bare branches of the trees lining the road, thin and skeletal, snapped back and forth, at times clicking as they brushed against one another. He could smell rain in the air, and knew before long it would be pouring.

And his mood had become as dark as the night. Away from the raucous company of the men, away from the bright candlelight, away from the liquor, alone on an empty road, home yet miles away, his only companion his thoughts, his mind turned elsewhere.

He recalled another night such as this one, blustery and cold, and so very dark. A night . . . almost two years ago.

He settled deeper into the depths of his cloak, seeking what warmth he could find. The cold seemed to seep to his very bones. His hands trembled even though they were gloved in heavy leather. He sought to control their tremulous motion, but failed. He uttered a curse under his breath. The animal, sensing his unease, began to snort and plunge, tossing its head, the whites of its eyes showing, and for the next few minutes Drummond's mind and body were solely occupied with quieting the beast.

Animal and man fought, each one seeking mastery, but at last the horse's agitation ceased. He stroked the horse's neck and softly called him by name. The beast whickered in response.

'Twas the past, he told himself roughly, and urged the animal on to a canter. The past. Dead . . . dead and gone. Past and buried.

He forced all thoughts from his mind, and threw back his head and felt the wind sting his eyes, his cheeks . . . the scar on his forehead.

His lips curled as he recalled Lord Alford's ill-bred curiosity about the origin of the scar. Fool to believe it had been caused by a rosebush. No, it had not been anything quite so domestic.

That, too, was in the past. Its angry soreness had healed and it rarely gave him any pain now. Rarely. If only other matters . . . other concerns . . . other scars . . . would heal so easily.

But the one in his mind only seemed to fester with the passing of time.

"I told you not to wait up for me," Drummond said curtly as he entered his study, the door slamming shut behind him. A window rattled from the force.

A middle-aged man who had been dozing in a chair by the roaring fire scrambled to his feet. "My lord, I told you I would."

"Thomas, you're a great fool."

"That I am," replied his lordship's valet agreeably. Thomas studied Drummond's face, saw the ugly expression there, and whistled soundlessly. "It was not a good evening?"

"No."

"You are most uncommunicative tonight, my lord."

"Yes."

Thomas knew it boded ill when Drummond resorted to one-syllable replies. He sighed inwardly, straightened his coat, and crossed to his master, who, one hand resting high against the frame, was staring out a window. Thomas peered past his master's shoulder but saw only darkness. He feared that was all his master saw as well.

"Do you desire anything?"

"A drink."

Thomas nodded, bowed though he knew his lordship would not notice, and withdrew from the room. As he put together a tray he wondered what had happened at Squire Grey's to put his lordship into such a black mood. He hadn't seen him this way since . . .

Enough of *that*, Thomas Dentham, he told himself fiercely. 'Twas bad enough to have him so low without thinking of *that*.

He returned with the tray. Drummond remained at the window. He set it on the desk, cleared his throat, waited. Still his lordship did not move.

"Your lordship, I have a tray waiting for you."

At last the viscount turned around, and the firelight played across the planes of his face. His eyes were damped coals, his cheeks sunken in, and the scar across his brow livid, almost as if it were afire. If Thomas had been of the Roman faith, he would most certainly have crossed himself. Tonight Drummond looked to be the very Devil.

Drummond reached across for the bottle and a glass without bothering to thank his servant. He did not even check to see what the liquor was. He uncorked the bottle, poured a glass, swallowed the burning liquid in almost one mouthful, poured a second glass. This he drank more slowly—three mouthfuls

Thomas watched as the contents of the bottle slowly disappeared into his master. When the bottle was finished, Drummond picked it up and turned it over. A single drop of amber liquid squeezed out and plopped down on the surface of the deep-grained desk. He stared at it wordlessly for a moment, then looked up at Thomas.

"Another." His voice was not yet thick. From past experience, Thomas knew it would take far more than one bottle to see his master under the table.

He nodded, knowing he could not disobey, and left. When he came back, he found Drummond seated in front of the fire, booted legs outstretched carelessly, staring intently into the depths of the flames, almost as if he wished to fling himself into them. Thomas shuddered. His master was haunted by a ghost, and there was nothing he could do. Nothing but wait. And in time . . . time would heal all, would heal this inner wound of his master's . . . in time—if only the wound did not fester and kill him.

He watched silently as the second bottle was drained, then he returned to the pantry for a third and a fourth. He was curious about what had happened at Squire Grey's, but would say nothing until his master volunteered to speak about it.

When he was half finished with the fourth bottle, Drummond stood. One hand was clasped about the neck of the bottle, the other held his empty glass. There was no expression on his face.

Thomas watched with concern to see if his lordship was unsteady on his feet. He was as secure as ever. He strode purposefully across the study, turned back as he reached the door.

"I am going there tonight," he announced in a low voice.

"I . . ." Thomas hesitated. "I don't think that's a good idea, my lord."

"I don't give a fig for what you think, Thomas."

His lordship poured more of the liquid into his glass, managed to open the door, and left.

Thomas opened his mouth to call Drummond back, changed his mind, and sat. All he could do now was wait.

* * *

He knew where he was going; had been there many times before.

Before. Not after.

He shuddered, swallowed more of the burning liquid, and continued walking. He did not pause to light a candle. He had no need of one. He knew his way there in the dark.

He went down a corridor lined with shut doors, all of them like silent watchful eyes, all of them leading into equally silent rooms, and at last he reached a double door, locked. He cursed out loud. He had forgotten the lock. The keys were in his rooms; he did not wish to retrieve them.

He kicked at the door and its lock, once, twice, again. The sound was monstrously loud in the silence of the unused rooms. The lock broke free, and one of the doors swung inward.

He stepped over the threshold, paused to look around. Evidently the wind had swept the clouds from the face of the moon, for the deserted room was bathed in pale moonlight. Dustcovers, draped over the major pieces of furniture, formed grotesque shadows on the floor and walls. Row after row of dusty books bore silent witness as he walked across the moldering carpet, stirring up clouds of dust. With each step he heard the distant echo of sprightly laughter, and he felt as though a mighty fist were crushing his heart.

At last he reached the fireplace, a great affair with a marble mantel, and plaster frescos surrounding it. An immense firescreen of ornate brass stood in front. Above the fireplace hung an oil painting set in a gilded oval frame.

He stared up at the picture. His eyes welled

with tears, and he dashed down another glass of liquor, then whirled and violently threw the glass against the far wall. It smashed into thousands of slivers glinting like diamonds in the moonlight. Dumbly he stared at the glass fragments, then at the bottle in his hand. His fingers, growing suddenly numb, opened and the bottle fell to the floor, breaking and splashing his boots with brandy, which pooled, unnoticed, around him until he seemed to stand in a sea of liquor.

Once more he stared up at the portrait, at its subject, a young woman whose eyes were so lovely, so filled with sadness, and the sorrow and horror of the night two years before rose up in him once again. He gave himself up to it.

FOUR

THE FOLLOWING MORNING AGATHA ROSE at her usual early hour, and after washing her hands and neck and face, slipped on a plain bodice and skirt with the assistance of Nettie, who pressed with unbecoming curiosity for details of the previous evening. Agatha, who had not been able to sleep because of the nightmarish scene in her father's study, only shook her head.

"Not now, Nettie," she said hoarsely.

The rough condition of her throat had resulted from the tears that had flowed for hours after she had finally gotten into bed. She had lain there on her bed, awake, staring at the shadow patterns on the ceiling, thinking, seeking a way out of her predicament, and when the fire had at last died down to a bed of embers and when the first rays of dawn had spread their light in her room, she had realized she was truly trapped.

It was then that the tears had come, and it was only shortly before she arose that they had stopped.

Even now she felt them threatening to spill over and course down her cheeks. She tried to keep them in check because she did not want Nettie to see her sobbing.

Nettie, though, knew something terrible had happened. Her own brown eyes filled with tears, and she dashed at her nose with the back of one hand. She stared wordlessly at Agatha.

Agatha, seeing the sympathy on her maid's plain face, could endure no longer. Her resolve to be brave in front of the servants crumbled, and the tears spilled forth. She collapsed into Nettie's arms, and while the maid rocked her, she reported all that had transpired the night before. Before long, both girls were sobbing loudly.

It was Agatha who gained control first, and had to fish a white silk handkerchief, its edges delicately embroidered with tiny forget-me-nots, from the linen box to hand to Nettie. Nettie choked, thanked her mistress, blew her nose loudly, and then stared miserably at the sodden handkerchief.

"This be your best hankie!" she wailed, and her tears started anew.

"Here, you goose, it doesn't signify."

"Oh, yes, it do. It was one of your mother's!"

"Now come, Nettie, do take hold of yourself," Agatha said gently but firmly. " 'Tis not the end of the world, you know."

"Might as well be." Nettie sniffed again, once more blew her nose. A large fat tear escaped one watery eye and rolled down her cheek. "Whatever will become of you, miss?"

"In time I shall . . . shall marry, and I will be a wife, and t-then a mother, and that is all." The thought of Lord Alford coming to her at night, demanding what was his by law . . . *touching* . . . her . . . brought waves of sickness rushing over her. She put a hand to her mouth and once more thought she would be ill. She managed to recover, and once the nausea had receded, she stood, albeit somewhat unsteadily, and said quietly, "I must go to breakfast now, Nettie."

Nettie jumped to her feet and held out the crumpled handkerchief.

Agatha shook her head. "You may keep it."

"I'll wash it, and press it, and——"

"No. It is yours now."

The girl managed a wan smile and thanked her mistress.

Agatha stared into the mirror. The face staring back out of the silvery depths was even more of a stranger than that of the previous night. This stranger possessed reddened eyes, with great black smudges under them, and looked as though her heart were broken. She retrieved another handkerchief and soaked it in cold water, then pressed it to her fevered eyelids in an attempt to reduce the swelling. When, after a few minutes, she decided she no longer looked as dreadful as before, she announced she was ready to go downstairs.

She dabbed rose water on her wrists, letting the sweet scent rise around her to give her some confidence. Taking a deep breath, she left her bedchamber. Nettie waved a tearful farewell.

She had no qualms about facing her father this early in the morning—why, it was not yet eight o'clock and he never rose before eleven, except when he intended to go hunting with his friends. And she knew he had planned no such venture this day.

She reached the dining room and had just seated herself in her customary place when her father stumbled in.

"F-Father!"

Bleary-eyed, he glared at her and plopped down into his chair at the head of the table. One of his hunting dogs, a young hound named Bruno, followed him and lay down beside the chair. It placed its head on its paws and stared woefully at her.

"You needn't look so surprised, girl. I have at times arisen early." He grumbled below his breath, put a rough hand to his forehead, and squeezed his eyes shut. "The truth of the matter is, I haven't gone to bed yet. Been up all night celebrating." One eye opened and surveyed her at the convey ance of this information.

If he had hoped to see her cry and perhaps beg him to reconsider, he was sorely disappointed for she did neither. Instead, Agatha stared down at her hands, clasped in her lap, and held her tongue. It was hard for her, but she would not be tricked by him into behaving like a hysterical female. *That* she behaved like in the privacy of her own rooms, but there was certainly no need for him to know.

"Cat got your tongue?"

She looked up at him now, aware that Temple had silently entered and was busily preparing their plates at the sideboard.

"No, sir."

He seemed puzzled, obviously remembering the

earlier schemes for her marriage and how she had always managed to talk him out of them. "Don't you have anything to say, Agatha?"

"Further protest would be futile. You convinced me of that last night."

Temple silently slid a plate in front of her father, marched to where she sat, and handed one to her. She took it and looked up to see his sympathetic expression. His support heartened her somewhat.

"That so?" her father grunted. Apparently the squire's all-night drinking bout had done little to dispel his appetite, for he attacked his beefsteak enthusiastically. The blood welled out as he sliced into it and jammed a great chunk of the nearly raw meat into his mouth.

Agatha glanced away, then down at her plate, and began half-heartedly to pick at her eggs and sausage.

Temple had set a pint of sour before the squire, while she indicated she desired only a cup of plain tea. A few minutes later she realized she had no appetite, and pushed her plate away. Temple saw, crossed to the table, and retrieved the plate. She picked up the teacup and wrapped her hands around it. The warmth felt good against the chill of her skin.

Silently she watched as her father devoured the beefsteak, called for a second, then polished it off. When he had at last finished three of the steaks, and a kidney pie as well, he pushed away from the table and belched loudly. The dog stirred beside him and he tossed a hunk of meat left on the plate to the animal. The dog swallowed it in one gulp.

"I have only one thing to ask, Father," she said, at last gathering the courage to speak.

"Eh?" He was on his fourth pint already, and cocked an eye at her. "What?"

"Why?" She tried not to sound plaintive, but suspected she failed.

"Why? Damme, I'll tell you, girl!" With a resounding crack he brought his hand down on the table. His plate, his daughter, and his dog all jumped. "Why?" he repeated. "Because I say so, Agatha, and that's sufficient. My word is law in this house. You've known that since the day you were born." He stood up, the chair falling backward, and the dog scrambled to its feet, wagged its tail once. He whirled, stumbled over the dog, too eager to please its master, and drew his foot back.

"No!" she shrieked.

If he heard, he gave no indication. The foot, shod in a heavy riding boot, followed through and landed on the ribs of the dog. There was a dull thunk, a high whine, and the dog flew across the room to lie by the sideboard.

Temple dropped the plate in his hand and stared. Crying from dismay and anger, Agatha stood up and rushed across to the dog. On his way out of the dining room her father paused to look down at her kneeling by the dog, and he laughed harshly.

"You always were a soft one, puss."

He left with a clatter of his heavy boots, and she focused her attention on the poor dog. Temple knelt to one side.

"He does not seem to be hurt, thank God," she said after a moment when she had finished running her hands over the length of the dog's body, checking for broken bones. The dog lifted his head and licked her hand.

"I think he is only bruised—and has had the wind knocked out of him, of course."

Outside, they could hear the squire shouting, demanding his horse be brought out to him. Temple rose and crossed to the window. The noise continued until the animal was brought forth, and with a great curse, Squire Grey leaped up into the saddle and dug his spurs into the horse's sides.

Temple returned to Agatha, who was gently stroking the dog's head. One hand cradled the dog's muzzle; its eyes were closed.

"He's gone."

She nodded, relieved, and stood, brushing her hands off on her apron. The dog slowly got to his feet, shook himself, and followed her as she headed for the door.

"I think, miss," said Temple, a smile creasing his features, "that you have a new friend."

She looked down at the dog, who wagged his tail in a small circle. "Indeed, I do, and I think," she finished softly, "I am in sore need of one."

After she left the dining room she went to the library, the dog patiently following her. She entered the intimate room, tastefully furnished with a green brocade settee, a large comfortable chair, and two tables, and gazed at the numerous volumes in the bookcases lining two walls and surrounding the fireplace of the room. While her father was for the most part sorely unlettered, he had a secret admiration for those who possessed greater learning and maintained an extensive library for show. But never once in her life had she seen him enter the room and open a book.

He had also been exceedingly careless of Agatha's education, but she had always been an intelligent child with a great curiosity, and when she was old enough Temple and Mrs. Howard had taught her her letters, and one day, when the squire was out, Temple had given her an introduction to the library.

She had fallen in love with it instantly, and it had always been her dream to read each and every one of the thousands of volumes there. She touched the binding on one of the books, marveling at the softness of the morocco leather.

Poetry. The classics. Law. Religion. History. All her good companions through her youth. She trailed a hand across the spines of the books as she walked toward the window. The dog, having laid down, picked himself up once more and followed.

She laughed as he plopped himself down at her feet once more and let out a long sigh. Gently she stroked his head. "Poor fellow. I'm sure you'll be glad when I settle in one spot."

He seemed to understand for he picked his head up and wagged his tail, with his tongue lolling out. He reached up and licked her hand. She continued to scratch behind his ears.

She had to stay here today. This was her retreat—it always had been. Nothing harmful could reach her here. Here she could heal a little before facing her father later that evening. Here she would not have to think of the dreadful future. Here she could retreat to the past, forget everything else.

She winced, and reached to select a book.

What was she in the mood for? Something light, perhaps. Certainly nothing serious. No moral treatises for her today.

She settled at last for a volume of French verse and curled up in the comfortable chair. It was close to the fireplace, so she could keep warm. The dog lay down by the chair and, rolling over onto his side, fell asleep. From time to time his legs twitched in his sleep, and she wondered what he dreamed of.

She closed her eyes, and in her mind she saw the puckered scar of the somber man, and wondered how he had received it. He had seemed so kind, so ready to rescue her from Alford, and then he had forgotten her. And her father . . . Alford . . . all of them.

She shuddered. Her dreams were nightmares. She would not think about them. Not now, not for a little while.

Forcing her attention back to the book on her lap, she began to read.

She must have fallen asleep for the next moment she heard Temple's voice calling to her.

"Miss Agatha, Miss Agatha."

She opened her eyes. "Yes, Temple, what is it?"

"Miss Lucille Wilmot is here to see you."

"Lucy!" She sat up. "Send her in at once!"

He bowed and left the room.

What a sight I must be, she thought. She ran a hand quickly through her hair, aware of how mussed it must look from her nap. She wondered how long she had been asleep. Perhaps hours. She glanced out the window. The sky was grey, as though snow or rain were imminent, and she could not tell what hour of the day it was. It was little wonder she had surrendered to sleep when the night before she had not managed to shut her eyes.

The door flew open, and Lucy Wilmot briskly preceded Temple into the room.

"Miss Wilmot," he said, announcing her after the fact.

"Agatha!" Lucy squealed, and forgetting dignity, ran across the room to her friend. They hugged one another, and Lucy kissed her friend's cheek, then drew back and studied her. "You look perfectly dreadful!"

Agatha gave a mock sigh. "Lucy, what a terrible thing to say to me."

Temple coughed discreetly.

"Yes, Temple?" Agatha said, favoring him with a smile.

"Is there anything else you will be wanting?"

She glanced inquiringly at Lucy.

"Well," Lucy announced loftily, "I have been traveling for absolutely *hours* and am practically *famished*—nay, starved to the *bone*!"

Agatha grinned at her friend, who was as plump as any partridge.

"A tray with tea and biscuits, please."

"And jam?" Lucy asked hopefully.

"And jam."

"Very well, miss." He bowed and left the two friends alone.

"Oh, Agatha, you must tell me all that is new, for I trow I've not seen you in a dog's age, and speaking of dogs, what is this creature doing here?"

Wrinkling her nose, she sat in a chair Agatha indicated and stared at the dog, who wagged his tail.

"I have . . . inherited . . . him from my father," she said, not wishing to say more of the matter.

"Oh." Evidently Lucy sensed more to the story, but for once showed some little self-control and did not push for an explanation. "Here, doggie. Here."

The dog strolled over to her and licked her gloved fingers. She laughed and patted him on his head. His tail wagged furiously, but his heart had obviously been given to Agatha, for he returned to curl up at her feet.

"Lucy, you are dressed quite smartly today. What is the occasion?"

Lucy wore a cherry pink bodice with a full skirt of vertical white and pink stripes. The hem was edged with ruched lace, and her underslip had tiny pink roses on it. Lucy, two years Agatha's junior, stood half a head shorter than she, and was a good twenty pounds heavier, but had the sweetest face Agatha had ever seen, and was possessed of a lively and endearing nature.

It went without saying that Squire Grey detested Lucy Wilmot.

Even now Lucy was grinning at her friend. " 'Twas no special occasion, my dear. I simply had to get out of the house. I had been cooped up for so long—literally weeks—that I could endure it no longer, while my poor aunt was quite out of patience with me!"

Agatha joined her friend's laughter, just as Temple entered with their tea service.

Lucy stared hungrily at the wide array of biscuits and at the honey and marmalade.

"You will stay for lunch, won't you?" Agatha asked.

One eye on the tray, Lucy said, "Oh, I couldn't——" She stopped. "I would love to!"

The girls laughed again, and Temple, no longer needed, bowed out.

For the next few minutes they occupied themselves pouring tea and securing biscuits on the china plates. Lucy had piled hers quite high, and Agatha smiled as she watched her friend precariously balance the overloaded plate on her lap. Three biscuits disappeared into Lucy before the dark-haired young woman spoke again.

"Ah, in truth I am feeling better already."

"I think," Agatha teased, "the only reason you come to visit me is to sample Cook's pastries."

"Not so!" Lucy protested. "Still . . ." She popped another in her mouth.

Agatha laughed.

"Do you have news for me, Lucy?"

"As always." She frowned thoughtfully, tapped a foot briefly. "Now let me see if I can organize my thoughts. I vow they lie scattered across my brain. Ah," she ate another biscuit for inspiration, then said, "The Duke and Duchess of Avalon's daughter has been brought out into London society this past autumn. She is a most pretty girl and takes after her mother, except for the hair, of course."

"Go on."

Agatha had never gone to London, and could

only faintly imagine all the sights Lucy must see when she stayed at her aunt's townhouse.

"Oh yes, and a certain lord has found it most expedient to leave the country for a while, and they do say there will be a birth soon at the household of the de Kleivens."

"You think then that . . . ?"

"Of course! I am most convinced—as is half of London—that the child will be born with the most dashing widow's peak. Oh—" and her face grew more serious— "there was a terrible fuss before I left London to come to the country. The daughter of a good family was found roaming a country lane. She talked of devils and men in masks, and terrible ceremonies. It's said she's been scared out of her wits, and now rests with her family."

"That's horrible," Agatha said, shuddering. "Devils?"

"Yes. I don't think they're real, of course. But there are those men—I know this is talked of far more in London than out here, my dear—in certain clubs, who raise more hellfire than the very Devil himself."

"Hellfire clubs? I've heard of them, but thought they were for the most part harmless."

Lucy shook her head, the mass of dark curls shimmering. "No. The Queen is most angry and has ordered her men to find these clubs out and to bring the ringleaders to her." She paused to sip her tea. "But enough of this dreary talk! Let me see what else I can tell you."

"It is amazing how much you learn while you're in London." Agatha smiled at her friend.

"I listen," Lucy said simply. "I think you should come with me to the City sometime."

Agatha's smile faltered.

"Have I said something amiss?" Lucy looked with concern at her friend. She paused with a biscuit halfway to her mouth.

"No," Agatha replied slowly, "I have but recalled . . ."

"Recalled what?" Lucy finished the biscuit, reached for another.

" 'Tis nothing, my dear." She forced the heavy thoughts from her head and tried to smile as warmly as possible. It was no easy task, but she did not wish to ruin her friend's visit with unpleasant thoughts.

Lucy stared thoughtfully at Agatha as she spread a thick layer of marmalade on a biscuit. She nibbled part of it, then said, "If you need to talk, you know I shall always be most willing to listen."

Agatha glanced down at her hands in her lap. The fingers were twisted together, and she knew she must present the very picture of distress. She wanted to speak freely with her friend, and yet, if she spoke aloud of her burden, she feared she would once more dissolve into tears.

"Come," the plump girl coaxed, "tell me what weighs so heavily on your mind."

She drew in a deep breath, stood, and paced about the room. If she kept moving . . . if she did not allow herself to sit and think too long . . . then things would not be so bad. Would they?

She glanced once at her friend's sympathetic face, and then the words came tumbling out. "I am soon to be married."

A half-eaten biscuit dropped from Lucy's fingers, and she gaped at Agatha.

"Is this not rather sudden?" she asked, recovering the biscuit and setting it aside.

Agatha nodded. "It was decided for me last night." She knew her voice trembled, but she could not prevent it.

"That is why you are so pale today." Lucy rose. "Oh my poor dear." She held out her arms and Agatha rested her head on her friend's shoulder briefly, then sat. Lucy followed suit.

"When is it to be?"

"Father has not yet set a date. Or rather," bitterness now crept into her voice, "he has not yet informed me."

Lucy blinked rapidly. "W-Who is the groom to be?"

"Lord Alford."

The plump girl gasped and stared, open-mouthed, at Agatha. "But he—that is, I mean, he is a most prodigious rake. I have heard nothing good of him! You cannot wed him!"

"I am well aware of that."

"Oh, your father cannot be such a brute as to force you to marry that man."

"But he will, and as you know, Lucy, there is little I can do about it. In the past I have succeeded in forestalling my father, but this time I cannot."

"You must try!"

"He announced it to a roomful of his friends last night."

"Oh."

A grim silence settled over the library for the

span of a quarter of an hour. Each woman was lost deep in her own thoughts.

Finally Lucy stirred and announced, "You must run away!"

Agatha laughed at the absurdity of her friend's proposal. "You are forever suggesting that, Lucy, and I am forever telling you I have no place to go. 'Twould, I fear, be only the worse for me."

"You would have to work."

"As what? I am qualified only as a companion."

"Then you would have to be a companion!"

"Until I found such an opportunity, where would I stay? How would I live?"

Lucy drew her eyebrows together in a puzzled expression, then said: "You would stay with us, of course!"

"I thank you for your generosity, but I would not wish for your mother and you to be the butt of my father's anger. He could do much to harm you."

"Oh pooh," Lucy said, shrugging a careless shoulder, and yet Agatha saw a glimmer of fear in Lucy's eyes. The squire's awesome temper was well-renowned throughout the district.

"No," Agatha said slowly, "I thank you for your kind offer, but I fear I am trapped. I will have to marry Lord Alford."

Lucy's upper lip trembled and without further ado she burst into tears.

FIVE

THEY WORE BLACK MONKS' ROBES, and masks betraying only the hard glitter of their eyes, and their names were Seven: Superbia, Invidia, Avaritia, Acedia, Ira, Gula, and Luxuria.

The Seven sat upon a dais covered in bloodred velvet. Their chairs were heavy wood, and behind them on the wall of dank stone hung an inverted crucifix. A table before them, draped in a black cloth decorated with creatures of ill omen, served from time to time as an altar. This night it bore two candlelabra with black candles burning brightly. An immense book, its pages yellowed with age, held the position of honor in the center of the table.

"Brother Discord." One of the Seven, the man on the right end of the dais, spoke in the silence of the room. He seemed younger than the others. While no individual feature could be discerned beneath the robes and masks, his voice bespoke a man not yet in his prime. He looked toward a handful of men and women who stood some distance from the dais. The robes of the men, the monks, were black; the robes of the women, the nuns, were red.

"Yes, Father Avaritia." A tall man, his face likewise masked although in white, stepped forward. His robe too was of the purest white cloth.

"You have been with us nearly a year. The night of your initiation into our society grows closer."

"Damned be his name," the tall man murmured, inclining his head toward the desecrated cross.

"It has fallen upon you, as our novice, to select a sacrifice for our mass that night. You know the requirements for our lamb. She must be a virgin, have known no man, and as befitting our code, she must be of high birth. Is this understood?"

"Yes, Father Avaritia." If the novice was at all disturbed by his superior's impartation, his voice betrayed no sign.

"On Walpurgis Night—the eve of May first—we will celebrate the Feast of Saint Secoine," the first man said. "From thence onward, Brother Discord, there is no return to that other realm for you."

Brother Discord remained silent. His eyes, through the slits in the mask, watched the Seven.

"Now, let us drink of his blood." Father Avaritia caught the attention of one of the women. "Sister Hellborn, the cup."

A woman, the color of her hair concealed by a veil, broke away from the group and gracefully knelt before a low cabinet. From it she took a golden chalice, the sides of which were embossed with the figures of toads, bats, and owls. She crossed slowly to the dais, bowed low, and handed the chalice to Father Avaritia. She backed away, her head still bowed. He kissed its base, then waited as Father Ira handed a bottle made of heavy glass to him. Chanting softly, he poured liquid into the chalice, held it up to the crucifix, and bowed his head.

"Master of Darkness, inspire in others the terror with which knowing you has filled our hearts. We bless you, we exonerate you, we revile you. Damned be all those in his name."

Father Avaritia nodded toward the others on the dais. He passed the chalice to them and in turn each took a sip. Then it was time for the monks and nuns to drink of the liquid. Each knelt before the altar while Father Avaritia held the chalice to their lips.

Brother Discord was the last to go up to the dais. He knelt and opened his lips. The metal of the chalice was cold, but was quickly replaced by the warmth of the liquid. Its saltiness filled his mouth, trickled down his throat, and he swallowed.

He returned to his place with the others, reached up with a hand to wipe the corner of his mouth. His fingers came away red.

"The blood of an unbaptized newly born bastard," said Sister Carnal, leaning over to him. She smiled at him, and he returned the expression.

"Now we must celebrate, brothers and sisters," Father Avaritia announced. The candles on the dais were extinguished; others, in brass sconces on the walls, lit. Scents, heady and thick, floated through the air. The light in the room became golden, liquid, soft.

Almost languidly the nuns and monks kissed, embraced, paired off, retreating into the corners of the room, into the shadows. At length only one nun and one monk remained. The Seven still remained on the dais, still watched.

Sister Carnal turned to Brother Discord. Her smile was brazen: he responded with his own. She moved to him and touched him upon the chest. He took her hand in his, lightly kissed her fingers. She shivered and drew closer. Their lips met; she bit him, drew blood, and licked it away. Laughing, she backed away from him and with damnable slowness opened the front of her robe.

Beneath it she was naked.

Slowly, so very slowly, the robe slipped from her white shoulders and she came into his arms.

The days after Lucy's visit flew by all too quickly for Agatha and filled her with a secret fear that increased as each day ended.

When Lucy had begun crying, she had comforted her friend and soon thereafter they had lunched, and they had talked of many things, but not again did they touch upon the subject of Agatha's impending marriage. Agatha had invited her to stay for dinner, but Lucy regretfully refused, needing to return to her aunt's. In the late afternoon the two young women had hugged, and then Agatha was left alone, watching as Lucy's coach disappeared into the distance.

That night the squire came home in good humor.

"The invitations have been taken care of," he

said, pulling off his gloves and tossing them at Temple. He passed Agatha, entered his study. She followed.

She felt dizzy, almost as if she could not breathe, and yet at the same time as if she were being consumed by flames. She took a deep breath.

"W-When is the wedding to be, Father?"

He smiled, an expression which failed to reassure her. "April first," he said, and then laughed.

A month and a half left. She swallowed painfully. Too little time, too soon, too . . . She closed her eyes, and when she opened them, her father had left the study.

Agatha was little inclined to ready herself for the event, but unfortunately found her father most willing to handle most of the preparation. Toward the end of the month, when a shocked Reverend Lewis had been notified of the impending nuptials and when the measurements for the wedding dress had been taken, the squire invited some of his acquaintances for an evening of cards.

Among them was the man with the scar, Lord Drummond. She was startled to see him once more, for in the past month she had often found her thoughts turning to him. He smiled amiably when he saw her, and bowed slightly. She curtsied.

"I believe I have not offered my felicitations upon your wedding, Miss Grey," Drummond said, his eyes fixed on her face.

She paled. "No," she said, her voice almost a whisper, "you have not."

It appeared as though he desired to say more, but he had no opportunity for at that moment her father strode up to them, clapped Drummond on the back, and winked at his daughter and told her to be gone for they were to begin their gaming soon. She excused herself, nodded to the tall aristocrat and her father, and left.

At odds with herself, she wandered through the halls of the house and finally found herself outside in the rose garden. The sun was just setting, and a rosy light colored the air. Underfoot the white rocks crunched. Tiny purple and dark-blue violets spread in profusion in one gardenbed, while in an adjacent spot the green leaves of daffodils and tulips could be seen pushing up through the soil.

Gradually the light faded until greyness enveloped the garden. She grew aware of the coldness and she resolved to go back to the house. At that moment someone moved on the terrace outside her father's study. She peered through the gloom, but could not recognize the figure. The doors opened, then closed, and she was once more alone.

Shivering, she crossed her arms in front of her breasts and headed for the door. Someone had been spying on her. Why? Who?

Her father, perhaps?

Surely he would have called to her, would not have let her enjoy the solitude, and yet this person had said nothing.

So perhaps it was not spying. Perhaps it was simply . . . curiosity. Curiosity for the doomed, she thought dully.

She went upstairs and retired to bed and did not see the viscount when he left, even though Nettie reported that he had inquired after her.

She did not know what to make of that information, and because she could not allow herself to worry overly much, she dismissed it from her mind.

A fortnight before the wedding the squire invited Lord Alford and Lord Ruthen to stay the weekend. This was not the first time Agatha had seen Alford since the public announcement of their engagement. Every week he seemed to be at Grey's Manor, and with every meeting her loathing of him increased. He treated her with proprietary intimacy—as if they were married already, as if he were her lord and master. She said as little to him as possible, even though her father chided her for her lack of manners.

This night was no different. They sat in a salon for a while, the men talking, Agatha quiet with her hands folded in her lap. At dinnertime they retired to the dining room to sit down to a repast of roast beef and mutton, stuffed chicken, beef and pork pies, a roast goose, farmer's cheese, suet pudding, dried apples baked in wine, freshly baked bread, and wine and ale. The men all displayed hearty appetites, but Agatha's suffered greatly, and she was sore pressed to eat more than a bite of each dish.

The three men, again, talked of many things while Agatha listened. She tried to feign an interest when they spoke of their hunting dogs, of their horses, of the weather, and of the problems of tenant farmers.

She listened, and sipped her wine, and from time to time saw Alford regarding her over the top of his wine goblet. At one such time he caught her eye and winked broadly.

Feeling ill, she dropped her eyes and did not again glance toward him during the remainder of the meal. In a fortnight, one part of her whispered, in two weeks he will be your husband, and he will come to you and——

No! she almost shrieked out loud, and she jerked her hand, knocking over the wine goblet. She was thankful for the incident, embarrassing as it was, for it distracted her from her painful thoughts.

When they were finished at last, she asked in a quiet voice to be excused.

"No," said the squire, standing and stretching. He scratched at his belly. "We want your company tonight, girl."

This was not customary, and she knew he had done it simply so that she and Alford might spend more time together—something she did not wish. The quartet retired to the study, where she sipped more wine while her father and the two younger men called for bottle after bottle.

She spent the next few hours listening with increasing boredom to their boasts and bravado. They directed few of their comments to her, and she wondered why her father had desired her presence. Finally she rose.

"Father, may I be excused? I have a headache and desire to go to bed."

He smiled somewhat benignly, a result, she thought, of his excessive intake of liquor.

"Run along, Agatha."

She turned away and before she could prevent him, Alford had jumped to his feet.

"I shall escort your daughter, sir."

Squire Grey grinned at him, Lord Ruthen

winked, and before she could protest, he had opened the door for her, her hand tucked through his. He all but pulled her up the stairs, and then stopped abruptly in the hallway outside the room he was using this weekend.

"Really, sir," she said, "I do not need further assistance. I am quite capable of——"

"Oh, I know that, Agatha my dear, but I wish to be helpful to you. You know our wedding day is not so very far away, m'dear." He drew her closer to his body and raised a hand to stroke her breast.

She broke away from him. "In truth, sir——"

"In truth, m'dear, no one but us would be the wiser if we should celebrate our wedding a bit . . . prematurely."

"I beg your pardon?"

He released her hand and pulled her close. His breath was hot, and smelled of liquor and stale snuff.

"Come, come, Agatha, do not play the innocent with me."

"I assure you, sir," she said, in as cold a voice as she could muster, "that I do not know what you mean."

"This is what I mean."

He jerked her hands behind her back, her wrists pinioned in one of his hands, and roughly brought his mouth down on hers. His free hand sought the warm softness between her breasts. She was being crushed against the wall, and she winced from the pain.

She tried to jerk her hands away, tried to move her head, but couldn't. Finally he brought his head away to take a long shuddering breath, and he laughed softly at her expression. He licked his reddened lips, and his eyes were bright with lust. "Little virgin," he said in a thickened voice, "but not for long. My sword will pierce you through and through, until you beg for mercy."

He withdrew the hand from her cleavage and tried to open the door, and while he was doing that, Agatha managed to work her wrists free. She whirled away, but could not completely elude him. He grabbed her again, and threw her through the now opened door into his room. She landed on the floor, slightly dazed. He kicked the door shut behind him.

Now he towered over her, his hands resting lightly on his hips.

She had had no time to think, only to react, and her heart hammered under her ribs. He would have his way with her . . . if not now, then on their wedding night. And there was nothing she could do about it.

For a long moment, as she panted heavily, trying to recapture her spent breath, he stared at her, then began unfastening his breeches. Anger now replaced her earlier fear, and she leaped to her feet. Unsteady on his feet as he struggled with his breeches, he wobbled when she pushed him with her hands, and fell backward.

He rolled over and one hand shot out for her ankle as she leaped past, but his fingers closed on air. She kicked out at him and he yelled, cursed, nursed his bruised fingers.

She reached for her bedroom, slammed the door, and managed to shove a chest in front of it. She leaned against it, gasping. Her chest ached, and she was shaking from the experience.

There was a knock on the door.

She tried to quiet her breathing, said nothing.

The door pushed ajar slightly, no more than a fraction of an inch, and then stopped, the bulk of the chest impeding it.

"Agatha," Alford called softly. "Come here, girl."

Still she said nothing.

"Agatha, come to me now. Freely, and I will be tender with you." He waited and when she said nothing, he spoke again, but this time his voice had changed. "Very well, m'dear, I shall wait until our wedding night. But be well advised that I am not accustomed to being thwarted. I think that night a little touch of the whip will swiftly bring you to your senses." He chuckled. "Adieu, Agatha."

She listened as he walked away, heard him go down the stairs, and still she did not remove the chest from the door. She stared down at her hands, reddened by his rough use, and crossed over to the ewer and basin, drew water, and scrubbed her lips. She wanted to wash away all touch of him before she became tainted. She bathed her neck and breasts, her face, and changed her clothing. When her trembling had subsided somewhat, she sat on her bed and stared at the door.

She did not know if he would come back, but she would be waiting.

She must have fallen asleep staring at the chest, for the next moment someone was knocking lightly on the door.

"Who is it?" She could not keep the sound of fear from her voice.

" 'Tis Nettie, miss."

She leaped to her feet, ran across the room, stopped. "Are you alone?"

"Why yes, miss." She could hear the confusion in the servant girl's voice.

"One moment."

She pushed the chest out of the way, opened the door, and quickly pulled Nettie inside. The girl stared open-mouthed at her, then at the piece of furniture.

"Lord Alford," she explained, "came after me."

Nettie's eyes filled with tears, and then Agatha began to feel a reaction to her near-rape. Her eyes teared, and she huddled on the bed, rocking back and forth, wrapped completely in her misery. Nettie tried to comfort her, but there could be none for her that night.

The days passed all too speedily and it was soon the eve of her wedding. Agatha sat in the library, a cold cup of tea on the table beside the chair, a neglected book on her lap, Bruno asleep at her feet, and stared without seeing at the burning log in the fireplace. She had tried to read, and failed; tried to force her thoughts elsewhere, and failed again.

Tomorrow. Tomorrow I will be wed. To Rupert Norton, Lord Alford.

She shuddered.

She had thought—stupidly now, she realized—that somehow her father might change his mind, or she might be able to talk to him about it, but neither had happened and . . . tomorrow . . .

Well, she would have what she had desired for

years: She would no longer live in her father's house.

She would have cried, but no tears were left.

It was past late afternoon, almost evening, and her father had been gone since the night before. She knew he would be coming home later, in a rare mood. He would be drunk and loud, and he would laugh once more at her predicament.

She stood, no long able to tolerate idleness, and placed the book on the chair. She picked up a shawl, set it loosely about her shoulders, and went outside. Pausing on the terrace, she breathed deeply. The air was slightly cool, yet it felt good after the stuffiness of the library. Stone steps from the terrace led to a path of crushed white rock. She walked slowly along the path, studying the patterns. Flowerbeds made dazzling with violets and daffodils abutted the path and filled the air with their fragrance. She had made sure that the flowerbeds were planted in such a way that flowers in full bloom could be found there each month of the year.

The path ended with the rose garden. She passed an immense walnut tree whose limbs hung low over the other side of the wall. Long ago a bench had been built around the trunk of the tree, but that had been many years before and the paint on the bench was worn and peeling. She entered the rose garden proper now, and as she walked between the rows of green plants, she gazed sadly at them.

She would not see them bloom this year, not these roses which she had tended for so many years. She touched a leaf, tracing its delicate veins.

Perhaps she could plant a new garden at her husband's house. Her husband's house. How strange it sounded.

There was a rustling noise behind her but she ignored it. Birds come to find twigs for their nests, no doubt. She stepped past the sun dial, heard the rustling noise again, and turned.

Behind her stood a man dressed in grey breeches, grey coat, grey cloak. Agatha stared. Even more astonishing than the fact that this apparition was in the walled garden was the half-mask he wore over the upper part of his face.

He swept his plumed hat off with a courtly gesture she had not seen often in men of her acquaintance, and bowed low.

For a moment she could do nothing, then somewhat recovering her aplomb, she sank into a deep cursty. She looked up to find him regarding her intently.

"Good eve, Mistress Agatha."

His voice was richly modulated and deep, and the sound of it sent shivers down her spine. 'Tis the wind, she told herself, only that. Nothing more.

"How is it you know my name, sir? I must be thought ill-mannered for I have none to call you by."

"My identity shall be revealed to you soon enough, mistress."

She drew her eyebrows together. "How have you come to be in this garden, sir?"

"I climbed the wall."

"An arduous task to undertake for no reason."

"Ah, but 'twas for a very good reason. I wished

to see the fairest blossom in this wondrous rose garden."

Her cheeks warmed and reddened, and she wondered if he could see her blush in the twilight. She thought not. She hoped not.

"You flatter me unduly, sir," she replied.

"Flattery of beauty is never excessive. And 'tis not flattery, but the simple truth I speak."

She should order this intruder to leave, should call for a servant if he would not, should send him away at all costs. And yet . . . she was not at all displeased by his attention and by his kind words. She was frightened and lonely, and did not wish to think upon the morrow. His presence was . . . welcome.

"Do you stay long?"

"As long as the lady permits."

She half turned away to hide the emotions crossing her face. Never before had a man flirted with her in this manner, never before had a man expressed such interest in her. Never . . . until the eve of her wedding. It was a devilish irony. At the thought of her wedding, the memory of her recent encounter with Lord Alford returned. She shivered, drew the shawl up around her shoulders.

"You have not answered."

"Sir, 'twas not a question you posed for me."

"Indeed not, mistress, but only tell me you will not send me away."

He had stepped to her side now and taken one of her hands in his. He had removed his gauntlets, grey kid leather embroidered with fine silver silk, and it was his bare hand which clasped hers. Hers trembled ever so slightly. She stared at his hands.

Long, slender fingers. Gentle hands, yet strong. The hands of a gentleman. Shuddering, she remembered Alford's hands that had held her against her will.

This man is not like that, one part of her said.

He is a man, another answered, that is enough.

"Mistress?" He was watching her intently, seeming to sense her inner turmoil.

"I will not send you away."

"Good."

He released her hand and stepped back, and she was very sorry, for she wished his hand to hold hers once more.

"Your garden is quite extraordinary." He strolled to a plant which would bear deep crimson roses.

"Thank you. Willy and I have worked most diligently on it."

"Willy?"

"The son of our housekeeper."

"Ah. Your effort has paid off handsomely, though." He touched a stem.

"Be careful of the thorns!"

"Mistress, I am well aware of the dangers." His lips curved slightly, almost into a smile, and she thought that smiling did not come easily to him.

She wished she could see his face. His jaw was strong, his lips well-formed, though slightly thin. Yet how far better 'twas that, she thought, than the thick ones of Lord Alford. A moment later, she imagined the intruder's eyes, visible through the slits of the mask, were brown, but it was difficult to judge with so little light left.

"These will be exquisite when they bloom."

"Yes," and her tone was tinged with sadness. The blooms she would not see this year.

He glanced at her. "Is aught amiss?"

"No." She could not speak to a perfect stranger of her troubles, even though she was so burdened, even though he seemed so kind, so concerned.

"I do not think you are being truthful with me."

"Do you accuse me of lying, sir?"

"Not . . . lying," he replied evenly, "only of . . . dancing prettily around the truth."

She could find nothing to say to that. She sought the bench under the great tree and sat, carefully spreading her skirts. One booted foot swung up to rest next to her, and she stared at it a little uneasily. He was so close . . . too close. And she was too aware of his presence.

"I have disturbed you. I am sorry."

" 'Tis not you, sir," she said in as light a voice as she could manage, " 'tis another matter altogether. But I should not think of it while a gallant and handsome gentleman stands before me."

"Now you flatter me."

"Not at all."

"How do you imagine that I am handsome?"

"Why, when you have such well-formed hands and such a pleasant voice, you could be naught but handsome."

He stared at her for a moment, then began laughing. She smiled up at him.

"You are a cunning minx!"

"Pray sir, I am nothing of the sort."

"Do not deny the obvious, Mistress Agatha," he responded, his voice deepening. "With each denial you only appear more the minx."

She shut her mouth abruptly, then laughed. She had not felt so unburdened in months. With him she could almost forget tomorrow . . . almost.

"I think you are most unkind, for I am hardly a minx."

"If not a minx, then what are you?"

She thought for some seconds, then said: "A tabby cat, who delights in curling up before a fire."

"Ah, should I leave a saucer of cream to lure the tabby cat?"

She lowered her lashes and stared at her fingers, which were playing with the fringe of the shawl.

"Fool that I am! Pray forgive me, mistress, if I have said something which angers you."

" 'Tis nothing, sir. Be assured you have not angered me."

"Still, we shall speak of other matters." He turned away, stared up into the gnarled branches of the tree.

"Come, sir," she said, trying to recapture the light moment of before, "you have not said what it is that you would be."

Without hesitation, he replied: "A falcon."

"A bird of prey? Do you swoop down upon the unwary?"

"Sometimes." His words were cruel, but his smile reassured her.

For the first time she noticed that the light had completely fled from the sky, and the garden had been plunged into darkness.

"I must go," he said, as if he too realized how dark it was.

Disappointment filled her, but she forced herself to remember who she would be on the morrow. The thought brought no consolation, only sadness.

She stood, reluctantly.

Without warning he swept a strong arm around her waist. She put her hands to his chest to push him away, but before she could he was bending toward her, his lips touching hers. They were warm and gentle, and she could not resist him for this kiss bore not the slightest resemblance to Lord Alford's. Her lips yielded, and their breaths mingled for an instant. She pulled away, confused.

"Sir, this is most unseemly."

"Indeed, mistress, 'tis so."

She was trembling; one instant cold, the next hot. She touched her cheek with her hand, and the skin was warm, moist.

"I—I wish . . ." Her voice grew softer, then stopped.

"Yes, mistress, what is it you wish?"

"I wish I could see you again."

"Perhaps you will someday."

She half turned away, feeling the sadness come upon her again. "No," she said softly, painfully, " 'tis impossible, sir."

"Nothing is impossible."

He took her hand in his and for a moment stroked her fingers. His lips, feathersoft, touched the back of her hand.

He released her then, and sprang lightly up to grasp the top of the wall, swung one leg over, waved a jaunty hand, and jumped down, out of her sight.

For a moment she stood there, and from beyond the enclosure she heard the sound of a horse's harness. The horse wickered. A deep voice called out, and she heard hooves racing into the distance.

She could tolerate the suspense no longer. In one quick motion she stepped onto the bench, set one slippered foot in a bowl where three limbs met, and pulled herself upward into a precarious perch. She could just see over the wall, but disappointment filled her for all she could see was a glimpse of white fading down the road.

For some minutes she lingered there, remembering the touch of his lips. Slowly she eased herself down until she stood once more under the tree. She stared at the hand he had kissed, and a great spring of sadness welled up within her.

Tears fell as she left the garden.

PART II:

THE WEDDING

SIX

"SO, IT'S TO BE TOMORROW," the Squire said, staring blearily at her. He had returned, drunk, removing the possibility of even the small joy of quiet and privacy on the evening before her dreaded nuptials. "Never thought I'd see the day. Well, you'll be a married woman on the morrow, Aggie, and I'll tell you your new husband won't tolerate any nonsense. By God, I've seen I've been too lenient with you. Too lenient for your own damned good." He shook his head and headed in the direction of his study and more liquid refreshment.

Shortly thereafter she undressed and crawled into bed, still caught up in the strange melancholy caused by the visit from the man in the grey mask. Exhausted, she quickly fell into a deep sleep, only to dream of him. It seemed that they stood together in the garden again, but this time they were embracing as she had never consciously imagined embracing a man. For a timeless moment she was lost in her own shocking, thrilling response, when, suddenly, a band of masked men leaped out of the bushes toward them.

The man in grey spun around, sword in hand, but before he could thrust, a long darkly gleaming sword pierced him. She screamed as she watched him sink to the ground and the others fall upon him with swords and daggers. The man who had killed her stranger flung his mask aside and smiled at her.

It was Lord Alford.

She cried aloud, and sat up, trembling. Her cheeks were damp with tears and she could still see vividly the blood on his coat.

'Twas only a dream, she told herself. 'Twas not real. But another part of her mind questioned, could not dreams foresee the future?

She sank back into the bed, pulled the covers up, and closed her eyes, trying to sleep. Yet sleep did not come again that night, and the hours ticked away slowly as she waited for the dreaded morning.

When she finally arose it was still dark outside. She sat in the windowseat and watched as the sky slowly brightened. 'Twould not be a sunny day, for the air was thick with fog. She pushed open the window and heard faintly the sounds from the stable. The jingling of horses' harnesses and the clucking of the stablehands came to her with eerie clarity, and she shuddered as she stared at the dense fog .

She was still there when Nettie came in to draw

her bath. She rose from the seat and bathed for a long time, comforted somewhat by the warmth of the water, then set about to dress.

She took her time, not because she wished to be particularly careful but rather because she had no desire to hurry. When she finished, she lingered for a moment before the full-length mirror.

Pink and lavender and blue forget-me-nots intertwined on her white quilted petticoat. Over that was draped a full skirt of maroon velvet, hemmed with silver thread in the shape of scallops. Her bodice, of the same color and material as the skirt, was cut low, and bore ruched beige lace at the collar, and upon the sleeves. Her hair, which she had desired to wear unpowdered, had been curled, and gleamed from the many brushstrokes Nettie had given it. The maid had wound long strands of tiny pink pearls through her mistress's tresses, and tied at Agatha's throat a simple maroon velvet ribbon with a delicate tear-shaped pearl dangling from it. Agatha's gloves were made of plain kidskin, and she wore pink silk slippers.

She stared long at herself. She had to admit she did look well, far lovelier than ever before. There was, to be sure, an unnatural redness to her cheeks, as if she suffered from a fever, and her eyes were dark with tears, but the impression was one of vibrant beauty.

It was a beauty she hated. Alford, not the strange man in the garden, would be the one to see her this way. She bit her lip, trying to keep the tears back.

Nettie, seeing her mistress's expression in the mirror, began to cry, her hands over her eyes.

"Please, Nettie, do not weep. It is almost done."

Seeing that her sorrow only increased her mistress's agitation, the girl dabbed at her eyes with the corner of her apron, and at last blew her nose on the handkerchief Agatha had given her.

Agatha drew on a shawl of persian. There was no sense in further delaying her entrance belowstairs. She did not doubt that her father was already waiting impatiently for her outside. The wedding was set for ten; it was already half past eight. If she did not soon make an appearance, he would have no qualms about storming upstairs and dragging her out to the coach.

Sighing deeply, she retreated from the mirror.

"Will you not give me your best wishes, Nettie?"

The girl simply nodded, too overcome to speak.

Agatha left her bedchamber and went slowly down the stairs. Temple was standing in the front hall; his eyes and face expressed his sympathy for her.

"My father is outside?"

"Yes, Miss Agatha."

She headed toward the front door, but at that very moment it was thrown open, and her father, dressed in breeches and coat of brown velvet, strode in, a scowl on his face.

He went to the foot of the stairs and glared toward the second floor. "Damme, girl," he bellowed, not seeing her standing quietly in the shadow of the staircase, "when are you going to be ready? The horses are fairly chomping at the bit!"

"I'm already here, Father," she said softly.

"Eh?" He peered at her. 'What are you doing hiding there? Get outside."

She nodded and went past him, only looking once back at the house. Mrs. Howard stood next to Temple, and Nettie had come downstairs to wave good-bye.

She would come again to Grey's Manor, for the reception was to be held here, and she would have to return to pick up the trunks of clothing and other belongings Nettie had packed for her to take to her new home, but it would not be the same. She would not be the same.

The fog, still as thick now as it had been when she'd arisen, swirled around the coach. She could scarcely see the four horses in their harnesses, though she heard the ghostly sound of their stamping. The air was damp and chill, and she pulled her shawl closer around her.

Foster, the coachman, handed her into the carriage and she carefully arranged her skirts and petticoats. Outside, her father was yelling at Foster and Temple. Finally he climbed in, the door was shut, and he settled himself with a groan opposite her.

She saw the trio of servants by the doorway as a gust of wind swirled the fog away, and she raised her hand a little. Nettie returned the wave, and then covered her face with her hands once more. Mrs. Howard put a motherly arm around the distraught girl. Then the coach jerked forward with a bounce of its springs, and they were traveling down the carriage sweep, away from her home, away from her old life.

It was not a long drive to the church, and soon, too soon, they would be there, and *he* would be waiting and—she could think of that no longer.

When she glanced out the coach window, all was grey. Dark shapes, trees in the forest beyond, could be faintly seen. She closed her eyes for a moment, and leaned back.

She was aware of her father's scrutiny, but she could find nothing to say to him this morning. She had said everything already. Nothing was left. Nor would she think about the ceremony and what was to come later. Instead, she centered her thoughts on the visit of the gentleman the night before. She wondered, not for the first time, why he had come to see her that particular night. And again she wondered who he was, and why he chose to mask himself. Was it because he feared she might recognize him? Even if she did, what did that signify?

Grey, mistaking the smile on her lips, jovially patted her on the knee. "Ah, girl, you're being a good obedient daughter at long last. See how much better it is to be compliant, eh?" He shook his head. "Finally, after all these years of rebellion."

Wholly engrossed in her thoughts, she did not hear his words. In fact, she was deaf to all, and it was a matter of some minutes before she became aware of the sound of shouting coming from without the coach.

She opened her eyes and stared at her father, who was frowning with a mixture of anger and puzzlement. She glanced out the window and saw nothing but the swirling fog. There was a final shout, a pistol shot rang out, and the coach shuddered to a stop. Before either occupant could act, the door was thrown open and a man, his hat pulled low over his face and a cloth wrapped across his mouth and nose, stuck his head in and brandished an ugly-looking pistol at them.

Squire Grey, momentarily disconcerted, drew back, and in that brief moment the highwayman acted. He reached in, grabbed Agatha by the wrist, and dragged her from the coach. She struggled in his iron grip, but to no avail, and before she could open her mouth to protest, he had picked her up and thrown her across his saddle.

She landed with a thud on the hard leather, and finally found her voice. "Father, save me!"

"Come back here, you blackguard!" The squire started to emerge from the coach, when a second man, whom Agatha had not seen before, rode forward and kicked the door shut so that the squire had to fall back to avoid breaking his fingers. When her father tried to open the door, the second robber leveled a pistol at him. The squire shrank back.

Agatha tried to wiggle off the saddle, but suddenly felt a hand on her backside thrust her up again. She lashed out at him with her feet, but her legs were tangled in her skirt and she could scarcely move. Tears of frustration fell, unnoticed, down her cheeks. She lunged out with one hand, trying to reach the man. He simply pushed her hand away, swung up into the saddle, and picked up his reins. His companion edged away from the coach door, leaned over and slapped the rump of the lead carriage horse, fired a shot into the air, and the frightened animals bolted. The squire stuck his head out the window of the jouncing coach and shook his fist at them as he was carried away.

"Cowards—come back with my property!" he

bellowed. "When I catch up with you two, you'll be ridin' the three-legged mare!"

The two riders wasted no time listening to the squire's impotent threats. As soon as the panicked coach horses had leaped forward, snorting and plunging, the highwaymen wheeled their mounts around, taking off at a gallop across the fields, heading away from the road.

Agatha, still stunned from this turn of events, was too baffled by the strange performance to be scared. She could not imagine why anyone would wish to abduct her. Perhaps they were after money; but if they were, would they not have robbed her father of his purse and his rings? Or were these men simply planning to kill her when they reached their destination?

But why wait until then? It made little sense.

Yet the man who had thrown her up into the saddle had not been rough. Indeed, his touch had been quite gentle. . . .

As the questions piled up, her courage increased. She could not let them simply abduct her. She would fight them. She would try to escape!

Unfortunately, her ignoble position, draped over the saddle like a sack of flour, gave her little opportunity for impetuous action. Her ribs ached, her arms were flopping about, and no doubt her skirt was beyond repair.

She tried to lift her head, and saw for a moment the fog gusting by and beyond it what seemed to be tiny golden lights dancing in the mist, but her captor gently pushed her face toward the ground again. From this vantage point, she had a dizzying view of the ground speeding by and the horse's legs moving almost in a blur. Too, the saddle jounced constantly, rubbing against her stomach, and she was becoming ill from the motion.

Long minutes had passed since they had surprised the coach, and yet she heard no signs of pursuit. Even if Foster had been able to bring the horses quickly down to a walk, she thought, more time would have been lost unharnessing one of the horses for her father to ride. Perhaps he would wait until he reached the church, not far from where she had been abducted.

She could see the roots and trunks of large trees, knew they had reached the woods. The horses slowed now to a trot. She heard the distant call of a bird, nothing else, for the two riders did not speak to one another. She thought that odd. After a while the horses were urged to a canter, and then a gallop, and from the woods they entered the fens.

"Who are you?" she yelled over the sound of the horses' hooves, no longer able to maintain her silence. Then: "Help me!" she cried, hoping someone close by would hear and come to her aid.

But all her protest earned her was having her face pressed against the horse's sweaty shoulder. She shook her head, and the man drew his hand away so that she could raise up slightly to draw in fresh air.

Who were these men? she wondered, not for the first time. Both wore nondescript clothing that had seen better days, and low-slung hats and masks so she could not mark their faces.

She did not think their escape had been in a straight line. They had probably jigged and jagged through the woods in an effort to confuse any followers. Which meant, she realized bleakly, there would be little chance for her father to find her.

Perhaps the highwaymen sought to ransom her. The well-appointed coach had bespoken wealth, and perhaps in this manner they sought to gain a greater sum of money than her father would ordinarily carry on his person.

Perhaps.

And perhaps—her mind returned to a chilling thought—they would simply kill her.

The horses continued their grueling pace, and when they finally stopped, hours later, the bandits merely changed horses at a cottage, tossed her in front of the first man again, and were once more off across the fog-ridden fields.

Finally, when the fog had lifted a little and the sun could be seen as a dim orb in the grey sky, they reached a small cottage in the woods, set well back from any path. The riders stopped the horses and jumped down. The first man reached up and, lifting her off the saddle, carefully set her on her feet. She stumbled, unsteady after so many hours of being slung across the saddle, and grabbed his arm for support. Then, realizing what she had done, she shook his hand away.

His hand shot out to hold tightly onto her, preventing any sudden dashes into the woods, and he led her into the well-concealed cottage. There, in a large room, a kind-faced woman of ample proportions tended a fire. The woman stood up and grinned cheerfully as the trio entered. Her captor dropped her hand and went outside with the other man, and the two women were left alone.

Agatha glanced around curiously. There was just the single room with whitewashed walls, as far as she could see, though, surprisingly, it was clean. Sparsely furnished with a cot, table, and chair, it was lit by a full dozen or more white candles.

Forgetting her vow to flee, and failing that, fight, Agatha drew herself up proudly. Very aware of the dirt on her gloves and skirt, and of her hair straggling about her face, she rounded on the servant, her hands on her hips. In her most frosty voice she announced, "I am the daughter of Squire Grey. I demand to be told the meaning of this. Why have I been abducted? Where am I? And when shall I be restored to my father?"

The woman, not in the least impressed by Agatha's words or attitude, merely shook her head and continued smiling. For a long uneasy moment, Agatha wondered if the woman were simple-minded. Then the woman spoke.

"It's not for me to say, dearie. You'll learn soon enough, I warrant." She tossed a long twig into the fire, watched as it was consumed by flames.

"I am not your 'dearie,' " Agatha snapped, "and you will kindly refrain from being so familiar with me." Again the woman did not seem put into her place. It was disconcerting, for the woman did seem to be some sort of servant.

Well, she couldn't just stand here, Agatha thought. Without speaking again, she ran lightly, aware that she was still shaking from her ordeal, to the single window in the opposite wall, but it was set far up in the wall and was, she judged, too small for her to crawl through, anyway.

She whirled as the door opened at that moment

and a tall man entered the room. He wore grey clothing, and a mask concealing the upper portion of his face.

Taken aback, she could only stare for a long moment. It was her twilight visitor! What was he doing here? Had he come to rescue her? What providence had allowed his path to cross hers once more?

She rushed to him and looked beseechingly up. "Please, sir, you must save me—return me to my father before that highwayman comes back!"

He chuckled, and leaned over to wipe a smudge off her nose.

"Return you, my dear Agatha? I do not think it likely—for you see, I plan to marry you myself!"

SEVEN

"MARRY ME?" SHE SAID, STARING in astonishment at the man.

"Why yes," he replied as though there could be nothing more natural. He conferred a moment in a low voice with the other woman, then turned back to Agatha.

"Come here."

Anger replaced confusion. "I will not do your bidding, sir!"

"Indeed? I think you shall."

Before he could continue, they were joined by a second man attired in black and looking remarkably like a minister. A moment later he was followed by a well-dressed gentleman, also in a mask—no doubt, she thought, the man who had aided in her abduction.

The grey-clad man took her by the hand and led her to the fireplace. He tucked her hand firmly through his arm. She struggled, but could not, without causing a great scene, recover her hand.

The minister seemed not to be aware of her unwillingness and drew a small black book from a pocket. He opened it to a marked place and peered over the book at the man in grey, who nodded. He cleared his throat and began reading in a ponderous tone.

"Dearly beloved——"

"I will not marry this man, this—this ruffian, this robber, this——"

"Hush," the grey-clad man admonished in his deep voice, "so that the good parson might continue."

She could not—would not—be married to a man she did not know. With all her strength she twisted away, catching him unaware, and shot toward the door, but her abductor quickly followed, grasped her by the shoulders, and returned her to the spot in front of the minister. The minister, who had never lifted his eyes during this episode, began reading aloud once more.

She tried to get free again, but this time the man was prepared and would not let go of her hand. Finally she ceased her struggles and stood, dazed, listening to the words of the wedding ceremony.

In a matter of minutes it was finished.

She was married. To a man whom she did not know.

She had not even been asked if she would take this man as her lawfully wedded husband. Instead, the minister had looked to the serving woman, who had answered in her stead.

The second man drew out a bag of coins, which he pressed into the waiting hand of the minister. The two men left, quickly followed by the servant.

She stared at the grey-clad man, who walked to the table. He poured wine into two glasses.

Why? Why had he done this? It was true she had heard of certain men, rakes and profligates, who would upon occasion abduct heiresses to marry them for their fortunes. Surely this was not what had happened. Yet what other explanation was there?

"A glass of wine, my dear?" he offered.

She started to refuse, realized she did truly need a glass of wine, and nodded. He handed one to her, and raised his in a toast.

"To us, and our long life together."

She could not drink, even though her lips felt parched. "Why?" she asked numbly, her throat dry. When he did not answer, she swallowed some of the wine and let the cool liquid soothe her throat. It filled her, too, with new courage. She drew herself up proudly and raised her chin defiantly. "I demand to be taken home at once. You have no right to do this!"

"Return you?" he asked, staring into the depths of his glass. "To what, Agatha? To Alford—who wants to use you as a brood mare and cares only for your inheritance? Return you? To your brutal, uncaring father?" He shook his head, a rueful gesture. "No, my dear, I shall not return you, and I think you will soon come to thank me."

"Never!" And she threw the contents of her glass into his face.

Wine dripped down his mask onto the lower

part of his face, and his smile faded. He removed a handkerchief from his pocket and mopped at the liquid. He stared at the stained material for a minute, then tossed the handkerchief aside.

He stepped toward her, and she backed away. He reached to take her into his arms, but she raised her hand and slapped him hard.

"Get away from me." She backed away until a chair blocked her retreat. She was breathing hard from her anger and fear, and she roughly pushed back a wisp of hair fluttering in front of her eyes.

Surely he was some sort of monster—not only to wear this mask, but to have stolen her on her wedding day. It mattered little now that she had not cared to marry Lord Alford. That was not the issue in question.

She watched his eyes behind the slits, seeking a clue to his behavior, and was surprised to see a look of sadness in those brown depths. She quickly suppressed any sympathy. He was, after all, a terrible man for having forced her to marry him.

When he spoke again, his voice had changed, grown lower and less spirited.

"It will take some time, Agatha, but you will thank me in the end. Now come."

She had no choice but to follow him outside to a waiting large and expensively attired carriage. Four matching coal-black horses in silver trappings pulled it. She had not heard its arrival, so she assumed it must have quietly stopped in front of the cottage during the bogus ceremony.

She glanced around, but could not tell her location from what she saw. She was in the woods, but where, she had no idea. She saw no sign of the other three. It was almost as though they had never been there. But she knew they had.

She permitted herself to be handed into the coach, and he followed her, closing the door and instructing the coachman to drive on.

" 'Tis a short way to our home," he said.

She remained silent, looking out the window as trees and bushes flashed by. Her hands, tightly clasped in her lap, revealed the turmoil and confusion within her. She wrinkled her brow, deep in bewildering thought.

She was married.

She had set out this morning in her father's coach to be married, and by afternoon she had been married. But the man who had sought her hand was not beside her now. No longer would she have to fear Alford's brutality.

Yet that thought little comforted her. She was still not free, still married—and to a complete stranger.

"Falcon's Hall lies straight ahead," her new husband was saying, "beyond those trees." He pointed, and she listlessly stared in the direction he indicated. "It's a very old house, the oldest part being well over five hundred years old."

In the gathering twilight she saw tall brick chimneys rising above the trees, and the next moment the carriage swung past the trees and she could clearly see Falcon's Hall. What she saw filled her with dismay.

The house's size alone daunted her, for even from this extreme distance she sensed its immenseness. Three stories high, it had legions of windows in gables and peaks, and wing after wing.

All styles of architecture were here, as if the house had been added to, year after year, whim by whim.

"My ancestors," he added ruefully, noting her expression, "displayed little taste when it came to architecture. They did, however, build with great enthusiasm."

She nodded agreement. She had already identified what appeared to be a tower of the old times, saw one section possessing a distinct Tudor flavor, and saw another part that seemed to have been worked upon by an Italian architect of the classical school.

That last caused her to smile a little. He noted her expression and the serious set to his face relaxed somewhat.

"What of your mask, sir?" she inquired in a low tone. "Will you always wear it before me?"

"This?" He touched the grey mask. "Good God no! I'd completely forgotten it." So saying, he untied the string and drew the mask away from his face.

In the dying light of the day, she stared up into her husband's face, stared and uttered a small gasp of horror as she recognized the ugly white scar on his forehead and the man who bore it.

It was the Viscount of Drummond.

"My lady," he said, a mocking tone to his voice, and kissed her hand.

She was so stunned by the revelation of his identity that she did not attempt to draw her hand away from his, and so they continued until the carriage swung up the drive and at last rolled to a stop. The coachman sprang lightly from the box onto the ground and opened the door. She drew her hand away from Drummond's, stepped out, and the servant carefully handed her down. As her foot touched the bottommost step, she heard applause.

Startled, she looked up to find the servants of Falcon's Hall had assembled to await the master and the new mistress. In the torchlight she could see they were all smiling.

This did not accord with her notion of Drummond as a blackguard, for surely servants would not be loyal to someone cruel and unprincipled. Yet without exception they appeared unfeignedly happy for their master.

Confused, she shook her head a little. He stepped down after her and tucked her arm through his, and they walked down the line of the servants. She was glad they could not clearly see her—nor her torn raiment—in the shadows of the early evening.

Toward the end of the long line she spotted the kind-faced woman who had served as a witness at the ceremony. The woman, her face reddening slightly, bobbed a curtsy.

"Mrs. Gordon, my—our—housekeeper," he murmured to Agatha.

She greeted the woman with a slight nod of her head, and the woman beamed.

All of the servants she saw were well-dressed and healthy and seemed not at all displeased with their service. She well remembered the servants at her father's house. None of them would have lined up to applaud his new wife. Most perplexing.

She sneaked a glance at Drummond, saw his lips had twitched into a faint smile. The heavy gloom she had heretofore seen settled on his face had vanished, and charitably she thought he looked very handsome, despite the cruel-looking scar.

Darkness had fallen now, and a footman, resplendent in grey and black livery, opened the front door of Falcon's Hall as Drummond helped her up the steps.

Italian tile graced the floor of the immense entryway and the hallway leading from it, while overhead a five-tiered crystal chandelier, on which dozens of candles flickered, burned brightly. She stepped into the hall. To her left sat a marble-topped console table, its ornate sides walnut and gilt, and above it hung a square mirror.

She caught a glimpse of herself before they moved on. She did not look quite as bad as she had thought. Still, she would be relieved to change from her travel-stained clothes.

To her right were double doors paneled in the muted colors of a pastoral scene. She gazed at them questioningly.

"One of the salons," he explained.

At the end of the hall a broad staircase wound its way to the second floor. He escorted her down the hall to another door on the right, and opened it for her. She proceeded him and studied this salon. Its dominant color was green. The oriental carpet was green and blue, and showed a great fierce dragon. On the walls hung French tapestries from the sixteenth century. A fire roared cheerfully in the marble fireplace, so huge an ox could have easily been roasted within its confines. Several high-backed chairs and settees, all decorated in muted shades of green and gold, were grouped before the fireplace. Beyond them was a low table, inlaid with mother-of-pearl and brass.

She liked the room at once, recognizing the refined taste which had gone into its arrangement, and appreciating its calming influence. And yet . . . yet this was the home—her home now—of a man who had brutally abducted her, had forced her to marry him.

She could not reconcile the two aspects of his character, and perplexed, she pushed away the puzzle for the moment. Drawing away from him, she crossed to the fireplace to hold out her hands to the flames, and for the first time it occurred to her she was cold and tired and not a little hungry.

Something of this must have been relayed in her face for he said kindly, "I will have your maid show you to your room, my dear. There you may rest for a while and change. I will expect you to rejoin me for dinner."

"I have no belongings," she pointed out coldly, suddenly remembering her sad situation.

"I have provided for that contingency, Agatha."

Somehow, she was not surprised by this revelation. She continued to rub her hands together.

"Ah, here is Holly now."

He nodded at a young girl who had just entered. She possessed bright yellow hair and large blue eyes, and had a disarming air to her. She bobbed a sprightly curtsy to him and then to Agatha, then folded her hands in front of her starched apron.

"Holly, this is your new mistress, Lady Drummond."

"Ohhh," the girl breathed, staring wide-eyed at her, "she's beautiful!"

Agatha tried not to smile, but could not completely refrain.

"You must show Lady Drummond to her rooms now, for she is quite tired."

"Yes, my lord."

She bobbed another curtsy and waited for Agatha. Agatha cooly nodded toward Drummond, then took her leave. He did not again mention dinner.

The girl talked the entire time it took them to go up the stairs and down the hallway of the second floor. By that time Agatha had learned what was to be found on each floor, how large and marvelous Falcon's Hall was, and how truly advanced was my lord's thinking, for he had even had designed indoor bathing rooms—could my lady fathom that!—and there was a great marble tub with running water,—if one did not mind a cold bath!

When she finally reached her rooms, Agatha felt as if she were intimately acquainted already with the house, and once more tried not to smile. But her maid's good spirits were far too infectious, and she failed.

Holly paused in the midst of her one-sided conversation, dramatically threw open a door, and Agatha stared, wonderstruck.

Her rooms were a suite at the end of the hall, and the first room she entered was a private sitting room which faced the front of the house. On its wooden floors lay a thick carpet of dusky rose. The walls had been painted a matching color. The tall mirror directly across from the door, and the other accents of candlelabra and sconces, were of highly polished silver.

The furniture was constructed of walnut, fragile in appearance, and had obviously been selected with some consideration.

But it was not any of these fine details which first drew her notice. What commanded her attention was the roses. Roses in vases and bowls were everywhere, an overwhelming profusion of color and scent. She entered the room and stared, bewildered, at the flowers. Crimson and pink, coral, sunshine yellow and white, all the hues, delicate to dazzling, were represented, and the room was thick with the sweet perfume.

She stepped to a low table and stroked the velvet soft petals of a bloodred rose.

"Who did this?" she asked, puzzled.

"Why, his lordship, Lady Drummond," Holly responded cheerfully. She grinned at her mistress.

And at that moment Agatha understood something somewhat unnerving. For, if her father had been wealthy, then her husband was as rich as a prince. It was not yet the time for roses to bloom, and these extravagant flowers could only have been grown by the most costly of methods: a hothouse.

And if he possessed a sizable fortune, he need not be abducting and marrying an heiress, which meant—— She frowned. What did it mean?

Holly led her farther into the room. "Here, now, your ladyship, you must be fatigued. I've run a bath for you, and you can soak as long as you wish."

The girl helped her from her travel-stained clothing and showed her into the bathing room, all white marble. She stepped into the tub filled with warm water, slid under its depths, and felt the aches easing from her body. The water was fragrant with cinnamon, and the soap was a very fine, imported one.

Mirrors lined one end of the room, and she stared at herself, then blinked sleepily. The ordeal of her day had suddenly overtaken her, and she felt so very tired, so very sleepy. She mustn't fall asleep, she told herself, for she might drown, and yet she could scarcely keep her eyes open. She yawned, splashed a little in the comforting water, and sighed.

She could hear Holly humming a lively air as she selected her mistress's clothing in the dressing room. She was a good girl, Agatha thought, and hoped she would not miss Nettie as much as she had dreaded. She stirred in the fragrant water, shifting so that her back could soak. She wiggled her toes and sighed, unable to feel as unhappy as she knew she should. Certainly the servants seemed pleasant; and certainly her rooms were more than adequate; and certainly she would live a life she had not imagined in her wildest dreams.

With a sudden clarity she realized her future did not seem as dreadful as it had two hours earlier. If she did not love her husband, well, had she loved the man to whom she had been betrothed? She shook her head sleepily. Of course not. This man, even though he had abducted her from her father's coach, was much more polite and more of a gentleman than Alford.

And more handsome.

She smiled faintly, stretched languidly, yawned, closed her eyes, and was soon claimed by sleep.

"Ah, Paul, you did come back."

Drummond had entered his study to find Paul Sterling there. He nodded, watching as Sterling stirred within the depths of the chair, stretched, and stood. He was not as tall a man, nor as solidly handsome as Drummond, but his face was more than passing pleasant to gaze upon, his hair a bright shade of light brown, and his hazel eyes normally holding a merry look in them. In mood he was quite the opposite of the somber Drummond. Presently, though, Sterling was frowning, his mouth turned down in what Drummond thought was a most unbecoming expression for his friend, and his eyes were not at all merry. Absently, he smoothed a fold in his moss-green coat.

"Did I wake you?"

"No, no, not at all. Of course, I returned, Richard. Where else should I have gone? Too," he said, sighing deeply in feigned exasperation, "I confess that I am a fool and possessed a rather lively curiosity to see if the bridal coach arrived safely. From her expression in the cottage I would have thought the bride would have gladly throttled you."

"Well, as you can see, we arrived without incident." Drummond stepped over to a table. "Care for a drink?"

"Yes, thank you." Sterling, accepting the glass, stared at its contents for a moment, then said: "I had reservations about leaving the two of you alone.

I thought surely she would try to bolt the minute we left."

Drummond slowly sipped his wine. "So did I. It came as a great surprise that she did not. She did, however, ring a fine peal over me." He returned to stand in front of the fireplace. Sterling followed.

"Do you regret your—er—actions?"

"Not at all." He crossed to the fireplace and stood in front of it, facing his friend. "I will still maintain that what I did was completely necessary."

Sterling shook his head, stared thoughtfully at Drummond. "I don't know. Seems to me there could have been another way."

"No," Drummond said shortly. "There was none. Not for my purposes."

"If her father should find out . . ."

"I trust he will not."

"Well, damme, *I* won't be telling him," Sterling said, "so there's no fear 'pon that head. You know I wouldn't go near the animal, after all the tales I've heard." He sipped his drink. "They are not exaggerations?"

Drummond laughed, a brusque sound. "No." He glanced at the fire for a moment, his brows drawn together in a frown, then back at his friend.

"What of the servants? A loose mouth there——"

"Fear not for their indiscretions. There will be none. You know my help is loyal."

"Ah yes. Would that all servants were so devoted."

"Would that all masters were willing to treat their servants as people."

"True, true."

"Will you stay for dinner?"

"Ah, thank you, but I think not. I should soon

be on my way. Perhaps another time . . . when your lady is more settled."

"Very well."

They talked for a few minutes more while Sterling finished his drink. Then, refusing a second glass, he shook hands with the viscount and left the study.

Drummond regarded the greedy flames lapping along the log as he finished his wine. He poured another glass and drank it quickly, his thoughts solely of the woman abovestairs, the woman he had married.

He *had* done what was right. That he knew without question.

Yet a lingering doubt remained, a doubt that nothing good could come of this match, that nothing good would come of a man who had robbed another of his bride on the precise day of the wedding. That nothing good could come of *his* marrying the girl.

He shrugged with seeming indifference, and continued his sober contemplation of the flames. This was hardly the worst of his crimes.

EIGHT

WHEN SHE WOKE THE WATER was icy cold. She shivered, raised up from her reclining position, lathered herself with the soap, rinsed, and leaped from the tub to rub dry. Holly scratched at the door at that moment.

"Are you ready, your ladyship?"

"Yes, Holly." Wrapped in the linen she'd used to towel herself, she opened the door and stepped out into the dressing room. She shivered slightly, and the maid quickly slipped a robe across her mistress's shoulders. Agatha belted the robe, then padded over to the wardrobe to see what her maid had selected for her to wear that evening.

She had slept well, despite being in the tub, and she wondered how long she had been there. Certainly she was feeling refreshed. She had washed away the soil of her unorthodox journey, and she must admit, albeit somewhat reluctantly, she was feeling quite comfortable at present.

"I picked the sapphire bodice and skirt, your ladyship," the girl said. She held it up for Agatha's inspection.

Agatha nodded, pleased with her maid's selection. " 'Tis a fine choice."

Holly smiled broadly.

The maid hung up the robe Agatha handed to her, then helped her mistress into the corset. The chemise and a quilted petticoat quickly followed.

"Do you have family here?" Agatha asked as Holly buttoned her bodice. Why else would someone as charming and hardworking as this girl stay with such a creature as her husband?

"Oh yes, your ladyship. We all work for my lord and have for quite some time, y'know. My father is the gamekeeper for my lord, and my brother, Tom, helps him. My youngest brother, Ben, takes care of my lord's favorite horse. There, your ladyship, how's that?" She hardly gave Agatha time for more than a brief nod. "My uncle works for a duke, and has gone 'round the world with him. Can you imagine that, your ladyship? Why," she continued, her eyes growing dreamy, "I would surely like to travel to exotic places. Wouldn't you, your ladyship?" Agatha opened her mouth. "But I don't know about that. My family, well, it's always been in service, you see. Still, who's to say about the future. Isn't that right, your ladyship?" she asked cheerfully.

Agatha's restrained smile widened. "Yes, 'tis true enough, Holly." The sapphire of her outfit made her skin appear all the more translucent. She fingered the material. Silk, and costly by any measure. "Who had these clothes made, Holly?"

"Why his lordship did, your ladyship." Her expression clearly implied she was quite surprised at my lady's question.

"Oh."

"He personally selected all the materials. Took quite an interest in it, he did, your ladyship. He has right good taste, y'know, not like some. Just because a body's born above the salt doesn't mean they have good taste, begging your pardon, my lady. It's true, to be sure."

Amused, Agatha said, "I have little doubt of that." She slid her feet into matching silk slippers. She flexed her foot, and light glinted off the diamond buckle.

Holly turned away to straighten up.

"These clothes must have been long in the making."

"Oh, but your ladyship has a personal dressmaker. Straight from France, she is. A bit uppity, if you ask me, your ladyship."

"Holly, please do not call me 'your ladyship.' "

"It's your title, your ladyship."

"Yes, I know, but . . . well, I am not yet accustomed to it. Could you not call me 'ma'm,' or 'mum'?"

"Why, yes, your l—ma'm, I could indeed." Holly grinned, and swiped some imagined dust off the satin bows upon a pair of slippers.

The viscount, Agatha thought, had been most thorough in his selection of her trousseau. She glanced at the clothes in the wardrobe, then opened various drawers of a tall chest standing nearby to see what they contained. Scarves, shawls, mob caps, gloves—all of the finest materials, the latest styles.

Everything the wife of a viscount could want—or possibly need. It would seem no cost had been spared.

"Will you be wearing jewelry tonight, your l—ma'm?"

"What selection do I have, Holly? I was not . . . able . . . to bring any of mine with me." She did not think the girl caught the irony in her voice.

Holly turned back from the wardrobe with an immense jewel case in her arms. She staggered over to a table, dropped the case on its surface, and opened the lid. Agatha gasped as she stared at the contents carefully placed on the velvet lining.

Diamonds and pearls and sapphires, rubies and gold. More gems than she had ever seen—nay, imagined—in her life. She reached out, hesitantly touched the pendants and earrings, the rings and necklaces, with wonder, as though expecting them to disappear any moment.

"Most of it's his mother's," Holly explained in a soft voice. "She died two years ago, after—well, she just died—and it was her fondest wish, ma'm, that these went to her son's wife."

His mother's . . . her mother's . . . Suddenly a great sadness welled up in her as she thought of all of her mother's belongings that she had left behind. She doubted she would ever be able to recover them. They were lost to her forever. No doubt her father would destroy them now.

"Is something amiss, ma'm?" the girl asked, her face taking on a concerned look.

"No," Agatha replied slowly, "no, 'tis nothing."

"What is your wish, ma'm?"

Her wish? Her wish was to return home. To be

wed to a man of her choosing. To be rid of the unhappiness that had cloaked her. For now there could be none of this.

"I shall wear the diamond and sapphire necklace," she announced, pointing to an exquisitely delicate fabrication toward the front of the case.

Holly placed it against her throat and latched it. Then she set about adding the finishing touches to Agatha's hairdo. In the case she found matching diamond and sapphire pins and put them neatly in her mistress's hair. Agatha walked to the mirror and when she turned her head, the diamonds sparkled with the candlelight, and it seemed as if tiny stars gleamed in her hair.

"How do I look?"

"Oh, just beautiful," Holly breathed. "Like a princess."

She laughed, a sad little laugh. There could be no further delay. "Now where may I find his lordship?"

"In the dining parlor, ma'm. It's on the first floor, back on the left behind the stairs. I could show you if you like."

"Thank you, but no, Holly. I shall manage to find it on my own."

Within a matter of a few minutes she found the dining parlor. A footman opened the door for her and announced her.

The viscount stood staring at her for a moment, as though suspended in time, then crossed the room in three long strides and bowed low over her proffered hand.

"Madame, you are most beautiful tonight."

"Thank you, my lord."

He escorted her to her place at one end of the table, and then returned to his, opposite hers. The table was not long, for it was designed for intimate dinners of fewer than five couples, and for that small blessing she was pleased. A large table, which would have isolated her, would have made her all the more unhappy. The table was agleam with shining silverware and polished china, and in the center stood a Chinese ebony vase filled with crimson roses.

She said nothing as a second footman began serving the beef, roasted chickens, and succulent duckling. A third servant filled their goblets with a rich dark wine.

She was all too aware of her husband's dark eyes upon her, but she suddenly felt too shy to lift her own eyes and meet his steady gaze. Indeed, when she could look at him, it seemed all she could stare at was the scar. How had he come by the disfiguring mark? What had he done to merit such hideous punishment? Or, perhaps, was it the outward legacy of the sorrow she had glimpsed in his eyes?

"Are you rested now, my dear?"

"Yes, thank you."

"The clothes are to your liking?"

"Yes, thank you."

"You find your rooms are quite sufficient?"

"Yes, thank you."

"Holly serves you well?"

"Quite well, my lord."

He set his knife down with a clatter on his plate, and she glanced up, startled.

"Have you nothing to say to me, Agatha?"

"No, my lord, I have very little to say to you."

"I see." He narrowed his eyes, picked the knife up once more, and sliced through the roast beef.

For a few minutes there was no further conversation, then: "I thought perhaps we could go riding tomorrow." The tone of his voice gave her no hint of his feelings.

"If you so desire, my lord."

He stared into his glass, slowly swirling its contents. "You could select your horse in the stable first."

"As you wish."

"My friend, Paul Sterling, comes to dine with us 'pon the morrow. He is a good soul, full of merriment. I think you will enjoy his company."

She smiled politely.

He tapped his fingers upon the linen tablecloth, looking not at all pleased.

"I wish you to be happy, Agatha. I have your best wishes at heart."

"Yes."

The one word was filled with irony, and she noticed he looked away then.

They finished their first and second courses in silence, the only sound being the click of plates as the footmen removed them from the table.

"Agatha."

"Yes, my lord?" She looked up from the dissection of her fruit tart.

"Could you not now call me by my given name?"

She shook her head. "No, my lord, I do not find it possible." She met his gaze steadily. "I think you well know the reason why." She glanced down, and returned to her tart.

When the footman had removed the last of the dinner plates and had set plates of sliced fruit and cheeses in front of them, Agatha paused, playing delicately with a piece of cheese.

"I am free to come and go about the house?"

"Yes, excepting that wing which is locked. I would wish you do not go there."

"Outside?"

"You may not leave the grounds without a servant or myself riding with you."

"Then I am a prisoner."

"No, not a——"

"Yes. A prisoner. You are my jailkeeper. And this house, as beautiful as it is inside, is my prison. Forgive me, my lord. I fear I must excuse myself. I find I have a headache." A footman leaped quickly to pull her chair out for her. Drummond stood as she left, but she did not look back.

Returning to her rooms, she found them quiet, for Holly had already left. She crossed to the window in the sitting room and looked out. Because it was quite dark, she saw only the blacker shape of a tree outside. A branch swung back and forth. The wind was blowing, and she had not even heard it.

She was thankful she would not have to listen now to Holly's chatter, for as entertaining as she had found it earlier, she wished to be by herself this night. The dinner had not been too unpleasant, but when she had discovered she was a virtual prisoner, all her unhappiness had returned. She drew in a deep breath, almost a sob, and turned away from the window. She undressed quickly, pulled on a soft nightgown, and crawled into the bed. It was cold for a few minutes, but when she had warmed the sheets, she snuggled down and closed her eyes. She would rest, try not to think any more tonight, and perhaps in the morning, things would not appear as bad.

The strain of the day quickly took its toll, and she slipped into sleep, undisturbed even by dreams, until she heard a quiet *snick* some time later.

Her eyes flew open. What was that sound? 'Twas simply the wind, she reassured herself, or the sounds of an unfamiliar house.

Something made a slight rustling on the carpet.

She sat bolt upright, with the covers pulled up to her chin. She frowned. It could not be Holly, for surely the girl would have knocked before entering. Too, she thought it unlikely that the maid could move so stealthily. Then she remembered the night when Lord Alford had tried to force himself upon her.

Her heart was pounding quickly, and she was trembling slightly. Her mouth was dry.

"Who goes there?"

A slight breath, something or someone brushing against her bed, and then the person sat down.

"It is I, Agatha."

Him.

"Oh." She drew in a deep breath.

"Did I frighten you?"

"Of course not." She pushed the hair out of her eyes, but could only make out a faint shadow in a room black with night.

"I see." She thought his tone held amusement, but she could not be sure.

"What are you doing here?"

There was a moment's hesitation, then: "It is our wedding night, Agatha."

Their wedding night. How stupid she had been to forget, to not even consider. It was his right by law to come to her, to take what was his—what is *mine*! one part of her cried out silently—to make her his wife in body as well as name.

"No," she said.

"Agatha, please reconsider."

"No."

"My love——"

"I am not your love," she responded harshly.

"No, perhaps not, but you are my wife."

She moved away from where he sat to the other side of the large bed. She licked her lips. She would not—could not—admit the fear she felt. He was a man, larger than she, stronger; he could take by force what she would not surrender.

"Agatha," he murmured. "I will not hurt you. Only let me hold you."

She said nothing. Her breathing rasped in the darkness.

"I promise I shall not touch you in that manner until you so desire."

"Promise?" She laughed with no humor. "You give your word?"

"Yes."

"The word of a blackguard, a thieving scoundrel who steals girls away from their family, who——"

"Once!"

"What?"

"You talk as though I make a common practice of . . . stealing . . . maidens."

"I did not know if I were the first," she replied stiffly.

"Yes, my dear. You are the first—you will be the only."

Suddenly he reached across the space between them. She tried to rise from the bed, but caught her legs in the sheets and fell back. She opened her mouth to scream, but he softly placed his hand across her mouth.

"Please," he whispered, "there is no need to cry out."

She struggled in his arms, but to no avail. His grip on her was firm, yet strangely gentle. He removed his hand and touched her cheek. She jerked her face to one side.

"I will not hurt you. I give you that promise. That is my word as a gentleman, and though you do not believe me to be one, I am."

One of his hands brushed her shoulder and under the thin material she shrank away from him.

"Do you not remember our kiss in the garden?"

"Yes." She did. And could not associate that intriguing man with this villain.

"Then could you not kiss me again?"

"No."

"Why not?"

"That was different. It was . . . special. This is . . . cruel."

"Cruel? But I have done nothing to you!" he cried.

"You have stolen me from my family," she said angrily.

"Stolen you yes, and saved you as well."

"So you have alleged before, my lord, and yet I do not believe you."

"Would Lord Alford have played the loving husband with you? The night of your father's party he talked with Lord Ruthen after you left, saying he would break your spirit. It was Alford's greatest desire that he should quickly get you with child. He also expressed a hope that you would die in childbirth so that your inheritance might be his at once."

It was too hideous . . . even to believe of the loathed Lord Alford. She would not believe it; it could not be true. "No."

"Yes. I do not lie. He would have used you ill, Agatha, as your father did all these years. Is that what you want?"

"No!"

"I will not abuse you, my dear. It would please me much if you would grow to like me. It is my fondest hope that someday you could love me, but I do not demand it of you. I would care for you, and look after you, find in you a true companion . . . a friend . . . a lover."

She squeezed her eyes shut. His voice, so deep, was too seductive. It was lulling her, making her want to believe him, willing her to give in. Too well did she remember that kiss in the garden. Too well did she remember how the touch of his hand had confused her.

"No," she said again tremulously. "Please, leave me."

"Very well, my love."

He bent swiftly before she could prevent him and kissed her upon the lips. She started to push him away, but found she wanted him to keep kissing her. His hand stroked her forehead, and her cheek, and his touch was feathersoft. She felt a warmth growing inside her, stirring at the level of her abdomen, and she did not know what it meant, only that it excited her. His hand caressed her collarbone, slid to the roundness of her breast, and there her hand caught his.

"No," she said huskily. "No, please, no, you go too quickly."

He withdrew his hand to the relative safety of her shoulder, reluctantly drew his mouth back from hers, and breathed words into her ear so softly she was not sure she heard them.

"Until another evening, my dear."

He stood up, and crossed without hesitation to the door. It closed quietly behind him.

She stared into the darkness for a long time before the strange warmth and feelings receded from her body. She could not help but think of his kiss, of the feel of his hands on her body, and she almost wished she had not sent him away.

Almost.

She shuddered, rolled over onto her side, and tried to force all thoughts from her mind so that she might sleep peacefully. But she was not successful, and when the first rays of dawn entered the room, Agatha, Viscountess of Drummond for less than one day, still lay awake.

NINE

"WHAT IS HER NAME?" AGATHA asked the groom. He had introduced himself as Ben, and she had recalled Holly saying her brother worked in the stables. He looked like an older version of the maid, for his hair was just as yellow, his eyes just as blue—and his manner just as disarming.

"Tally's Fortune, ma'm," he replied, stroking the tall chestnut's neck with real affection, "or Tally, as we call her here." The mare turned around and blew gently at him. He grinned with pleasure.

She walked around the mare, studying the horse's legs, line of back, arch of neck, the various aspects of equine confirmation.

"I see you've been taught the finer points of horseflesh," Drummond said in an admiring tone as he watched her circle the horse.

She nodded absently, running her gloved hand down the mare's leg. It was strong, sound, straight.

"My father wished me to know what he considered the refinements of life. He also taught me to shoot and hunt, much to the shocked sensibilities of most every inhabitant in the district."

"He believed in a wide education?"

"No. He simply wanted to upset his neighbors. He delighted in that, you know." She shook herself. "Why am I telling you this? You well know my father, being, as you are, a friend of his."

"A friend. Yes."

She glanced at him. Had she not seen him in the study the night of the announcement? Yet there had been a strangeness to his voice when he had said "friend." And if Drummond were a friend of the squire's, why would he steal her away? Was he not a friend, then, of her father's? If he were not, if he wanted to hurt her father . . . Enough of this nonsense, she told herself. 'Twould lead to naught but a headache.

The mare shook herself, and at the sound Agatha brought herself back to the stable in mind as well as body.

"Would you care to see another one, your ladyship?" Ben asked.

"No, Ben, I'll take Tally's Fortune." She turned to her husband. "That is permitted, is it not, my lord?"

She could not read his expression. "Of course, my dear, that is why I brought you to the stables. I am well pleased with your choice. She's a sound mare, and provided with a good nature as well."

"Will you be takin' them out now, my lord?"

"Yes, Ben. Have them saddled."

Ben called out and two boys, both in their teens

and who, from their wide grins and the color of their hair, looked to be cousins of Ben's and Holly's, rushed out to receive their instructions. They ran to the tack room to return in a matter of seconds with the saddles. While one boy saddled Agatha's horse and the other boy stood with the second saddle draped over his arm, Ben headed into the stable. Within minutes he came back with one of the most magnificent animals Agatha had ever seen.

The horse was tall, Ben's head just coming to the creature's muscular shoulder. It was the silvery color of moonlit-snow, and it pranced toward them, its strong neck arched, its head tossing with excitement. His mane and tail were black, and thickly luxurious, and the full tail nearly swept the ground behind. His shoulder was well-muscled, and he had the look of a racer—endurance as well as speed—about him.

Drummond whistled softly and the horse's delicate ears pricked toward him, listening.

"He's beautiful," she said admiringly. "I've never seen anything like him—and my father had many fine horses."

Drummond gazed at the animal with a mixture of pride and affection. "He has the blood of the desert in him. I bought him from Lord Godolphin, who with the Duchess of Marlborough has been bringing these animals into the country."

The stallion, who had been tossing his head and dancing nervously, now calmed as Drummond laid a hand upon his side. The horse nuzzled him and whickered softly.

Agatha frowned a little at this show. Animals, it

appeared, well loved the viscount, too. Animals and servants; they were those who should least love and most fear an ogre such as her husband.

A dog barked as it raced across the stableyard, and Agatha thought of poor Bruno, the dog she had left behind. She wondered how he was, and hoped her father would not mistreat him.

Drummond, scratching the stallion's hard-muscled neck, noticed her expresson. "What is the matter, my dear? You seem quite sad."

She nodded toward the dog, a setter, now snuffling in the bushes beyond the stableyard. "I had a dog, sir, that my father was wont to abuse. I tried to protect him—he was only a pup—and I—I was just wondering how he fared. I hope that my father will not harm him now I am gone."

Homesickness swept over her. How could she bear to be away from Grey's Manor forever? It appeared that her husband would never allow her to visit her home again. Would her father someday find her? Would he then come after her? Could she perhaps get word to him of her location? Did she desire to do so? The thought sent a shiver down her spine.

She watched as Ben saddled the grey horse. He helped her mount. In turn she watched Drummond swing easily into the saddle. He looked good upon the big stallion, she thought. They looked as if they belonged together, as if they understood one another by some sort of secret communication.

She flicked the reins, and they rode out of the stableyard.

She glanced over at Drummond. "What do you call him, my lord?"

"Grey Sir."

"Grey Sir?" She arched an eyebrow. "You wear grey often as not; you possess a magnificent grey horse; you name him 'Grey Sir.' Most intriguing."

"I am most partial to things Grey."

She felt color tingling in her cheeks and pointedly gazed toward the road, just framed between her horse's ears. This was the first she had seen of the surrounding countryside in the daylight. Around them were mile after mile of gently rolling hills, and beyond she could see a dark smudge of woods. She did not know where Falcon's Hall was, nor how far they were from her home.

"You have not spoken of your riding habit. Do you not like it?"

She drew her thoughts away from the landscape, returned her attention to Drummond. "It is quite lovely, and I thank you, my lord." Her tone was polite, as always.

She had, in truth, been quite pleased to find the outfit in her wardrobe when she had gone to change. The riding jacket, sewn along the lines of a man's coat, with pleated side vents with brass buttons and a small turned-down collar, was far superior to the riding habits she had worn at Grey's Manor. On her new habit the collar and sleeve cuffs were faced with a dull gold satin contrasting well with the russet of the outfit. The waistcoat too followed the line of a man's. The petticoat was long and full with an inverted flounce. She wore riding gloves of kid, had tied a Steinkirk at the neck, and a smart three-cornered hat of Flemish velvet perched atop her head.

His own riding coat and breeches were severely

cut of black damask, the cuffs faced with grey material, and his linen cravat was a startling white by contrast. His boots were high, coming well above his knees, and were so highly shined she could almost have used them as a mirror. His appearance, she thought with a small shiver, was intimidatingly correct. At least, from where she sat she could not see the scar, and for that she was thankful.

"You are looking most fetching, Agatha."

"Thank you . . . my lord."

She heard him sigh, then he said no more. He urged his horse to a trot, and she followed.

They had breakfasted in relative silence, and afterward he had asked if she would care to ride with him. Concealing a spark of hope, she had said yes with a show of indifference. At no time had they mentioned the night before.

She raised her head, and the wind blew back her hair to trail behind her. It felt good to be outside in the fresh air and the sunshine. If she did not glance around, she could almost believe she was back home riding on her father's estate.

Almost.

She glanced sideways at her companion. Drummond, absorbed in his own dark thoughts, seemed to be paying scant attention to her. She looked down at the reins clasped lightly in her hands, set her jaw, and sharply turned the mare to the right. She kicked the horse in the flanks, and the mare shot forward. Soon they were galloping across the open field. She glanced once behind her and saw him pursuing her.

"Hold on!" he shouted.

She smiled grimly to herself. So he thought she

had a runaway horse, eh? Well, he would soon learn otherwise. She bent forward, patted the mare's shoulder, and spoke into her ear, coaxing her to greater speed.

It was a race now, mare against stallion, woman against man. She was in the lead, she was winning, she was escaping. Above the sound of the wind whistling and the thumping of her heart and her rasping breath, she heard a deeper sound, the thundering of Grey Sir closing quickly behind her. Her heart pounded faster. She had to get away! She brought her crop down once on Tally's flank, and the mare stretched her stride.

Soon she would outdistance him, leaving him far behind, and she would be free, free to go home.

A flicker of movement out of the corner of her eye caught her attention. It was the tip of Grey Sir's nose! She saw his nostrils flare with each deep breath he took; the sound of the horses' hooves slammed inside her head. She brought the crop down again.

The mare nudged slightly ahead, lost some distance on her lead as she stumbled across a sudden rise in the ground. Agatha glanced back and saw Grey Sir, hardly laboring under the strain, open up, his stride almost seeming to double. He was racing alongside her mare now, and Drummond's arm flashed out toward the mare's bridle.

Agatha brought the crop down on his hand, and he withdrew it with a curse.

Then Grey Sir was edging into her mare, crowding her, and the mare stumbled. Drummond reached out again, and Agatha raised the quirt to strike him. He knocked the crop from her hand, caught the bridle, and hauled back on the mare, while slowing his stallion. She struggled to pull her mare away from him, but could not without pitching out of the saddle. Gradually the horses slowed to a canter, then to a trot, and finally when they were almost to the fringe of the woods, he brought the two animals to a stop.

Their sides heaved from the effort, and they were flecked with foam, the mare more so than the stallion. Tally chewed at her bit, while Grey Sir tossed his head and rolled his eyes.

She did not look up from her contemplation of the reins in her hands. She could not meet his eyes, although she knew he was watching her. He said nothing, but she could sense his disapproval, his hurt.

He still held her mare's bridle, his arm and body very close. She could almost stretch out a hand and touch . . . She trembled then—reaction, she told herself fiercely—and gnawed anxiously on the inside of her lip. She waited for him to yell as her father would have done, to strike her across the face as her father had done.

He did neither. He did not say a word.

Instead, he released the bridle, shifted his grip on the reins, and turned the horses, directing them back toward Falcon's Hall. She was as tired as the horses suddenly, the fight gone out of her, and she did not resist.

When they were within sight of the stable, he spoke for the first time, in cool clipped accents.

"That was foolhardy."

"I——"

"Tally could have stumbled in a hole, broken her leg, and I would have had to put her down."

Put the mare down! The horse could have been hurt! He had never once considered her safety, been concerned that her unhappiness had driven her to escape! She flashed an indignant look at him.

To her great chagrin she saw her withering glance was lost on him for he was not even looking at her. Instead, he was watching the mare, no doubt for any signs of lameness.

To run the mare that way had, yes, she would admit it, been foolhardy—and desperate. But desperate she was!

With these thoughts in mind, she kept her silence. When they reached the stableyard, he jumped down off the leggy grey. Ben rushed over to help them.

"Tally ran away with Lady Drummond," he said shortly. "Please check her to make sure she's not lame. Look Grey over too, Ben."

"Yes sir."

He did not help her down, but instead walked away, already pulling his gauntlets off.

Ben, an unreadable expression on his normally open face, lifted her out of the saddle and set her on the ground. She was shocked at the worn condition of her mare. She patted Tally's wet neck, promised her a treat later, and hurried after Drummond. Although his back was to her, she was acutely aware of his anger, and feared it the more because she knew it was justified. She wished he would give her a chance to apologize; she wished she could say something to him, but she could not.

He did not speak to her again until later in the afternoon, when he reminded her that Paul Sterling would be dining with them that evening. She nodded, he withdrew from the library where he had found her, and she was once more left alone with her thoughts.

After the disastrous ride, she had changed into a simple bodice and skirt of grey cloth, and had sought the comfort of the library. This room was far larger than the one at home, and the volumes appeared well read. It was not a room for show, she knew.

She curled up in a chair with a book of Greek plays and thumbed through the pages slowly, but she could not keep her attention on the words. The print blurred in front of her eyes, and she closed them.

She had hurt him by trying to run away. She couldn't help that, though, could she? Was she not obligated to make an attempt to escape? After all, would he not think her a pale, feeble creature if she meekly accepted her imprisonment here? She frowned. What did she care for what he thought? 'Twas of no importance.

She was startled by his appearance at the door though she listened quietly while he spoke of dinner, and when he left, she looked at the book again without seeing it.

For a long time she sat there. Finally she stood, the now forgotten book falling from her lap. She circled the room several times, each circuit showing more agitation than the last, and when she grew tired of that she crossed to the large window and stared out. In the distance she could see a horseman riding up the carriage sweep.

Was this Paul Sterling, her husband's friend? She wondered if he, too, were a friend of her father's. Would he have been there the night her engagement was announced? His name was not familiar to her, but that scarcely mattered. She watched as he grew closer and at length dismounted, tossing his reins and a coin to one of the stableboys. His horse was fine, but not of the superior quality of her husband's.

Sterling—if it were he—was dressed in yellow breeches, a bottle-green coat, and gleaming black boots. He looked like a pleasant enough fellow, hardly the sort of man she would have thought to be found consorting with her father and Drummond.

Appearances, however, could be deceiving.

If her husband's guest had already arrived, she had best go upstairs and change before *he* came seeking for her again.

The door opened and Merton, the butler, stepped into the room and bowed formally. She did not think the servant liked her. He was nothing short of polite to her, but his eyes, a light shade of grey, seemed ever frosty in her presence.

"My master sent me to find you, my lady. Mr. Sterling has arrived."

"Thank you, Merton. Tell his lordship I shall be down shortly."

"Very well." He nodded stiffly and left.

What would dinner be like, she wondered? Would the two men talk, leaving her to her silence, or would this mysterious Sterling attempt to draw her out? Well, she would have to wait and see. In the meantime, she must change.

She ran upstairs and rang for Holly, who appeared so quickly she must have been standing outside.

"Mr. Sterling is here," said Agatha, "and I must change."

"Oh, Mr. Sterling," the girl said breathlessly, "is he not the most handsome of men?"

"I can scarcely judge, having never been close enough to view him."

"So kind, too," the girl went on, as if she had not heard her mistress's wry comment, "and always a good word for everyone."

"The burgundy, I think," Agatha directed her maid patiently. Holly faithfully pulled out the rich bodice and skirt, trimmed with beige eyelet lace.

In a matter of minutes Agatha was dressed, her hair arranged carefully. She left her bedchamber and went downstairs. She heard men's voices coming from the study and she walked to it, prepared to knock on the door, then paused.

". . . going tonight?" an unfamiliar voice, obviously Sterling's, was asking.

"I think not," replied her husband's voice.

"Will they not grow suspicious over your continued absence?"

"It has only been two days since I was last to the abbey, and no ceremony was planned, so I think that doubtful."

"Still, I would be careful, Richard."

"Thank you for your concern, Paul. You know I have a healthy regard for my own neck."

Sterling snorted. "Indeed, I know quite the opposite, old friend."

She drew back, frowning a little at what she had overheard. Of what were they speaking? What was this abbey? This ceremony? Her husband was surely not a Roman, so why would he visit an abbey? Most strange.

Merton walked past in his careful tread and glanced at her.

She realized how odd it must appear for her to be standing outside the study with one hand lifted to knock, and how much it must look as if she were eavesdropping.

Which she was, she thought a little guiltily.

She knocked soundly on the door.

"Ah, that must be Agatha now."

She heard footsteps coming to the door, and then Drummond threw it open. He did not smile at her, but did take her arm.

"Come in, my dear, and meet my good friend."

She found Sterling standing by the fireplace, a glass in one hand. She curtsied and he bowed low, and then she had a chance to study his features. Holly was right in her assessment—he was handsome, though not as classically handsome perhaps as Drummond. Nonetheless he was goodlooking, and had a pleasing manner.

"My wife, Agatha. This is Paul Sterling, the best friend a man might have."

"I am pleased to make your acquaintance," she murmured in her most polite manner.

Sterling smiled expansively. "Delighted, ma'm, to meet you. I've heard so much about you, y'know." He grinned at Drummond.

She lifted one eyebrow. "Indeed?"

Sterling's grin widened. "Indeed."

She glanced covertly at Drummond, wondering what he could possibly have said, but his back was to her and so he did not see. Sterling, however, did not miss it.

Merton entered at that moment before further conversation could ensue.

"Dinner is served, my lord."

Drummond gave his arm to his wife, escorting her into the dining room. Sterling followed a few steps behind.

"A generous repast, as always," Sterling said as he sat. He stared hungrily at the courses set upon the sideboard.

"You must learn, Agatha, that Paul is an outrageous flatterer. He has been after my chef for these many years."

Sterling grinned at Agatha. "I eat a poor fare until I dine here, ma'm."

"Pooh," Drummond responded. "You have a cook, come all the way from Paris."

Agatha looked to Sterling. "Is this true, Mr. Sterling?"

"Well . . . yes . . . but he is not half as fine as your own chef." He paused. "Please, I would find our dinner more comfortable if you were to call me by my first name."

"Very well . . . Paul. And you must call me by mine."

"Thank you, Agatha. I think we shall be famous friends." He winked at Drummond.

Dinner passed more pleasurably than Agatha had thought possible, for Paul kept them entertained with stories, and anecdotes, and little bits of information he had gleaned from she knew not where. In many ways he reminded her of Lucy. Those two, she thought, would get along well. In another place, under other circumstances, she would have played at matchmaker, but it seemed she would never see her friend again. If Drummond would not permit her to leave the grounds, he surely would not permit her to invite Lucy to visit them.

As they were finishing their cheese and fruit, she realized with some surprise that Drummond had scarcely spoken a word all evening. She had said little more, except for when Paul had directed a question her way.

They retired to the viscount's study afterward to sip wine and converse further.

Paul raised one eyebrow questioningly. "How do you find Falcon's Hall, Agatha?"

"What I have seen of it, I have found most remarkable." She did not look in her husband's direction, uncertain how much Sterling knew of the manner in which she had been wed.

"Have you taken her into the village yet, Richard?"

"Good lord, man, we only arrived yesterday."

Sterling was not one whit crestfallen. "Oh, to be sure. If he does not find time to escort you, Agatha, I shall be more than happy to."

"I confess," she said in what she hoped was an innocent tone, "I do not know the name of the village."

Sterling glanced quickly at Drummond. "Oh, er, Oxton."

"Why, thank you very much for that information," she said sweetly, with a triumphant smile.

"Well, yes, Richard tells me you're a fine rider." Sterling, seeming a little nervous, obviously wished to avoid any unpleasant topics.

"My lord is much too kind."

Sterling's eyebrows shot up at her "my lord." "Perhaps some afternoon when you are not busy, we could go riding."

"I would enjoy that." She smiled at him, finding she genuinely liked the man. He did not weigh upon her spirits as did Drummond, and she wondered at the two men being apparently such fast friends.

They continued to talk of the latest fashions, of the victories abroad by the Duke of Marlborough and Prince Eugene, and of the Queen's latest illness, till at last when the clock on the mantel chimed two, Sterling looked up, startled.

"Good God—I hadn't realized it was so late. I'd best be taking my leave now. I have some distance to go yet, and do not wish to wear out my welcome."

He could not be convinced to stay for another glass of wine, protesting he'd be a sorry sight on his horse. He stood at once, bowed over her hand, thanked her for the dinner, and the two men strolled out of the room. She could hear Drummond speaking now, and she wondered at his previous silence.

Not knowing what else to do, she left the study and went upstairs. Holly, obviously intending to wait up for her, had fallen asleep on a stool in the dressing room. She bent and gently shook the girl's shoulder.

"W-what? My lady?" She rose, rubbed her eyes, and yawned.

"Go to bed, goose. I shall manage by myself."

"Are you sure?"

"Yes. Now run along."

Holly nodded, yawned, and bobbed an unsteady curtsy. She quietly closed the door behind her.

Agatha removed her clothes, pulled on her nightgown, and went to the window in time to see Sterling mount his horse and ride off. Drummond remained outside, his hands resting on his hips. She watched him for some time, and when he did not seem likely to move, she went to bed and snuffed the candle. She pulled the covers up to her chin.

It was so quiet in the house. Yet she knew Drummond would have come back into the house by now, and might even have returned to the study. Would he be surprised to find her gone? Or had he expected her to leave while he said good-bye to Sterling?

She liked Paul Sterling, and she was glad he would be coming often to the house. At least, she would have one friend in her new life.

She closed her eyes, then jerked them open as she thought she heard a noise. Was he returning? Coming to her as he had last night? She burrowed further under the covers, as if that would hide her even better.

She waited, heart pounding. Nothing. She listened, and waited, and finally she fell asleep, for he did not come to her that night.

TEN

NOR DID HE COME TO her for the remaining week. A feeling of puzzlement mingled with her inner protestations of relief. Was she not his wife? Why did he not demand that right of her? Her father and his close friends—had they been in such a position—would have thought nothing of coming to her and forcing themselves upon her.

Yet he did not, and she told herself again she was glad, though she knew his patience would one day grow thin. Still, she recalled the touch of his lips on hers, and they seemed to burn at the memory.

One day he brushed by her, politely begged her pardon, and continued down the corridor. But she could not continue on her way, so shaken was she. The touch of his hip against her had left her breathless. In the next moment she berated herself for being such a goose.

In the evenings they were the model of husband and wife as they sat together and read their separate books. Little conversation passed between them, and yet often Agatha would find herself watching him over the top of her book. She would read a page, pause to look up at him, then turn the page and resume reading. If he was aware of this scrutiny, he gave no indication. Some evenings they would play chess, sharing a fondness for the game. That, too, required little conversation.

Still, as the days passed he seemed to be softening in his attitude toward her, relaxing the stiff formality with which he had treated her since the afternoon she had tried to escape. She also found her opinion of him changing, for he did not seem now the complete monster she had thought him when they were first married.

When they had been married a sennight he asked if she would go for a stroll in the garden with him. She agreed, and what she found delighted her.

"It's beautiful," she said, staring in amazement. Drummond remained silent. Lifting her skirts slightly, she moved away from him. To her left stood a giant of a hedge, thick and already very green for so early in the season. She rounded the corner and found herself at the mouth of a long green tunnel. She stepped in a few feet, and saw an opening at the far right. A maze! She quickly ran through the verdant corridors, coming to deadends, turning around, retracing her steps, and at last she found the very center of the maze. In it sat a marble bench and a sundial. She paused, listening, and heard only the cheerful warbling of a robin. It was as though she were the only one on the entire estate. She breathed deeply of the fresh spring air and began retracing her steps to the start of the maze.

She found Drummond patiently waiting by the maze. He was staring off into the distance and did not seem to hear her approach.

Beyond the maze she discovered a pond, filled with rainbow-hued fish and lily pads. A wide wooden bridge spanned the bubbling stream which fed into the pond. She crossed the bridge, one hand gliding along the smooth railing, and on the opposite side she found a formal garden with crushed stone paths bisecting the garden beds. In these she found an amazing variety of spring flowers, most of them blooming or about to do so. A low stone wall, one she could easily sit upon, circled the entire garden, separating it from the immense park beyond. Although her movements were restricted to the house and grounds, she found she did not feel as closed in here as she had at Grey's Manor.

A most curious circumstance, she thought as she sat on the wall and stared at the colorful profusion of violets, tulips, and daffodils.

"Your garden is complete except for one rather necessary item, my lord," she called to Drummond, who had just crossed the bridge.

"Oh?" He raised one eyebrow as he joined her.

"Yes, you have no roses. A most unfortunate oversight," she chided.

"Perhaps we should do something about it. Hmm. Come let us find a spot where a rose garden could go, my dear."

She obediently followed him back across the bridge into a section of the garden she had not yet seen. It was enclosed by a brick wall with a pretty little gate in it. He opened the gate for her, and stepped aside. Once in the garden she stopped, unable to go on.

In front of her were row after row of rose bushes, all preparing to bud. She quickly began counting, lost track in her excitement, and began again. Surely there must be over a hundred bushes here. Perhaps closer to two hundred.

"How . . . ?"

"How did they come to be here? I had them planted here when I knew you would be my wife."

She could think of nothing to say and only continued to stare at him. All the trouble and expense . . . for her. For his captured bride. It did not make sense.

She roused herself enough to profess her heartfelt thanks.

" 'Tis something you may take an interest in, Agatha, so you will not be bored." His face displayed no emotion, but she thought she sensed some hurt. Before she could speak, he continued, "There is a greenhouse beyond." He pointed to a structure past the roses. "That will no doubt be of further interest to you."

She nodded and started toward it, then looked back at him. He had not moved.

"Will you not come, my lord?" she asked softly.

"Only if you wish."

"Yes, I do."

He nodded, and followed her to the greenhouse, the largest she had ever seen. Inside she found a small white-haired man repotting a plant. He bowed when they entered.

"Agatha, this is Willem Vandiivort, our gardener. Willem, this is your new mistress."

Willem peered at her, and smiled, revealing a gap between two bottom teeth. "Goot. Glad to meet you, my lady. You like the roses, ja?"

"Yes, I like the roses very much."

"Goot." He grinned again, and turned back to the flower. "Here the roots are twisting on themselves. I put this poor little violet in a larger pot. Ja?"

She stepped closer to the counter so she could watch him better, and Drummond strolled away to peer at something on a shelf farther down.

Time passed quickly as she listened to Willem's learned discourse on plants, and it was only when the light in the greenhouse had grown faint that she realized how much time had elapsed.

She thanked Willem for his patience, and left. Outside she found Drummond sitting on a bench a few feet from the greenhouse.

"My lord, have you been waiting all this time for me?"

"Yes." He stood.

"You should not have," she said, suddenly feeling shy at his thoughtfulness.

"I wanted to."

"You should have reminded me of the time."

He shrugged. "You were enjoying yourself."

She smiled slowly. "Thank you for this garden. It is a lovely present." Without thinking, she stood on her toes and kissed him on the cheek.

She began walking back to the house, well aware

of the surprise on his face, and well aware, too, of the surprise she felt.

Why had she done that? He had been kind, it was true, and thoughtful, as well, but—but she could not think of this for now. It was much too confusing.

Once more in her bedchamber and planted before the mirror, she brushed her long luxuriant hair, frowned at her image, and thought again of her foolhardy action.

Why had she kissed him?

Out of gratitude? Would not her thanks have been enough? No, she thought, not this time. But, she told herself firmly, she would not kiss him again. It would simply encourage him, and after all, she did not love him. . . .

She need not have worried, for at dinner Drummond was the same toward her, polite and faintly interested, but slightly reserved, as if he did not wish to grow any closer to her. If her chaste kiss had encouraged him in the least, he certainly did not indicate it. When at length, long after the meal was finished, Agatha excused herself, pleading fatigue, he did not follow.

As she changed into her nightgown, crawled into the bed, and closed her eyes, she thought he was truly the most perplexing man she had ever known.

In the study, though, the subject of Agatha's drowsy thoughts occupied himself with drinking glass after glass of wine. When he had finished nearly half a bottle, he stood and took a turn around the room.

His thoughts had been in turmoil all day, and Agatha's kiss had hardly helped steady them. He rubbed his chin and stared into the flames of the fire.

He had wanted to seize her, crush her to his chest, and smother her face with kisses—all of which would simply have served to drive her all that much farther from him. No, she could not be handled impetuously. Agatha would have to learn to trust him, and that would take time.

Time. More time gone by. The days and the nights, gone, as he waited, waited for so many things. Waited for——

He had to get outside, had to ride, let the fresh air clear his head and heart. He rang for Merton.

"Have Ben saddle Gray Sir," he instructed the elderly servant.

The butler did not seem at all surprised at this request, despite the night's late hour. He simply nodded. "Very well, my lord."

Within minutes Drummond slammed out the front door, found his stallion being led up, and sprang lightly into the saddle. The stallion, not having been exercised in over a day, was more than eager to convey his master, and he broke at once into a lively trot.

There was a ghostly half moon out, and the light it shed was for the most part obscured by wide clouds. He knew there was little chance of anyone seeing him. Once away from the house, he urged the horse into a canter. He took the back roads, and cut-offs and twisting turns he knew so well by heart, and within a short time he was nearing the spot. He noted, without seeing, the lonely countryside he rode through.

At last he found the path, overgrown with bushes and low-hanging branches. He eased Grey Sir to a steady walk, patted the stallion on his shoulder, and finally brought him to a stop. Sliding off, he tied the horse's reins to a conveniently low branch, and pushed through the tangled brush.

He made his way slowly, for he wanted to be quiet. He didn't know if anyone would be there. It wasn't the time, but still . . . He passed the giant oak tree marking the outer reaches of the property, paused with one hand resting on the trunk, and listened.

There was nothing to hear but the sighing of the wind in the branches above his head. Still he waited. He heard no other sounds, and more importantly, he saw no one. He pushed on until he reached the fringes of a clearing. The clouds scuttled past the face of the moon and in the faint light he could see the crumbling building surrounded by thigh-high grass.

The abbey.

Its windows, bereft of the stained glass that had once graced them, stared at him like dark sunken eyes. They seemed to jeer, defying him to enter. The roof still covered most of the second floor, and only one wall had begun to crumble. Tangled bushes, covered with ripe blossoms, grew around the abbey, and ivy inched its way along the walls, seeking crevices between the bricks, slowly, inexorably bringing destruction to the centuries-old building.

Above, the three-story bell tower stood empty.

A century before the great bronze bell had been taken down and melted to be used as cannonshot against the Puritan armies of Oliver Cromwell. To one side a rock shrine had stood for years, but all that remained was a ring of rocks grown green with moss. A statue lay half-buried in the earth next to it.

A few hundred feet past the building a path wound through the remains of an overgrown garden. It crept down the face of a cliff to end on the beach, a mile distant. There, a narrow strip of sand and rocks faced caves carved by the pounding of the water.

The abbey had been built, he knew, in the early twelfth century, not long after Stephen of Blois had seized the English throne upon Henry I's death. Generation after generation of monks had conscientiously preserved the numerous writings of the Norman culture, but disaster had befallen in the mid-sixteenth century when a rapacious Henry VIII had dissolved the religious order, ordered the execution of the two hundred and twenty brothers and its prior, and appropriated the abbey's hefty coffers for himself. Its confines had remained deserted since then.

A bloody history, but the strangeness had not stopped there, for there had been passed down tales of dark doings by the brothers even then, stories claiming that what the good brothers had done was not God's work, but the Devil's. There had been odd disappearances of children and animals in the area, strange odors emanating from the abbey's chimneys, and few had regretted the dissolution of the brotherhood.

Century after century then the abbey had slowly dissolved, becoming less a place of man and God, and more a place of wild beasts and things that crept at night.

God and Satan . . . there was no place for the former here, he thought, staring at the dark abbey. Only evil, the work of men.

Soon, very soon, it would all be over. Soon he would no longer have to come to this place. Soon he would be free from the ghost of two years past.

Thunder cracked over him, and he glanced up, startled. In the time he had taken to stare at the abbey, large awesome clouds, bloated with rain, had filled the sky. He started toward his horse.

Evil. Was he not perpetuating it by what he had done? He should never have abducted her, should never have married her. It was a mistake, he knew now, a mistake from the moment he had noticed her at the party that night. She had been like a spring flower in the midst of a weed-choked midden, and he had known he must transplant her to a proper setting, lest she be trampled. But he had thought to enjoy her himself, thought to see her bloom and turn to him as her sun, her source of light and warmth and . . . Fool, he cursed himself. Fool for trying to save her from the squire and Alford. There could be no saving. Not in the end. For after all, they were both cursed, both doomed.

The thunder woke her, and for a long time, she lay there, her heart pounding, not knowing what it was that had awakened her. Then it boomed again, and she knew, and chided herself for giving in to such childish fears. Yet she could not immediately go to sleep. Yawning, she pushed back the covers and sat up.

The fire had long ago died down, and the embers now glowed a faint red. She crossed to the fireplace, held out her hands and warmed them, before she went to the windowseat in the sitting room and watched the progress of the storm.

The clouds seethed through the midnight black sky, large and ominous. Lightning, fierce and yellow, jagged through the clouds, as though piercing their very fabric. From time to time she caught a brief glimpse of the moon, but all too soon it would disappear behind the roiling clouds. Thunder reverberated, causing the glass to rattle. She pushed the window open to smell the air, and heard the distant echo of a horse's hooves.

Who was abroad on a night such as this? A foolhardy traveler, indeed, to risk a drenching and subsequent chill.

As she listened, the hoofbeats sounded louder, as though the traveler were coming closer to the house. A visitor? she asked herself. Surely not. It could be no more than four in the morning, scarcely the time for social calls to be made. She waited, and watched as the first fat drops of rain began falling.

Through a break in the trees she saw a horseman approaching. He grew closer, until at last Ben, or at least she thought it was he, carrying a torch, ran out from the shelter of the front door. He helped the rider down, grabbed the reins of the horse, and headed for the stable.

In the brief moment the torch's yellow light had

flickered across the rider's face, she had identified the man.

It was Drummond.

A chill shook her body, and she pulled the window shut. She made as if to return to her bed, changed her mind, and went to the door. She pressed her ear against it, listening.

After some time she heard his steady footfall as he ascended the staircase. The footsteps continued. She counted them. One, two, three . . . twelve, thirteen, fourteen . . . and still they came on.

He was coming to her room. She swallowed the lump in her throat and backed away from the door, staring fearfully at it. He would push the door open, and he would stand there, the rain still dripping from his hat and clothes, and he would kick the door shut, and——

The footsteps had stopped just outside her door. She put one trembling hand to her chest, one to her mouth lest she make some noise, and waited for what seemed an eternity. Her throat constricted, making it difficult to breathe, and she could scarcely hear for the pounding of the blood in her ears.

She saw the latch turning slowly, ever so slowly, and the door opening——

No. She heard footsteps. Fading, going away from her room. Down the hall she heard the quiet opening and closing of a door, then silence.

Swallowing rapidly, she went back to her bed and pulled the covers up, burrowing down in the warmth.

He had come to her room, but something had stopped him from entering. Something had made him return to his own room.

She forced her eyes to shut, even though they wanted to stare at the door, still waiting for it to swing open. She must sleep.

But no matter in what position she lay, no matter how much she tried to will herself to sleep, she found it impossible, for all she could see in her mind's eye was the horrible look of agony on her husband's face as he dismounted.

ELEVEN

AT BREAKFAST HE SAID NOTHING to her of his early-hours excursion, and she did not broach the subject to him. All day he remained secluded in his study, emerging only when Paul Sterling was announced. Agatha, talking to Sterling in the salon, had prevailed upon him to stay for supper, and he had readily accepted.

"Paul, how glad I am to see you," Drummond said with a smile as he joined them.

Sterling stood up to shake hands. "Your wife has kindly asked me to supper."

"No doubt you begged."

"I did nothing of the sort!" he responded indignantly. "I did, however, drop one or two powerful hints, which she could scarcely ignore."

Agatha laughed at that. "You are beyond reason, Paul."

"I truly hope so."

Drummond said, somewhat formally, "Excuse me, my dear, for stealing Sterling away, but I must talk with him privately."

She responded with what she hoped were spirited words, but the moment she uttered them she heard their flatness. "Very well, I shall forgive you this once. However, I demand his attention after supper."

"That, Agatha," Paul said, bowing low over her hand, "you shall have. Undivided."

The men left the salon, but for a while longer she remained. What weighed so heavily upon her husband's mind? What—or who—disturbed him so? What was it that kept him away from her now? She had found, to her complete surprise, that even during this brief withdrawal she had missed him.

She frowned. Had she grown so accustomed to him in such a short time? Did she not remember that this was the man who had abducted her from her father's coach on the way to the church where she was to be wed, torn her from her home and friends? Was she not still angry at his presumption, his cruelty, his imprisonment of her?

To be perfectly honest, she thought, no. For whatever reasons, her anger had dulled over the past sennight, lost its sharp edge. As the days had passed, she had found she missed her home less and less. Her father and her bridegroom-who-would-have-been she missed not at all. To be sure, she longed for the company of Lucy, and would liked to have once more seen Nettie, and Mrs. Howard and Temple, and of course, poor Bruno.

And she would have liked to have her mother's belongings with her.

But time dulled the memories and longing, and each day she found something new to which to devote her time and restless energies. Life at Falcon's Hall, after all, was exceedingly pleasant.

The problem was, she was growing complacent. That was it. Like many a prisoner sentenced for life, she had given up, lost her spirit and her will to fight.

Well, perhaps that was not precisely the problem, she conceded fairly.

She was happy. For the first time in her life. She no longer feared rising in the morning as she had when she lived with her father. She did not fear that this man would raise his hand and strike her, as her own father had. She did not fear that this man would bring home loutish companions, who would mock her, as her father had.

She was allowed the complete management of the house and the numerous staff, and the servants, with whom she was now getting acquainted, were only too eager to assist her. Her husband was kind and gentle and considerate in all ways, and was always a gentleman, and if inside she still did not trust him for what he had done, it was surely not a poor marriage.

What more could she ask for?

Love.

She wanted to love.

She remembered how her father had laughed when she said she wanted to love her husband. He had claimed it wasn't important, but he was wrong. 'Twas true many women did not love their husbands when they married, and that many husbands never loved their wives; and yet the couples well suited each other, but that was not for her.

She felt an emptiness, a longing that could only be fulfilled by love. She wanted to love Drummond, but feared to do so, feared she would give him her love, and he would reject it, hurt her, destroy all this new-found happiness of hers.

He had seemed so distant to her recently, so unlike the first few days of their marriage. A dark cloud had settled over him, filling his eyes with unhappiness, leaving him brooding, and she wanted more than anything to know the source of his sorrow. If she knew, then somehow she might be able to dispel the darkness.

For only then, she knew, could they begin to love one another.

"I went there last night," Drummond said quietly, almost to himself.

Paul earnestly searched his friend's face and what he found there was not at all to his liking. "Was that wise?"

"No. I couldn't stay away, Paul. I have tried—God knows I have—but it called to me, and I went. I rode back in the rainstorm. I was drenched by the time I got back." His lips twitched at the thought.

"Ah, the wages of sin."

"At least I have not taken a chill."

"Small blessings." Sterling laced his fingers and looked over at Drummond sitting in the chair by the fire, his legs outstretched, his head leaning back against the chair. "Does she know?"

Drummond shook his head. "No."

"When will you tell her?"

"God knows. I suppose I should, but . . ." He shrugged. "This is not so easy, you know."

"I well know that, Richard, for I have been with you through all of it."

"I am sorry. Selfishly I think only of myself in this matter."

"As is natural, with what has happened. Still, I do counsel you to tell Agatha—tell her before it is too late. Do not fear I will speak to her before you. Upon that you have my word."

"Thank you, Paul." He leaned back in the chair and closed his eyes.

Sterling watched the shadows play across the sharp planes of his friend's face. Drummond looked tired tonight, tired and defeated, and more somber than he had ever seen the man.

How the past followed them, haunted them, bedeviled them, caught them like a dog with a fox and shook them until they had no strength left. Was this fox vanquished, or did he still possess some wits? Sterling asked himself. Only time, he supposed, would provide the answer.

Drummond opened one eye. "You are staring at me," he accused.

Paul spread his hands. "After a fashion."

"You are worried."

"Of course! You know I am fretful by nature. All who love you worry, as would your wife, if she knew. And since we speak of your wife, we should not leave her alone over long else she shall give up on us and dine by herself." He paused, a hesitant expression on his face. "But perhaps you desire me to leave. . . ." He half rose from his chair.

"Stay, Paul. We'll dine now, and retire later to the salon and talk until all hours of the night. Perhaps my shadow will depart for a short time."

They persuaded Paul to spend the weekend at Falcon's Hall, so the three stayed late in the salon with good wine and conversation, and all rose late the following day.

Agatha, dressed in sprightly colors of green and rose, was the first to find her way to the dining room and have breakfast. Paul soon joined her.

"Good morning!" He smiled cheerfully at her and sat down in an adjacent chair.

"Good morning to you, Paul, although it shall shortly be afternoon."

He feigned a yawn. "I believe I am all talked out, although if Richard were here he would scarce believe that." A footman placed a plate in front of him, and he fell to cutting the beefsteak. "How are you this morn?"

"Fine, thank you."

He stared with mock dismay at the toast she was eating. "Is that your breakfast?"

She nodded.

"An appetite like a bird. Heavens! You shall preserve your figure, while I shall soon be too large to mount my horse unassisted."

"Nonsense, Paul, you are not yet fat. Merely plump."

He stared at her for a moment, then laughed.

She smiled.

"You are a rare one, Agatha."

She said nothing, but stared into her cup of tea.

"What shall we do today?" Paul asked after a moment.

"I had thought I would walk in the garden this morning. Would you be interested in that?"

"Yes, madame, I would. And later?"

"Perhaps we three could pack a picnic lunch, and go for a ride."

"Sounds delightful. I shall surely need to take the exercise if I continue to eat in this unbridled fashion!"

So saying, he turned his attention to finishing his beefsteak, followed it with a meat pie, and washed it down with ale. Agatha had finished long before he did, but remained at the table.

"Was my lord stirring when you came downstairs?"

"Richard? Don't know. Didn't hear him. We talked some time after you left last night—this morning," he amended with a faint smile, "and I'm sure that with all that has been on his mind——" He stopped, aware he had revealed too much. "That is, he probably stayed up late. Needs the rest," he finished lamely.

" 'With all that has been on his mind.' Pray, sir, what does that signify?"

"I have spoken unwisely, Agatha. Please do not press me."

"Very well," she said, letting the subject rest. But her curiosity had been piqued, and she turned Paul's words over and over in her mind. What could be on Drummond's mind to cause him to lose sleep? Was it the darkness she saw in him? What was that darkness? She had to know. 'Twas obvious Paul was too loyal to her husband to tell her. She would have to learn of it from her husband, and 'twould be no easy matter to coax this intelligence from him, at least not until she gained his complete trust.

"Shall we go for the walk now?" Paul suggested.

"I would love to."

Once on the terrace, they paused to admire, from a distance, the garden and the park beyond. Sterling breathed deeply and smiled with satisfaction at the lovely spring day.

"Beautiful, simply beautiful," he said.

"I think there could be none finer."

Without agreeing on a general direction, they began walking toward the rose garden. When they arrived, Paul stared wordlessly at the rows of roses. He stopped to admire one of the bushes, whose tiny buds hinted at a white flower.

"They should bloom in little over a month." She touched one of the buds.

"Simply astonishing. Never did any gardening myself. Couldn't make a weed grow."

They circled the roses, following the path toward the bridge. There, Paul paused to look back. He frowned slightly.

"You know, I don't remember Richard having a rose garden before."

"He didn't," she said softly. "He had it designed for me."

"Oh." Sterling stared at her for a moment, then offered his arm as they crossed the bridge.

Thereafter they said little of consequence, touching lightly on the weather, the fineness of the garden, their horses, and once again on the weather as a slight breeze sprang up.

"I hope our picnic shall not be ruined," she said, gazing up into the sky for any sign of clouds. There was none.

"I daresay it would not do something so impolite as rain." He paused, looking back toward the house. "I wonder if Richard is about yet."

"We should find out."

They began walking back, but were met halfway by Drummond, who nodded to both.

"In answer to your unspoken question, yes, I have been up for some time, but did not come downstairs at once. Satisfied, Paul?"

Sterling laughed. "Yes."

"I thought, my lord, that we could have a hamper packed and ride out to picnic." She watched him, fervently hoping he would agree.

For a moment he seemed as though he were about to refuse, then he nodded. " 'Tis a fine idea, Agatha. Let us return to the house. You inform Cook, and I shall tell Ben."

In little over an hour the trio had rejoined in front of the house, now quite prepared to set off on their adventure. The men had changed into comfortable riding clothes, while Agatha had donned a mauve habit. A long white plume on her hat added a soft touch, curling around her face, its tip barely touching her cheek.

Sterling thought she looked enchanting, and declared so. Drummond concurred, although he was more restrained in his praise.

"Cook was most distressed that I gave him so little time in which to prepare a meal," she said as she mounted Tally.

Drummond, already astride his grey stallion, looked over at her. "Indeed?"

"Yes, I kept insisting this was only a picnic, not a banquet. He maintained I should have given him a full day's notice. At last I persuaded him that all we wished was a simple fare."

Paul chuckled and urged his mount forward. Drummond held the basket in one arm, and Agatha rode alongside him.

She watched the muscles in Drummond's thigh, little hidden by his breeches, work as they rode. She studied his hands, with their long slim fingers, as he clasped the reins. She imagined those fingers caressing her cheek, touching her neck, her naked breast and inexplicably found herself warmer than the day warranted. Looking up, she caught Paul watching her with undisguised interest. She blushed slightly and looked straight ahead.

"I know a spot ideally suited for a picnic," the viscount said, happily oblivious to any undercurrent. "It is some miles distant, but well worth the ride."

"Ah, anything for a perfect picnic," Paul said, laughing at his friend.

This was Agatha's first opportunity to study the countryside, for she had not yet ventured away from Falcon's Hall. She found it little different from the land surrounding the Grey estate, although there were more woods to be found here, and Drummond had said the coast lay not so many miles distance. The woods, though, were deeper, darker, appearing far older than those she had played in while a child, and not a little frightening.

It took well over half an hour for them to reach the spot Drummond had suggested, but when they saw it both Agatha and Paul avowed aloud that the ride had been well worthwhile. He had brought them through a copse filled with tall trees between which little light managed to enter, to the wide openness of a grassy knoll, dotted with wildflowers and rolling gently to the banks of a quicksilver stream.

They dismounted, tethered the horses so they might graze on the lush grass, and Agatha spread a white linen tablecloth in the shade of a giant oak. Quickly she began unpacking the basket.

Paul stared with surprise as she laid dish after dish on the cloth. Spiced eggs, and baked apples. Cold meat pie and baked capon. Bread with two kinds of jam, wine, and a cake.

Wordlessly, Drummond helped her with the china and the glasses and soon they were ready to eat. She spread her skirt carefully, and handed plates to the men.

"Simple, eh?" Paul asked as he tore off the wing of a capon he had appropriated.

"Well, of course," Drummond replied somewhat mockingly, "you will note he did not send the best china!"

The trio laughed, and hungrily attacked their meal. Afterward they talked, until Paul's eyelids began to droop.

"I believe," he said, barely restraining a yawn, "I shall take a short nap. Only a few minutes, though. Don't let me sleep too late."

"Of course," said Drummond, amused. "Shall we walk, Agatha?"

"Yes."

"Leave all this," he indicated the ruins of their repast, "to later."

He gave her his arm as they strolled away from their picnicking area. They followed the course of the river, its water dark with green tangled weeds. Occasionally Agatha saw a flash of gold or silver as a fish swam close to the surface.

"This is a lovely spot," she said softly. "Thank you, my lord, for sharing it with me." She was very aware of his arm under her hand, aware of him next to her.

They reached the fringes of the trees, and now he drew her into the woods, well away from the eyes of Paul, if he should happen to open them unexpectedly.

"Please, Agatha, could you not find it possible to call me by my name now? We have been wed over a sennight."

"Yet we are not man and wife." She blushed at her own words, wondering what had prompted them, and glanced away.

He touched her cheek. "That is not as I would wish." He gently brought her face around so he could look into her eyes.

She stared up into his dark brown eyes, and saw his passion there. Its intensity frightened, yet intrigued, her, and instead of drawing away from him, she drew closer. He bent his head, and their lips met. She closed her eyes, and was transported back into her father's garden and that night when he had kissed her for the first time. She seemed to tingle at the merest touch of him.

Wrapping his arms around her, he drew her closer, and she could feel the pounding of his heart through his coat. Hers began to beat more quickly, and she found it difficult to breathe. She lifted her arms around his neck; it seemed they moved of their own accord. Her lips opened under the slight pressure of his, and his tongue darted in, caressing her mouth. She quivered and pressed closer to him.

She had never felt this way. Never . . . so wonderful! Her body had awakened with urges she had not known existed. She ran one hand through his hair, feeling its softness, her breathing ragged now. One of his hands strayed along her waist, then ranged steadily upward. He touched her breasts with his fingers, and she moaned softly.

"Agatha, Agatha," he whispered, his voice hoarse, "I've wanted you for so long." He buried his face in her hair and continued to stroke her breast, the nipple hardening under the attention of his fingers.

"Oh, Richard."

He brought his head up and stared down at her.

"Is aught amiss?" she asked, concern on her face. Had she done something wrong?

"You used my name."

"I shall call you it once more . . . Richard." She raised her face to be kissed, and she lifted her hands and slipped them inside his coat. He swallowed quickly.

"Indeed, madame." Quickly he bent, picked her up, and kissed her on the lips. "We shall find a more secluded spot."

One arm draped behind his neck, she rested her head against his shoulder. It seemed to her it fit exactly, and that she had done this more than once. Certainly it seemed so very *right* to her, and she wondered that it had taken them so long to come together. So many wasted days . . . and nights, she sighed to herself. How very foolish they had both been. How foolish to have wasted all this time together.

A twig snapped behind them.

"Oh, I say, I am sorry."

Drummond looked back.

Paul stood a few feet behind them, his face extremely red.

"I—I woke up and didn't see you, and thought I'd look for you, well, er, um . . ." He lapsed into embarrassed silence.

She sensed the disappointment and brief anger from Drummond; felt it herself, as well. But she quickly recovered.

"I hurt my ankle," Agatha explained when Drummond did not speak, "and Richard was kind enough to help me." She kept her eyes downcast as she spoke, unable to meet Paul's gaze.

"Quite so." Obviously Paul did not believe her, though it seemed he would have liked to. "Well," he said, a false heartiness in his voice, "I'll return to the picnic area—feeling a bit hungry, you know—and see if we left any crumbs."

Drummond glanced at Agatha out of the corner of his eye and she nodded, almost imperceptibly. There was no sense in attempting to recover the mood; it was lost to them both. "We'll go with you, Paul."

"Oh, look, you don't have to."

"It's late. We should be riding back now." So

saying, he headed back toward the picnic area, Agatha still firmly clasped in his arms.

She comforted herself with the thought that he would come to her again that night, and she would be waiting.

At her usual hour she retired to her bedchamber, and had Holly run a bath for her. She discouraged the girl from chattering, for tonight of all nights she did not wish the maid to linger. She dismissed Holly, and soaked a long time in the warm water. She took special care in arranging her curls, changed into a delicate nightgown edged with the finest of lace, slipped into her bed, and waited.

She was aware of the growing inner excitement, the strange feelings that caused her to squirm, the tinglings within that needed soothing. They had started that afternoon on the picnic, had quieted somewhat during dinner and the hours following, but the moment she had stepped across the threshold of her rooms, they had been rekindled.

She watched as the fire died down, watched as the embers slowly lost their angry redness. Watched until they were grey with ash.

Watched and waited until it was almost dawn.

He did not come.

Finally, as dawn streaked the sky with light, she fell asleep, tears of anger on her cheeks.

TWELVE

"WELL?" SQUIRE GREY DEMANDED HARSHLY. He glared at the stocky man standing awkwardly in front of his desk. "Did you find her?"

The man, his brown head bent so that he was not looking at the squire, shuffled his feet and cleared his throat hesitantly. "No, sir," he responded in a low voice.

"What's that?" the squire thundered. "Can't hear you, boy!"

"No, sir," the man repeated in a somewhat louder tone. His hat was in his hands and he toyed with it, running its brim through his fingers. He had not been a boy for more than twenty years.

"Damme!" Squire Grey brought his hand down on his desk with a loud smack and the man winced. "Where's that girl taken herself?" He stood and paced to the window, his hands locked behind his back. "Where did you search?"

"We went far afield this morning, sir. As far as Bradford, and we talked with the Danvers and visited Miss Lucy Wilmot again. She was still real upset about Miss Agatha's disappearance. We be goin' to Falcon's Hall today, then to Oxton's Manor."

"Perhaps Drummond will know where she is," the squire mused, still looking out the window. He hunched his shoulders. "He's a knowing sort."

"Yes, sir."

The squire shifted, then squinted at the man. "If you find you must go farther, you will do so. Do you understand?"

The man nodded quickly.

"Continue hunting for her, Potter. It's been over a sennight now. I want her found."

"Yes, sir."

Potter began edging toward the door.

"Potter," the squire said. He was smiling at the man now in a way that failed to cheer the servant.

"Yes, sir?"

"I don't want damaged goods. Do you understand?"

Potter nodded quickly, bowed low, and left, shutting the door quietly behind him.

Squire Grey scowled at the closed door, his heavy grey eyebrows drawn together.

So the little bird thought she could elude his net, eh? Perhaps she had for a while, a short while. But he was confident he would find her—it was only a matter of time. And when he did, he'd rip the clothes off her back and strap 'er like he should have done when she was smaller. That would teach her a thing or two! She would be right docile when she went to her husband.

In the week-long—over a week—absence of his daughter he had been far from idle. He well remembered the day, and his lip curled as he recalled Reverend Lewis's horrified face when he arrived and announced to the stunned wedding party that his daughter had been abducted not more than ten minutes before by two highwaymen. And though the minister had little love for Agatha's intended groom, he had called for her to be found at once. An astonished, then increasingly angry Rupert Norton, who had no doubt seen his soon-to-be fortune flitting away, demanded immediate action, and the men of the wedding party, all in their finery, had ridden out in search of the two riders and Agatha.

But, as the squire had thought from the beginning, it had been a fool's errand. The two abductors had had too much of a head start and could have gone in any number of directions. Too, the dense fog had not helped the searchers, either, for Ruthen, in helping, had become turned around and ended up in the river and had to be fished out like a drowning kitten.

As the squire rode through the grey countryside that morning he knew the two blackguards could be anywhere now. Indeed, they could be hiding in any one of the farmhouses they saw, or barns, or even within the woods. They might well have passed within feet of them, and in the fog they would not have known it.

The day had ended with the father of the bride, the groom, and his best friend returning to Grey's

Manor where they proceeded to try to drink their way through bottle after bottle. Alford declared himself inconsolable at his loss, Ruthen tried to comfort him with an additional bottle, and Grey damned them both.

He'd waited through the next day to receive some word from the abductors. Surely they were holding his daughter for a large ransom, which he would duly pay so he could hand her over to her groom. But the day had come and gone, and no word had been received, raising his suspicions.

The next day he prevailed upon his servants to aid in the search for his daughter. None refused, though more agreed out of love for Agatha than fear of her father.

Each day thereafter the servants left the estate early in the morning and through the day they searched the surrounding countryside, questioned the residents, both high and lowborn, searched outbuildings and deserted farms. And each night they returned to Grey's Manor without the girl.

It seemed as though his daughter had vanished into thin air. Impossible, he told himself. When he found her, ah, when he did. . . .

He had first thought she was innocent of the matter, but as the days wore on he thought longer on it, and now he little doubted that she had planned this from the beginning. He didn't know how she'd arranged it, nor with whom, for she knew scarcely a soul—especially a soul that didn't fear his wrath—but he was heartily convinced she had masterminded it, simply because she did not wish to marry Lord Alford. Desperate to avoid the match, the girl would have gone to any length.

At first he had thought she might have sought shelter with Lucy Wilmot and her aunt. He had ridden over there, demanding to see his daughter. The damned mealy-mouthed females had claimed she wasn't there, but he hadn't believed them, and against their strident protests, he'd searched the house, to find—nothing. He had left without a word to the Wilmot women.

Oh yes, he would find Agatha, and punish the damned girl. By God, he'd make her suffer, too, suffer the way he had in the past sennight.

And he had suffered mightily. For was he not the laughingstock of the district?

There's Squire Grey—he's lost his daughter. Can you fancy that?

He knew his neighbors talked and laughed about him behind his back. They thought he'd been bested by a mere slip of a girl, who'd finally managed to get enough backbone to run off. They thought it amusing that she'd finally shown him a thing or two. Well, they were wrong, and he'd show *them* a thing or two.

Lost his daughter, and if that wasn't bad enough, one of the damned dogs had gone and run off. Damned animal wasn't worth the thought, though. Never had amounted to much.

He returned to his desk, picked up the full tankard, and drank deeply of the ale in it. When he was finished, he wiped his mouth on the back of his hand. His eyes narrowed, and he smiled unpleasantly.

Oh yes, he did indeed anticipate the day they found Agatha.

* * *

"Good day to you, Mr. Temple." Potter nodded to the butler.

Temple stopped, glanced around the hallway, then beckoned for Potter to follow him. The stocky man obeyed, and they withdrew to a room down the hall, some distance from the squire's study.

"How goes the search, Potter?"

Potter smiled grimly. "We haven't found her yet."

Temple's face relaxed. "That is good news. Of course, we all hope Mistress Agatha is safe."

"Of course, Mr. Temple."

He nodded toward the study. "What did he want?"

"To know where we'd be going today."

Temple watched Potter, no emotion in his brown eyes. "And if you should find her?"

Potter shook his head and idly scratched his arm.

"Well, you know, Mr. Temple, it's an odd thing. We men have been searching for Miss Agatha for some days now. And it's a big country. She could be just about anywhere. She might even be in London by now. Or even sailed across to France."

"Indeed."

"I just don't think we'll be finding her. You ken?"

Temple nodded, then hesitated. "If you should discover her, Potter, please send her my regards."

"Why, of course, Mr. Temple, that is, if I see Miss Agatha again, which I highly doubt. A man can get worn to a plain nub, lookin' through all the countryside." He paused. "The master's in one rare temper today. One of his huntin' dogs has gone astray. He's not happy about that, I can tell you."

"Curious," Temple said softly. "First his daughter. Now the dog."

"It's hard put anyone is to say which is making him madder."

"Caution, Potter," Temple said in a slightly warning voice.

"I beg your pardon," the servant said, but his face did not reflect his apology. He breathed in deeply and set his hat upon his head. "Well, I've got to be goin' now or he'll be getting suspicious."

"Good day, Potter. And good luck."

Potter stopped at the door of the salon, winked in a conspiratorial manner at the butler, then left.

Down the hall he heard a door slam, and knew the squire was leaving to go riding. He waited until he saw Grey up in the saddle before he found Mrs. Howard to tell her the news.

Thomas Dentham was cleaning a pair of his master's boots when Holly ran upstairs to find him. She was out of breath and could scarcely be understood. He made her sit down until she could talk right again.

"Oh, I ain't got the time," she said, jumping up. "There's men coming, and Ben sent me up to fetch you because Mr. Morton's not here. Men that come from Grey's Manor, he says."

"Indeed." Thomas set the boots down, wiped his hands on a cloth, and thoughtfully stroked his chin. As the servant closest to the viscount, he held a unique position, and when something happened requiring a decision to be made by the staff, they all turned to him. Not even Merton in his superior position as butler was accorded the respect given to Thomas.

"Well, thank God the master and mistress are out today, or there'd be the devil to pay!" He stood and stared thoughtfully at the maid. "Now, how far are these men, and how did Ben come to know?"

"One of the boys at Oxton come riding over with the news. They were still there when he left, and Ben says they'll be here within the hour."

"Hmm."

"Oh, Mr. Dentham, please stop hmming and do *something!*" She clasped her hands, and pleaded with her wide eyes.

He could almost have laughed had the situation not been so grave.

She flew to the window to look out. "Oh, that wretched boy lied. Those men are coming already! Whatever will we do?"

"First," he said, taking her small hands in his and shaking her a little, though very gently, "you'll calm down and act not a bit out of the ordinary. We don't want to be tipping our hands to them before they're scarcely on the grounds, now do we?"

"You're right as always, Mr. Dentham." Holly breathed deeply, patted back a stray strand of hair. "I'll be all right."

"Of course you will be. Now let's go downstairs."

In the front hall they found a somewhat apprehensive Merton waiting for them. Thomas assured the butler that all would be handled smoothly. The three servants watched as the group of riders, four unsmiling men, rode up the carriage sweep.

Thomas took a deep breath and stepped out. The door was left open behind him, and he knew Merton and Holly were behind it, listening. He shaded his eyes with one hand. "May I help you?"

"We're lookin' for Lord Drummond," announced a stocky brownhaired man on a dun horse.

"He is not at home at present."

"Is his wife here then? We understand he's been married recently."

"Indeed he has, and where did you hear that now?"

The stocky man nodded with his chin toward the woods. "Oxton."

Damn them at Oxton for opening their mouths, Thomas thought. Still, it was news that could hardly be a secret for too long.

"Why did you wish to see my master and mistress?" he asked. "Is it a matter in which I can be of assistance?"

"We're in the employ of Squire Grey of Grey's Manor, some miles west of here. His daughter was abducted a week ago on her way to her wedding, and our master's sent us out to hunt for the girl."

"On her wedding day?" Thomas shook his head. "A terrible thing. Why, though, does your master look to the estates?"

"He thinks brigands might have taken her." The man paused, seemed to feel he could take the valet into his confidence. "The truth of the matter is, there's been no ransom, and so he thinks she's run away. Thinks one of the families around here could be harboring her. We been travelin' the countryside searching her out."

"Indeed? Sounds like hot work. Come in, why don't you, and have a pint with me?" He thought he heard a squeak from Holly behind the door and hoped no one else had heard her. "All of you come in," he said, beckoning to the dusty-looking men. "You look like you could use a bit of a rest."

" 'Preciate it," said the speaker, smiling.

Thomas waited until they'd dismounted, and entered the house, then led them to the kitchen, where they sat at a table and he fetched them drinks.

"I'm curious to know why Miss Grey might be running away from her father," he said in what he hoped was a neutral tone.

The speaker, who'd given his name as Potter, looked to his companions, then shrugged. "Her father's not been good to Miss Agatha. All what lives around the Manor know that. It's a wonder to all that she didn't run off long before this." He drew on his ale.

"Why did she choose this time to leave?"

"Bein' married off to a huff-cap, man she loathed. Her father played a dirty trick on her and announced the engagement in front of folks." He shook his head sadly.

"A sad situation."

"Aye."

There were a few minutes of silence as the men finished their ale. Thomas found more for them.

"If you should find your master's daughter, what will you do? Will you drag her back to her father?"

Potter shook his head, and Thomas managed to conceal his surprise.

"No. We'll make the search because it's what the squire ordered. But none of us fellows—" he looked to the others, who nodded— "want to see her returned. He'd just go and strap her, and get her married all the faster to that nan-boy."

"Aye," muttered one of the other men.

"I see," said Thomas. He believed Potter's words, too, for the man did not seem the type to deceive.

"Well, we'd best be going." Potter stood, and the others quickly scrambled to their feet. "I don't suppose your master and mistress would be comin' back soon."

"I think it highly unlikely."

"I see."

Potter paused, his hat in his hand, and stared for a long moment at Thomas. "You seem a honest type, Mr. Dentham."

"Thank you for your confidence, Potter."

"I have a message for you to convey . . . if you should happen to see Miss Agatha sometime."

"I think it highly unlikely——"

"Well, just in case, you understand."

"Yes."

"Tell her we all care mightily for her and miss her, but wouldn't have her come back for anything. Tell her there's cruel men in the world who'll do all they can to hurt someone like her. Tell her we'll not give her away, but others the master hires might not be so caring. You tell her?" He peered up at Dentham.

"If I should see Miss Agatha."

"Aye."

With his silent companions following, Potter left the kitchen. Thomas trailed behind and watched as they mounted and turned their horses around. When he no longer saw them, he headed back toward the house and met Ben running toward him from the stables. A few moments later Holly appeared on the front steps.

"Is the mistress safe?" she asked anxiously.

Thomas stared at the cloud of dust left by the riders on the road. "I think so. For now at least. They'll not say anything to her father. But I fear," he paused, stopped.

"You fear what, Mr. Dentham?" the girl asked, her hands clasped.

"I fear that's not the last we'll be hearing of Squire Grey of Grey's Manor, and I fear it's only evil that'll be coming our way from this time on."

THIRTEEN

THE CHARCOAL SKY DAMPED ALL efforts of the sun, and bloated clouds glowered on the horizon. All around her the snow fell in leaden silence. What light there was was rapidly dying. She was running, and her boots were soaked, her feet chilled. Somewhere she had lost her bonnet and her cloak had almost been torn from her. Out of breath, she paused, and glanced fearfully over her shoulder. Something rumbled behind her, waves of the deep noise shuddering outward to ripple the ground under her feet. She drew the tattered cloak around her more firmly and began running again. Counterpoint to her own tortured breathing she heard a rasping panting. In the uneasy gloom something brushed by her ear, and she whimpered from fear. A dark shape, long and thin, glided out of the skeletal trees and flew past her. She stopped, startled. Darkness completely surrounded her now, and the deep breathing increased in volume until its source seemed to stand at her very elbow. The rumbling ceased and she heard another sound, muffled through the ever-falling snow. The pounding of a horse's hooves. A horse being ridden faster and faster. The hooves drummed along the road, and it shuddered with each stride of the horse. She glanced over her shoulder, saw something through the veil of snow, then turned back, but too late saw the log. She fell, landing in a snowbank on the other side, and could not move. The hoofbeats grew louder. Terror drove her to her feet, but she was still unsteady. She brushed snow from her cheek, her hair. She began running. She did not know where she was going. She was lost. And still the horse drew nearer. The shape loomed out of the darkness, a blacker black than the night snow. The horse, ebon with dark red eyes, reared, its forelegs striking out at her. She jumped back, but not quickly enough, for one of its hooves grazed her on the forehead. Sparks flew from the hooves' impact, and in the brief moment of flickering golden light she saw the horse's rider, a man swathed in a billowing cloak. His silver spurs shone with the light of the sparks. She stared upward into his face, and saw the mask across his features. The horse shrieked, reared to its full height again, and struck out. Screaming, she fell back into blackness, and fell and fell and——

Something cold pressed against her outflung arm and she recoiled, remembering her dream. Again the coldness touched her skin. She curled her fingers into a fist, struggled to open her eyes.

Lightness instantly assailed them, and she lowered her lids with a groan.

Again the coldness was there, a third time, but now it was accompanied by a low whine. Her eyes flew open and she frowned up at the ceiling. She rolled her head to the side.

Large brown eyes gazed soulfully at her. She blinked, and the eyes came into focus. She sat up, the sheet falling to her waist.

"Bruno!"

The dog wagged his tail and stretched, his front paws resting on the coverlet. She leaned over to hug him. He jumped onto the bed, knocking her back against the pillow. Excitedly he licked her face, his tail a blur. Laughing, she managed to extricate herself from him and sat up once more.

"Now how did you get away?" she asked the dog. "And particularly, how did you come to be in my room?"

In reply, he leaped up to lick her face again. She laughed again, hugged him, and looked toward the door.

Drummond stood there, the door shut.

"My lord—Richard, I mean—how long have you been there?" The fear of her dream returned to her, and she shivered.

His eyes did not miss that, but he smiled lazily. "For some time."

Aware suddenly that the sheerness of her nightgown did little to conceal the roundness of her breasts, she reached to pull up the sheet.

"Don't," he said. His eyes locked with hers, and she paused, her fingers touching the sheet. "We have been husband and wife now for a sennight and a half. You need not cover yourself in shame."

She blushed, but did not say anything. Bruno raced around on the bed, stopping from time to time to flop over onto his back to have his stomach scratched, in which she happily obliged the hound.

Drummond crossed the room in three easy strides, then settled upon the end of the bed without awaiting her invitation.

She was mute. She wanted to speak, but could not find the words. For a few minutes more she played with Bruno, so obviously overjoyed to see his mistress once more, while Drummond watched her. Finally the dog settled himself contentedly next to her pillow.

"I thank you for bringing him to me," she said at last.

"You are most welcome, Agatha."

"How did you come to have him?"

"I remembered what you had said of him, the affection you had for the dog, and so I sent a servant to see if the dog could be coaxed away. He was only too willing to leave the estate."

" 'Twas most kind of you—I have been sorely worried about him." She leaned back against the ornate headboard and stared down at her hands.

Drummond slid slightly closer.

She glanced up, her eyes wide.

He slowly leaned over her.

"Come now, Agatha, you know I will not harm you." He bent and kissed her full on the lips.

Her eyes closed and one arm slipped around his neck. Their combined breaths were warm and soft, and the last unpleasantness lingering from the dream faded. One of his hands rested lightly in the small of her back, and his fingers caressed her skin through the sheer material. She shivered, and he tightened his arms around her. She drew away for a moment, and stared up into the somber brown eyes. She rested her cheek on his shoulder, the cloth of his coat rustling against her skin. His hand continued its intricate pattern along her back, reaching from time to time to her trim waist, then darting back between her shoulders. A strange feeling crept through her, a tingling spreading through her arms, her chest, between her legs. She wiggled slightly, thinking that might ease the feeling, but it only increased.

He pressed his lips to her ear so he might whisper. "Agatha, let me come to your bed. Let us continue what we began."

She shivered, yet said nothing. Her heart was beating faster and faster, and she wanted him to hold her, to kiss her, to stroke her.

His lips kissed her neck, a feathery touch which sent a sharp shock running through her body. Her hands, gripping his coat in the back, tightened convulsively.

"Agatha," he said again, so softly she almost did not hear it. "Agatha, my dear, my love."

His hand strayed from her back, lingered for a moment at her side, then continued its way to its destination. He cupped her breast, and she shuddered delicately and languidly closed her eyes.

"My lord . . ."

"Richard," he chided her gently.

"Richard, I do not know . . . I . . ." She stopped in confusion. "I mean . . ."

His hand, during this exchange, was far from idle. His unrelenting fingers caressed her nipple, teasing the dusky aureole and tender bud to firm arousal. "You mean what?"

He was slowly picking her up, pulling her over onto his lap, against his chest, and she did not resist. Her head back, she stared up at him, into those dark brown eyes, and felt herself falling and falling——

Falling into darkness. She jerked, suddenly stiff, as he lowered to lie supine across the bed. She curled up, rolling away from him.

"What is amiss, my dear?"

The darkness of her dream had returned, the fear she had felt, the *threat* of it. She closed her eyes. She wanted so much to recapture the lovely moment before the fear had come back, the ugly all-consuming fear, but it was gone, swallowed by the darkness.

She slowly sat up, would not look at him. She raised her knees, circled them with her arms and laid her head on them.

"I had a dream." She spoke so softly he had to strain to hear her words.

"Yes?"

" 'Twas a strange dream that disturbed me."

"Do you wish to speak of it, Agatha?"

She shook her head, her hair brushing against her arms. "No, not yet."

A gentle hand grasped her upper arm; it was warming and a little comforting, but she did not move.

"I will not press you, my dear."

Still she said nothing.

He leaned down, kissed the top of her head, and walked away. "I will see you later at breakfast?"

"Yes." Her voice was muffled.

"Until then, my dear."

She nodded. He patted the dog, who opened one eye briefly, and then walked out of the room. The door closed softly behind him.

For a few minutes longer she sat there, then slowly she relaxed and rolled onto her side. She reached out to stroke Bruno. He licked her hand and his tail beat against the coverlet.

Tears began coursing down her cheeks, and she buried her face in the pillow, trying to swallow the lump in her throat rising to choke her. But she could not. The tears continued, unchecked, as she cursed her fear.

Paul watched the couple as they ate their breakfast in relative silence. He frowned thoughtfully, tapping one finger against the back of the other hand. He would have sworn yesterday when they'd gone on the picnic that these two had discovered at least the bond of passion. Yet today—while they were quite polite to one another, and Drummond called her "my dear" and she called him "Richard" rather than "my lord," something was amiss.

Definitely amiss.

He sipped his ale and watched them closely.

"Richard."

He glanced up from his plate. "Yes, my dear?"

"Would it sometime be possible for me to invite my friend, Lucy Wilmot, to stay with us?"

"She is no chatterbox, is she?" Drummond's eyebrows drew together. "I would have no wish for her to run to your father to tell him where you are."

"Oh no. She little loves my father, nor he her. She would never tell."

"Then I see no harm in it."

She smiled at him. "Thank you."

Drummond shrugged lightly. "I do not think you need wait months, either. Indeed, invite her to come visit the last week of April."

Paul glanced up at him, but Drummond's face was bland. He could read nothing there.

"The last week of April? That's so far away," she said.

"Not so distant as you would think," he murmured in a tone so low Paul did not think Agatha heard. More loudly, he said, "I am sure she will have much to do to ready herself for the journey, and I am sure she will welcome the additional weeks."

"Very well." She returned to her breakfast.

The room was silent except for the clicking of silverware against china.

Paul leaned back in his chair, watching Drummond for a few minutes

"Yes, Paul?"

"What?"

"You were watching me, and wished to ask me something."

Damned man had eyes like a hawk, or a falcon, Paul thought with an ironic smile.

"No, no, my friend, just staring off into space."

"Then kindly direct your gaze into a space not occupied by myself, thank you."

The words, almost snapped, remained just this

side of rudeness, causing Sterling to raise an eyebrow in puzzlement. Surely the obvious answer was a lovers' quarrel, a spat between newlyweds.

Surely it was nothing to worry about. At times he even caught them directing secret glances at each other, although only when the other was engrossed in the meal. There was longing in her eyes, and something akin, but more so, in Drummond's as well. Hurt, perhaps? Or anger? No, it was not the latter. As for Agatha, she looked as though she had been weeping. Still, it was strange—he had heard no raised voices earlier.

Most perplexing. He would, of course, have to patch matters up. Such a charming couple could not be allowed to quarrel. 'Twas true he had expressed many misgivings about the entire scheme when Drummond had laid the plan out before him, but now that he knew Agatha he thought she was plainly delightful, and would do more than well for his friend.

How vividly he remembered those misgivings, too, for they had been serious. He had thought Richard's plan, to rescue a girl he scarcely knew, hare-brained. He had said it was none of Richard's concern, in truth, and that he needn't bother, but Richard, his eyes hardening, had claimed she was being mistreated.

Always the gallant, always the idealist. Always the one who was hurt.

"It could jeopardize everything you've worked so hard for," he had started to point out, but Richard's look had choked the words in his throat, and he had subsided.

" 'Twill jeopardize nothing," Richard had said, and that was almost the end of the matter.

To his dismay, he realized that Richard needed a helper for the scheme. He had been loathe to volunteer; abducting girls from their marriage coaches was scarcely an ability he wished to cultivate. Yet he could not see his friend stand—nor hang if they should be so unfortunate as to be caught—alone. Thus, in the end he'd given in, said he would go, and Richard, smiling one of his rare smiles, had said he knew he could count on Paul.

On the fateful day, he had left his estate, changed into rough clothes in the woods, and put on a mask so he would not be recognized. Then the two men had met at a prearranged spot, not far from Grey's Manor. Drummond had already earlier declined an invitation to the wedding, claiming he would be traveling on that date. For corroboration, he had his servants, who were quite willing to swear to anything their master requested.

They'd waited, without a word, until they heard the rumble of the coach. Paul's mouth had been dry, and his hands had trembled as he kicked his horse forward. Indeed, his dreams the night before had been filled with visions of failure, capture, and subsequent unmasking, and a visit to the three-legged mare. But they'd had a far easier time than he had imagined.

They'd whisked away the girl, straight from under the nose of her ogre father, Drummond had married her in a ceremony just barely the right side of illegal, and now they were lawfully—if not happily—married.

Oh yes, he had grown to like Agatha, and he

really felt she would do well with his friend. If only . . . if only Richard would let go of the past. He thought of the night two years ago, the night Richard had received the terrible scarring wound, and he shuddered.

'Twas a scar of body and mind, for he knew his friend still brooded about the events of that night. But that was the past, all was gone, and he could not change it, no matter how hard he tried.

Nor would dwelling upon it help matters. Perhaps Agatha could bring some healing power to Richard, salve the wound, allow it to heal naturally, and then he could forget.

A hand shook his shoulder. Startled, he glanced up to see Drummond.

"I called you twice, but you were sunk in your thoughts."

"Er, yes." He reddened. "What were you wishing, Richard?"

"Shall we go riding?"

"Of course." Drummond's hand dropped from his shoulder, and Paul pushed back his chair. Agatha had remained seated. He glanced to her, then to Drummond, then back at her. "You are riding with us, Agatha?"

Drummond spoke quickly. "Agatha expressed a desire to remain at home to talk with Willem."

"I see." He smiled at Agatha, bent low over her hand. "Until later."

She smiled wanly up at him, and he detected in her eyes the faint glimmer of tears recently blinked away.

The men arranged to meet in thirty minutes and Paul removed himself at once to his rooms to change into riding clothes. He did not see Agatha again, for when he later stuck his head in the dining room, she was gone. He met up with Drummond at the stables. Ben had already saddled the horses, so all that remained was for them to mount and head toward the woods.

"Agatha seems upset today," Paul ventured once they were out of the stableyard.

"She is merely overcome by my present."

"The hound?"

"Yes."

"You gave it to her this morning?"

"Yes."

"Oh."

The horses picked their way along an overgrown track, and Paul concentrated on watching the path. Drummond was disinclined to speech today, it seemed.

"But she *is* happy . . . with the dog?" he quickly added, when Drummond gazed at him.

"Yes, I believe so. She did thank me."

"Good, good."

Sterling paused to adjust a stirrup. He glanced at his friend's face, now set into an emotionless mask, and he wondered what Richard's thoughts were.

"Do you think it wise for her to invite her friend to come at that particular time?"

"Yes. I think it would be a most excellent time. I am aware of the significance of the date, you know, Paul."

"Oh. Well, if you're convinced——"

"I am."

Paul lapsed into silence, and concentrated on

watching Grey Sir as he tried to break into a gallop. Drummond's hands held back on the reins, the muscles in his arm bulging with the effort. Drummond, he thought, was a lot like the stallion. Both wanted to run all out, but Drummond would no more allow his horse to do so than he would himself.

Finally, he could tolerate the silence no longer. He *had* to know. "You have fought?"

Drummond looked again his way, and his eyes were darker than usual. "No, Paul, we have not fought. Come, friend, I know you are concerned. Do not be. I am confident this matter will work itself out."

"I hope so. I do like Agatha. Very much."

"And so," said Drummond softly, almost to himself, "do I. Too much."

With that, he kicked his stallion into a canter.

She watched from the window in her sitting room as the two horsemen reached the fringes of the forest. Paul seemed to be doing all the talking; Drummond appeared as silent as he had been at breakfast. Paul paused to adjust his stirrup, then said something. Apparently it did not sit well with her husband, for a short time later he kicked his horse into a canter. The stallion shot into the woods, and even from this distance she could see Paul's startled expression. He struggled to catch up, and then the woods swallowed them and she saw them no more.

Disappointed, she turned away, and hugged her arms around her body, trying to warm herself. She was so cold . . . so very cold. Tears blurred her eyes, and she sniffed. She could not prevent them from welling up, spilling over the rims of her eyes and running down her cheeks. Sobbing, she threw herself across the bed. Bruno jumped up next to her and poked her with his cold nose, but she did not respond. He whined a little at her inattention.

She was a fool, a fool for having ruined everything. This morning Drummond had come to her, and she had felt as she had the day before. She had been so very willing. She had wanted him to touch her, to kiss her, and in turn, she had wanted to caress him, to hold him in her arms. She had wanted all of this, and then stupidly she had remembered the dream and she had turned to ice.

He had been hurt. She had seen it in his eyes. She did not want that. She wanted his arms, his lips, his body, and yet her fear had paralyzed her. Her memories of past harsh treatment turned her traitor to her own desires.

Intuitively she knew he would not be patient with her forever. Not that he would ever be cruel—he would simply turn away, once and for all, and her heart would break. They would continue on as polite strangers, but as for love . . . there would be no chance of that. So, she told herself sternly, she must take hold of her fear, must not let it turn her cold, must not hurt him. For that was inexcusable; as inexcusable as all the hurt she had received in her life.

"One chance left, Agatha," she whispered aloud. Bruno, hearing her voice, licked her hand and she buried her face at his neck. "That's all."

PART III:

THE COURTSHIP

FOURTEEN

THE FOLLOWING DAY, PAUL LEFT, to Agatha's sorrow. Though she pleaded with him to stay longer, he declined, claiming he'd already overstayed his welcome, and that he must now return home to tend business. He thanked her profusely, shook hands with Drummond, mounted his horse, waved, and began the ride back to his own estate some miles to the north.

Following Paul's departure she and Drummond said little, and it was then she realized how often Paul had entertained them that weekend. She watched as Drummond closeted himself in his study for hours. She wondered what he did there, what he thought, what he read. Did he think of her, of their misunderstanding? Or did his thoughts delve deeper, into the darkness she saw enveloping him?

The hours passed in loneliness for her. When the walls began to close down upon her, she retreated to the openness of the garden. From time to time as she wandered she glanced back at the house. Once, as the sun's golden rays slanted low in the afternoon sky, she thought she saw a curtain fall back at one of the windows, but she could not be sure.

When the light had so faded from the garden that everything seemed to be colorless, she arose from the bench where she had been sitting. At last aware of the early evening chill, she rubbed her arms and wished she'd remembered to bring a shawl. She hurried inside to warm herself before a fire.

Restless even after her long walk, she wandered from hearth to hearth in the great house, but nowhere encountered Drummond. She wondered if he remained locked away in his study. She dined alone, the first meal she had spent thus, and her spirits were low as she sampled the soup and the braised beef. She ate little, suffering Merton's reproving eye upon her, and afterward retired to the library where she could find some comfort from the books and a cozy fire.

She crossed the floor and held out her hands to the flames.

"You have turned blue from the cold."

She whirled. Drummond was sprawled in one of the chairs, watching her. She had not even noticed him in the depths of the chair when she entered.

"You surprised me, my lord."

"Ah, we have returned to that, have we?"

She blushed a little. On the table beside him sat a silver tray. On it were a half-empty bottle and a glass filled with dark liquid.

"Care for a glass of wine, Agatha?"

She shook her head.

"What's the matter, my dear, cat got your tongue?"

"Indeed, it has not!"

"Ah, good, she *can* speak," he said, as if to himself. "I had feared all her words had left when Paul departed."

"I could not speak with you as you had shut yourself away, my lord."

" 'Tis true."

She folded her hands, waited. Her back was toward the fire, her face shadowed.

He studied her for a few moments, sipped more wine, then stood.

"You are displeased with me."

"No, my lord."

"Richard, please," he said urgently.

"Richard. I am not; 'tis you who are unhappy with me."

"No, Agatha." He came close to her. "I think we mistook one another's thoughts."

She smiled wanly. "I think so, too."

"Shall we begin anew?"

She nodded.

"Can you tell me now what it was that disturbed you, my dear?"

"A dream I had," she whispered, unable to meet his eyes. " 'Twas frightful, and when I thought of it again, I was afraid."

"There's naught to fear."

He was so close she could have reached out with a finger and touched him. Trembling, she looked up at him. His eyes were dark with shadows, while flickering light from the fire played across the planes of his face, accenting the livid scar. How like a bird of prey he looks tonight, she thought, and shuddered at the image.

He smiled slowly, and the image fled. He reached out with a hand made unsteady by emotion, and hesitantly touched her arm. She shivered.

"You are cold."

She nodded.

His arms slipped around her, holding her loosely. She was aware of his hands, his chest.

"I am sorry you are frightened."

"No longer," she whispered. Her lips parted, and he gently traced their outline with the tip of one finger. She shivered again under his touch.

"Your lips are very soft." His breath was warm against her ear, and tickled deep within her.

She said nothing, could find no words.

His fingers now followed the line of her jaw, caressed her cheekbones, swept along her arching eyebrows, softly touched the lobes of her ears.

"A determined face," he said in a low tone grown husky.

They kissed at last; his tongue gently probed her lips, and as she opened to him, he explored the soft depths of her mouth. She moaned softly, clung to him as her legs seemed to give way. Her fingers tightened until they became almost a part of his arms. Her breathing quickened, beating a tempo with his. The only sound in the room was the crackling of the fire along the logs and their combined breathing.

He drew back, and her eyes opened. His cheeks were red, and there was a curious light in his eyes, almost as if he had a fever. His arms tightened around her, brought her closer to him so that she was pressed against him. She could feel the hardness of his desire growing against her, and her pulse raced.

"Are you afraid?" he asked.

She nodded.

"You needn't be."

The gentleness of his tone reassured her, and she relaxed a little, only to stand stiffly as his hands played across the back of her bodice. One hook came undone, then another, then a third, until at last the bodice was loose. He pulled it off, let it drop carelessly to the floor.

Shyly she crossed her hands in front of her breasts, protecting them from his view. He laughed gently and disengaged her hands, wrapping them around his back. His fingertips brushed the smooth globes of her breasts, pushed up by the corset she wore, and trailed across the pale skin.

The new tickling sensation within her increased until her stomach was knotted with tension. She blushed, and the redness crept down her cheek, down her neck, down to the white expanse of her bosom.

He leaned down and kissed the top of one breast, his tongue just playing across it, the delicate touch causing her to sigh with pleasure. Her hands, still behind him, tightened convulsively. He cupped her breasts, brushing against their tips with his slender, whipcord-strong fingers. The tender red peaks rose and firmed at his incitement. She shifted, the tickling intensifying deep within her, sending a longing for she knew not what coursing through her body until she wanted to cry out.

She traced the scar which had once frightened her, her fingers feathersoft. Again she kissed him, and he returned the embrace, leaving her shaken.

He sank to the thick, soft carpet and slowly drew her down beside him. They were only a foot from the hearth. He unfastened her skirt, loosened her corset, painstakingly slowly removed all her clothes until she lay naked before his dark scrutiny. She shyly tried to cover herself, but he would not permit it. The flickering light gleamed on her body as his hands traveled down her slender neck, across her full breasts, past her narrow waist, down to the creamy lengths of her legs. She watched him from under half-lowered eyelashes as he propped himself on one elbow, leaned over to kiss her. She closed her eyes as his fingers idly caressed her stomach. The fingers fled south, seeking warmth, and she groaned with pleasure as he found the center of her womanhood. Her legs parted as he stroked her satiny inner thigh. He brought his head down to her breasts. His tongue flicked out, caressed the tiny rosebudlike nipple, and she seized his arm.

"Richard," she said hoarsely, and he smiled.

He turned away and began undressing. He pulled off the cravat, dropped it; it fluttered slowly downward. She watched wide-eyed as his maroon coat fell to the floor, soon followed by his waistcoat, shirt, and breeches. At length he, too, was naked, and he lay next to her, his chest barely just touching her hip.

She took her turn now to stare at him, at his

unfamiliar masculine form, and she found it beautiful. His shoulders were wide, his hips narrow, and he had the strong, muscular legs of a man who spent many hours on horseback. A mat of black curly hair covered his chest. She touched it, twisted a curl around her finger. Then she glanced shyly below his waist, blushing at what she saw. His hand guided hers toward his stiffening manhood.

"No," she said faintly.

"Yes, Agatha. For my pleasure—as I pleased you."

Her fingers brushed the solid flesh, curled, then reached out once more. She took his length into her hand, warm and throbbing.

"Ah love, 'tis wonderful."

She shook her head. "W-What do I do now?"

He leaned over and whispered into her ear.

Faintly, questioningly, she repeated his words. He laughed softly, and nodded.

"I could not. I mean——" She groaned as his lips sought one rosy nipple.

Her fingers moved instinctively, caressing the length of his manhood, finding the rhythm that caused him to groan deep in his throat. "Ah, Agatha!"

"My fear is gone," she admitted, smiling shyly.

One finger traced the line of her lips, then trailed down her pointed chin to her neck. He kissed the hollow there, his lips cool. "I will not hurt you, Agatha. That I promise you."

She nodded, her hair fanning out in dark waves across the carpet. He wound his hands through it, toyed with the gleaming tresses, watched as they reflected the light. She ran her tongue across her lips, and trembled at his touch. Then he rolled closer to her, his body half over her, and slipped one of his legs between hers, using it like his hand to caress the glowing ember of her desire into a flame.

"I will go slowly, for this is your first time. It is hardest then. I do not wish you to learn fear."

"I won't," she said softly, her voice husky with desire, "not with you as my instructor."

He showed teeth in a smile, then covered her face and neck, breasts and stomach and legs with kisses that burned. She moaned and gripped his hair in her hands, exclaiming softly with surprise, then murmuring his name as he rolled gently upon her. Her hand explored his shoulder, chest, back, as he continued kissing her. His breathing came now in short pants, and her legs widened. She moaned as he slid into her. She wrapped her legs around his, drawing his body closer to her, and he thrust deeply.

Biting her lip, she cried out, grabbing his shoulder. She arched her back as he thrust again, deeper still, and he moaned, a wild animal sound. Their bodies were slick with sweat. When he briefly pulled away, their skin seemed to have already melded. He kissed her face, her ears, her throat, and stroked her breasts, all the while murmuring endearments. She called him by name once, whimpered, then cried out as her center of delight opened. They rocked, thrust, slipped away, came closer together, became one living entity. She felt as if she were being cut in twain, and then an aching pleasure burst inside her, rippling wave after wave until she was shuddering with delight. He called out, his body rigid, and time slowed for them, kept them encapsulated in a perfect moment where only they existed. She stared up into his dark eyes and for the first time saw the brooding gone, and he stared down into her eyes, lost in the lapis depths. Then the moment was past, their eyes closed against the tempest of their ardor, and she was clutching at his shoulder, clinging to him, and sobbing, deep-throated in her passion. In another moment the passion had ebbed, the tremors stilled.

When her breathing was once more steady, she looked at him. He had rested his chin on one hand and was watching her. Her eyes were still moist with tears of joy. She dashed a hand at one so she could better see him. His arm went around her, a warm, comforting weight, and she gazed up at him.

"I——" she began, but he put his hand across her lips.

"No more, my dear."

He kissed her cheeks, wiped away the tears that had fallen, unnoticed, in the midst of their passion. Her swollen lips parted, and she felt his warm breath touching her face.

There had been no fear, no hurt—none beyond that brief instant—just as he had promised. There was only pleasure, and love, and warmth.

She snuggled closer in the depths of his arms. They lay there for long minutes saying nothing. They did not have to speak. Her eyes closed, her long black lashes sweeping down onto her cheeks.

A spark arched from the flames, landing on resin oozing from a log. The resin burst into flame and popped with an explosive sound, and her eyes flew open. She must have fallen asleep, she thought. She shifted her head slightly, glanced at Drummond, who lay with one leg draped across hers, his arm still cradling her. His head was pillowed on her shoulder; his eyes closed. His breathing was regular, and she knew he slept as she had. She studied him, saw his lashes were long and dark and thick. He did not look so brooding now, did not look as if he hid some secret. He did not look the hawk tonight. His face was almost innocent in sleep. The scar still was white against the tan of his face, and she touched a high cheekbone. He stirred, shifted slightly, but did not wake.

The happiness that had been denied to her for so long blossomed now into full flower. She stretched, seeking not to disturb her husband. Voluptuously, she raised her arms above her head, felt the warmth of the fire on her fingertips. She gazed at the flames and sighed contentedly.

It had begun as a nightmare, this marriage. She recalled her abduction from the coach, her sudden marriage to a stranger, then her arrival at her new home. But she had been so very lucky. Her husband had proved to be a gentle man, albeit a sad-eyed one, who wished to make her happy. The days had mellowed her anger, softened it into liking, and now—now . . .

It was so perfect.

She hugged herself and shivered, nodding her head. It was true.

She loved him.

She had not thought it possible, would not have believed it, but the impossible had happened. She knew as she looked back that it had all begun the night before her planned marriage to Lord Alford. Her love for Drummond had been planted in her father's garden, cultivated in the past ten days, and had flowered this night before the fire.

She glanced back at him. His eyes were open, and she could tell he had been watching her for some time. He seemed amused.

"You look quite happy," he said, reaching up to give her a gentle kiss.

"I am."

"Good," he said lazily, slowly rolling onto his back. He lay with his hands by his side, his fingers slightly curled. His eyelids lowered, but did not close.

She wanted to tell him of her new-found love, of the love that she had discovered tonight, but she suddenly felt shy and tongue-tied. She could not speak of this love, for she was unsure. No, she would say nothing. She would let the flower grow, and grow, and then she would see.

"What's that smile for?" He arched one eyebrow, a slightly teasing tone in his voice.

"This." She rolled onto her side, kissed him, then folded her arms, and laid her cheek on them. "Richard."

"Yes, Agatha?"

"Will you love me again?"

He shifted his head to gaze long at her then, and smiled, a gentle and sad expression, she thought. "Gladly, my dear."

She put her arms around his neck and pressed her lips against his, and sighed deeply. His arms brought her close, and once more he expertly showed her the ways of love. But this time he lingered, drawing her to higher peaks of passion, allowing it to last even longer than before until Agatha felt she could bear it no longer. His deep gasp of pleasure mingled with her sweet cry, and they collapsed, spent, their bodies shining with now cooling sweat, into each other's arms, wrapped around one another, their cheeks touching.

She knew her life would only grow better now. All the past unhappiness was at last gone.

FIFTEEN

THE FOLLOWING FOUR DAYS PASSED in idyllic happiness for Agatha. Drummond devoted his daily hours to her, as they rode through the woods, picnicked along the stream, or walked arm-in-arm through the rose garden he had had planted for her.

And each night he came to her. When the house was quiet and she had retired to her rooms, she lay awake and waited impatiently. Finally, the door would quietly open; he would slip into the room, and then the next moment he would be beside her in the great bed.

With each ceremony of love she grew more experienced, more deft with hands and lips, more able to give him pleasure, for she wished to do that. He gave her so much; surely 'twas only fair she return the favor, she reasoned.

He laughed softly the night she told him, and

declared her a delight. They kissed and embraced, and he stroked her dark curls, murmuring in her ear. The first night they slept many hours afterward. He woke first, and started to slip out of the bed.

She woke with the movement. "No, don't," she whispered, holding out her hand to him.

He looked down at her face, pale in the moonlight which came through a crack in the curtains, and she saw an expression in his eyes, part joy, part tenderness, and something more, something she might almost have called fear. But he stayed, and she told herself she must have been mistaken.

Thereafter he stayed with her, clasped in her arms, one morning stayed even until Holly crept in to wake her mistress. Eyes widening when she saw the sleeping couple, the maid crept just as quietly out so she would not disturb them.

The next four days, Agatha thought, were the happiest she had ever spent. They read together in the library, talked for long hours of books; she spoke of her life with her father, although he never spoke of his past. And while that might have proved to be a dark cloud in her sunny days Agatha did not dwell on it. She refused to see that the sad look had not completely left his eyes; she refused to believe that there might yet be some unhappiness. For she was deliriously happy, and in love, and cared not a fig for anything else.

On the first day he presented her with an exquisitely elaborate cage carved of yellowed bamboo—from China, he claimed. Perched inside was a small bird, its plummage brilliant blue—the blue of her eyes, he said—with a most melodious warble and a very bright eye. She threw her arms about his neck, thanking him with a deep kiss. With the ever faithful Bruno at their side, they took long walks through the woods, and there under the cover of the tall trees with their new leaves, he spread his cloak, and they made love.

On the second day he presented her with a new sadde for Tally. The fine leather saddle was tooled with exquisite designs and its mountings were of silver. She thanked him, but said she could give him nothing. He said he needed nothing.

The third day dawned as beautiful as the ones before, the sky a perfect blue with only a few wisps of clouds. The sun shone brightly, promising a perfect spring day. After they had breakfasted, he took her by the hand and led her to the hothouse. There he told her to close her eyes. She obeyed, and he led her in. When she once more opened them, she saw on the workbench a rose of a deep purple hue. In its center the petals were a blue-purple. For you, he said simply, and she cried.

On the fourth day he surprised her early in the morning with a picnic lunch, and when she struggled up out of the arms of sleep and tried to rise, he pushed her back onto her pillows. The picnic, he informed her, was to be indoors. He promptly unpacked the basket and spread the feast across her bed, and there they ate warm beef pies, spiced eggs, and toast with marmalade, and drank goblet after goblet of sparkling red wine. He toasted her, and she laughed with him.

Afterward, well after noon, he swept aside the carnage of their picnic, and pulled her to him, kissing her eyelids, her cheeks, her mouth, and there they made love. No one disturbed them, for the servants had their orders. When evening came, and he rolled out of the bed, he went to the door, opened it, and picked up the basket that had been left outside by a very busy Cook. He returned to the bed, drew aside the napkin, and they once more partook of a picnic dinner.

On the fifth day she awakened to a sharp crack of thunder, and the tattoo of rain on the window-pane. She rolled over to hug Drummond and to wish him a good morning, but instead stared, not believing what she saw.

She was alone in the bed.

She sat up and called for him, but he did not answer. The fire had died down hours ago, and a chill lay on the room. She shivered, hugging herself.

Pulling on a dressing gown, she rose and looked out the window. She could see nothing but greyness. Greyness out, and greyness in, she thought, for her spirits had settled low. Perhaps he had not wished to awaken her, she told herself. That was it.

She decided not to ring for her maid, dressing quickly by herself. Downstairs she searched for him in the study, the dining room, the library, and one of the salons. She asked Thomas if he'd seen his master. Thomas shook his head. She asked Merton, the housekeeper; she asked Holly.

No one had seen Drummond for hours.

She stood finally in the library, where a fire roared in the fireplace, and stared morosely out at the pelting rain.

'Twas late afternoon, and she did not know where her husband was. He had left no word, and she did not understand. Even before they had reached their newfound accord, he had been thoughtful in this regard, always leaving word for her of his whereabouts. She had assumed, after the closeness of the past four days, that he would have told her if he found it necessary to leave the estate for some time.

Perhaps he'd ridden off to arrange another present for her, and wished it to be a secret, she thought. But somehow she knew that was not the reason.

Her stomach grumbled a protest, which she ignored. She had eaten nothing, had sipped only a little tea earlier. She had no appetite.

Not knowing what else to do, and feeling lost and adrift, she wandered through the rooms empty of his presence. She walked around his study and gazed at the books, the objects on his desk, which was immense and built of a deep-grained maple. She studied the pictures on the walls, then her gaze wandered to the window and she went to it to see if she could see him.

She remained there until Merton announced the arrival of Paul Sterling.

Agatha turned to find him already in the room. For a moment she thought he watched her somewhat apprehensively. But then, smiling as usual, he was crossing the room to bow over her hand.

"Pray, Agatha, how are you today?"

"Fine, Paul," she said, although her tone belied her words.

He glanced at her, then away, straightening one lace cuff. "And how is Richard?"

"I don't know," she replied listlessly. She moved away, returning to the window to stare out the water-spattered window. "In truth, Paul, I have not seen him all day."

"Oh?"

She regarded him curiously. His tone had been quite sharp and she wondered at that.

"Yes. I woke late, and he was already gone. No one admits to having seen him, nor to know where he has gone. I do not think the servants tell the truth," she said. "I think they do not like me."

"They all adore you!" he protested.

She shook her head sadly. "No, they tolerate me for their master's sake. They do not love or respect me. I think Thomas believes I am not worthy of his master. Perhaps I am not."

"Come, Agatha, my dear, do not be so morose. Let me call for some wine to cheer you."

"Nothing could cheer me today."

"Perhaps we should repair from this room," he suggested.

"*His* room," she said.

Paul nodded, helped her from the study, and led her into a salon, where he saw her seated before the fire. Then he rang for Merton and ordered wine. He settled before the fireplace, his arms crossed against his chest, one boot resting on the grate.

"I am a sorry hostess today," she said with a sad smile.

"Doesn't signify," he said kindly.

"You have not said why you ventured forth this day in the rain."

"No reason, Agatha, only a desire to visit," he responded lightly.

"I trust the rain did not prove too troublesome to you?"

"Er, no."

At that moment Merton arrived with the tray, set it on a low table, and waited for further instructions. Paul waved him out of the room. He opened the bottle, poured, and handed her a goblet. Then he filled his. He studied the golden liquid for a moment, then asked, "What shall we toast, Agatha dear?"

She started to shrug, then said, "Happiness."

He winced. "Very well. To happiness." He took a long swallow, watched her as she sipped her wine.

"Don't worry about Richard," he said cheerfully after a moment.

"Why?"

"Why? Well, he's a resourceful fellow, and I doubt he's run into any trouble."

"Then why has he not returned?"

"Er, well, his errand might take many hours to complete."

She seized the opening. "Errand?"

"Figure of speech, my dear." He lapsed into silence, sloshed the wine in the goblet, stared at the hissing flames.

The minutes passed in silence. He filled her glass a second and a third time, and watched as she slowly drank the wine. Outside the light faded from grey to black, and the rain continued to fall.

At length, when the only light in the salon came from the fire, she stirred. "You will stay to dinner, won't you, Paul?"

"Love to."

She rose from the settee. "Let me inform Cook." She left the room, and he took a turn around it; glanced out the window, listened to the soft chiming of a clock out in the hall, finished his glass of wine, poured another. He waited for her to return.

"Dinner is in just half an hour," she said, coming through the door. Her quiet approach so startled him he dropped his goblet, spilling wine all over his coat.

He stared in dismay at the spreading stain. "How foolish of me." He pulled out a handkerchief and began ineffectually mopping it.

"Here, let me." She resolutely took the handkerchief away from him and soon most of the wine had been removed from his coat.

"Well, thank you, my dear. That's much better." He forced a nervous chuckle and smile. "Must be getting clumsy."

She handed him another glass of wine and stared at him speculatively. "Or nervous."

"Nervous?" He accepted the glass, and saluted her. "Me? Whatever for?"

She cocked her head slightly, watching him gulp his wine. "I don't know, Paul, I thought perhaps you could tell me."

"Nonsense, my girl. The day's made you skittish. That's all."

"Perhaps."

The door opened. It was Merton.

"Dinner is served, my lady."

"Thank you, Merton. We shall be in shortly."

"Very good."

He bowed and left.

"Pleasant fellow, isn't he?" Paul asked, searching

for conversation. He started for the door. Her hand on his sleeve stopped him.

"Paul." Her voice was quiet, yet forceful. He faced her.

"Yes, Agatha."

"Where is he?"

He looked at her, saw her blue eyes intent on him, and took a deep breath. "I don't know."

"You are telling the truth?"

"Yes."

"Very well. Let us go to dinner."

"After you, my dear." He bowed gallantly.

She flashed a brief smile at him and preceded him out of the room. As she left, he sighed deeply with relief. He did not know how much longer he could continue lying to her.

After a long and silent dinner, which Paul proclaimed excellent as usual and of which he ate more than his usual amount while she only toyed with her food, they retired to the library. Paul sat in the chair close to the fireplace. Her face intent, Agatha paced about the room, her hands clasping and unclasping.

He sipped his cherry cordial and watched her stop before the window to gaze mournfully through the water-specked glass. From time to time thunder, deep and menacing, rolled overhead, and she invariably started.

"Agatha," he called gently after watching her for what seemed the hundredth time, "do come and sit down, my dear. Your agitation won't bring him home any earlier, and I trow you'll only exhaust yourself."

"Where could he be?" she whispered, as if she had not heard Sterling's words.

He said nothing.

"What if he is lying on some road, his blood running out."

"Then Grey Sir surely would have returned to the stables by now. I believe he is a horse of uncommon sense." He had said the latter in a light tone, but she did not seem to hear.

"He could be dead."

"Agatha, Richard is not dead." His tone was quite firm.

She looked at him. "How do you know?"

He sipped the cordial, took time to select the proper words for his reply. "I think he is quite safe, for had he been killed—nay, even hurt with the merest scratch—I am quite convinced we would have somehow known it. We care for him too deeply not to know if something dreadful happens to him. Do you not agree?"

Though agreeing with a nod, she resumed her pacing, and Sterling leaned back in the chair with a heartfelt and weary sigh.

After a few moments he spoke again. "Do you wish me to stay the night? Would that be of some comfort to you, my dear?"

"You must stay, Paul," she said earnestly. "You cannot go riding out in that downpour. I do believe it is storming even harder than when you arrived." She paused. "Something terrible might happen to you." She faced the darkened window.

He said nothing, simply stared down at the toes of his black riding boots.

Out in the hall by the stairs the grandfather

clock struck twelve, a deep resonating chiming, and each count of the hour seemed to be a thrust of a sword in her. Her face grew even more wan.

"It's getting late," he said after the last stroke of the clock had faded.

"Yes. Very late." She turned back to him. "I'll have Mrs. Gordon show you to your room, if you wish to retire now."

He grinned and heaved himself from his chair. "No need to disturb Mrs. Gordon. I know the way." He took her cold hand in both of his, and held it for a long moment. "Now, please promise me you won't worry, Agatha. Richard is exceedingly resourceful, and I am quite sure he has come to no harm."

She just nodded once.

"I do not wish you to stay up very long, or you shall be quite exhausted upon the morrow. Perhaps if it is a fine day we could pack a bit of a picnic lunch and ride out to the stream tomorrow. What do you say?" he asked heartily.

"Yes, that would be fine," she said slowly.

He was convinced she had not heard a word he said. Sighing, he bowed to her, wished her a good night, and left the room.

She waited for a few minutes, then sat in the vacated chair. She waited, and heard the clock chime one. Her eyes blurred, and her head nodded forward, her chin resting on her chest. When she next heard the clock it was striking four. She jumped from the chair, rushed upstairs and paused outside Drummond's room.

She hesitated, then holding her breath, she knocked softly.

No answer.

Perhaps he had not heard. Perhaps he was soundly asleep, having come home and gone to bed while she dozed belowstairs.

She knocked again, this time a little more loudly, more firmly.

Still no response.

She grasped the doorknob, twisted it, and stepped into the room. She waited while her eyes adjusted to the darkness, then looked around. To her left stood a small table, on it a candle and flint. She lit the candle, holding it carefully so it would not drip wax on her, then raised it. She stepped into the room itself and stared at the bed.

It was empty.

With a cry she dropped the candle. Its flame flickered out and the candle rolled away from her, coming to rest under the bed.

She fled his bedchamber, ran down the hall, and slammed the door of her rooms. She flung herself onto her bed, but tears did not come.

Instead she lay there, and wondered where her husband could be so late in the night, so early in the morning, and why he had not said a word to her of his plans.

SIXTEEN

SHE AWOKE LATE THE NEXT morning, and quickly dressed in plain clothes. She searched for Drummond, but did not have far to look for she heard his voice coming from the library. She paused, heard Sterling's voice, hesitated, then knocked on the door and entered without waiting for a response from within.

"Ah, my dear." Drummond rose from behind the desk. He came around and kissed her cheek. "Won't you join us?"

"I don't wish to disturb you . . ."

"Nonsense. We were just talking of horses, weren't we, Paul?"

"Er, yes."

She glanced quickly at Paul's face, and saw a particularly bland expression there; her husband seemed in almost too jovial a mood. She did not think they had been talking of horseflesh prior to her arrival. But what they had been discussing she could not fathom. She was determined to say nothing of his absence the previous night. Let him be the first one to speak of it, she averred. Let him offer his explanation.

They retired to the dining room for the midday meal and spent a leisurely three hours there. Afterward the trio walked through the garden until Sterling, claiming he'd been too much trouble already, bade them farewell, even though they invited him to stay for dinner. If Drummond was surprised to find Sterling had spent the night, he said nothing to her.

After Sterling's departure, Drummond devoted all his attention to her at the meal. They talked of their horses, the garden, and the day's activities. Never once did he mention where he had been. It was as though he had never been gone and everything was as it had been.

She chided herself for her suspicious nature. Perhaps, she thought, his absence had been an accident, or perhaps he was readying a surprise for her. Perhaps he was simply waiting for the right moment to tell her.

Perhaps.

She had no sooner crawled into bed and extinguished the single candle than the door opened.

"Richard?"

"Yes, my dear."

The door scraped shut, and she shivered with anticipation. She could heard his footsteps growing closer. Finally he sat on the bed. His fingers reached out and stroked the fine hair off her forehead. She trembled at his touch. She could see him outlined against the light of the fire.

"Agatha," he whispered hoarsely. His lips eagerly sought hers, and he pulled back the covers and lay down beside her.

Her anger and worry were forgotten as she slipped her arms around his neck. He deftly pulled her nightgown over her head, and ran his hands across the hills and valleys of her body, arousing her to such a height within minutes that she clutched his shoulders and whispered, "Now, now, Richard, please."

He eased into her and she cried out with the intensity of her pleasure. They rocked together, kissing and stroking and searching, and when at last she felt the rippling shudders coursing through her, he cried out in a deep voice at the same moment. They collapsed into each other's arms and slept, undisturbed.

She woke early in the morning, expecting when she rolled over that he would be gone, the other side of the bed coldly empty. But he was still there, lying on his side, wide awake and watching her. She started to speak, but before she could say a word he leaned over and kissed her deeply, once more flaming her desire.

Afterward they dozed a little, then languidly rose to dress, and breakfast. Afterward, Richard left for the stables. Agatha retired to the library to write a letter to Lucy, inviting her to stay with them at the end of April. She begged Lucy to say nothing to anyone—not even her aunt—lest her father should find where she was. She sanded the letter, folded and sealed it, and rang for Merton, asking him when he arrived, to see that it was delivered at once to Miss Wilmot. He bowed and left the room. She looked through the bookshelves, found a book, made herself comfortable, and began reading, Bruno asleep at her feet. Unbidden, her worries returned. Drummond, she thought, might try to pretend all was the same between them, but it wasn't. Forcing those thoughts away, she concentrated on her book and lost track of the time until Merton entered to announce that dinner was served.

It was eight o'clock and Drummond had not returned. She dined alone, then retired to the library to finish her book. When she had turned the last page and closed it, she leaned back in the chair and listened to the clock chime midnight.

Drummond still had not returned.

She waited downstairs until four in the morning, as she had the other night, and once again she went to his rooms and checked his bed.

Again it was empty.

Feeling more perplexed this time, although no less hurt, she retired at once to her bedchamber, changed into her nightgown, and crawled into bed, knowing she could not fall asleep.

In the morning she found him poring over business accounts in his study. He was not in the good humor of the other morning. The dark brooding look had once again settled on his face, and shadows lay under his eyes. The white scar on his forehead was whiter than usual.

He looked up from the papers in his hands. "Good morning, Agatha. Did you sleep well?"

"Yes, my lord."

He winced at the formality of her address, then glanced once more at the papers. "Accounts for the tenant farmers," he explained, riffling through them.

She nodded, waited, hoping he would offer some explanation—some excuse—for his second absence. But the minutes passed as he talked of the farmers on his land and the progress of the spring planting, and how he had been able to drop the rents slightly this month. She stood patiently, her hands folded in front of her, her face smoothly blank.

At length he stirred, as if aware for the first time that she was not particularly interested in his discourse on agriculture. "But you do not wish to hear of this. No doubt it bores you, my dear." He attempted to smile. A slight raising of his lips at the corners; it failed, and made him look all the more grim.

Or unhappy. She could not decide which he seemed most today.

Still . . .

"Richard, I must speak with you."

"Yes, my dear?"

"I must know where you were last night." She carefully watched his face, watched for some sign that would betray him.

There was none. "Last night? I rode to see one of the tenants. We fell to talking and I lost track of the time."

"And did not return until well after four in the morning?"

"Did you stay up until then?" he asked.

She nodded her head.

"You should not do that again, my dear. You will wear yourself out." He stepped closer to her, and touched her cheek. "You already look quite pale. From lack of sleep, I would warrant."

"And worry."

"Do not worry yourself about me, my dear."

"I cannot help it," she said softly.

"I know."

He cradled her in his arms, and with her head resting against his chest, she felt quite safe and warm, and totally convinced of what he had said. He was right—she should not stay up so late. She was losing much sleep, and was so very tired when she rose in the mornings. Of course she should not worry so much! All would be right. Of that she was certain. She restrained a yawn, and he kissed her fingertips one by one.

"Now, let us ride together this afternoon. Would you enjoy that?"

"Yes, my lord."

"Richard," he corrected gently.

"Richard."

He kissed her, and they left to change for their ride. They spent the day in each other's company, the evening hours as well, and that night he remained with her in her rooms.

The following night he did not.

Agitatedly he paced the darkened room. Running a hand once more through his already unruly hair, he glanced back at the portrait. Had the eyes of the subject changed slightly? Were they less sympathetic than before? He did not know. There was scarcely enough light in the room to tell. The drapes were still drawn against the full light of day, and only a few stray beams managed to sneak past. Dust motes danced, whirling and drifting through the air. The faint light only served to emphasize the sadness of the room.

Too sad, he thought, by day, and vowed he would never return during the daylight hours. With the sun's light he saw too many ghosts of the past.

He stopped before the portrait of the young woman and stared up at her for a long moment. He seemed to be struggling with himself, till at last, the conflict ended and he spoke aloud.

"What are you thinking? Are you disappointed in me? Tell me!"

No answer came. But of course he'd known there would be none. What had he been thinking of, anyway? He had been a fool to expect one.

He looked away for a moment, feeling his weariness, his leaden spirits, then stared up into her beautiful eyes. "I should tell her. Yes, I know that. It is wrong of me not to say anything, to deceive her in this fashion. But surely, *you* of all people should understand this. I know I am a coward. But I mean well, and I do this for you." He turned away, feeling the heaviness settle even deeper in his chest, acknowledging the sorrow.

"And yes . . . I do this for me, and for that night two years ago. For this." He touched the white scar on his forehead. It throbbed under his fingertips.

"So much depends upon it," he whispered, his voice hoarse. Once more he wandered through the room. His boots left faint prints in the dust. His were the only set of footprints.

He passed the shrouded tables and chairs which rested like ghosts in the silent room, but he did not look at them. Finally he stopped by a tiny desk, its sides intricately carved of red maplewood, and he ran a finger across the top. It alone of all the pieces of furniture in the room had not been covered. Grey dust painted his finger, and he stared at it, then, uncaring, wiped it on his coat.

"Soon," he said, looking once more at the portrait, "soon it will be over. And then I shall be judged."

He walked away, not looking back, and as he left the deserted room the old familiar feeling of bleak weariness once more took hold of him.

Today, she announced to herself as she rose early on the seventh morning after Drummond's first disappearance, she would explore the house—something she had put off far too long. Here she had been mistress of Falcon's Hall for almost a month, and she had not even seen all of the house.

She ordered Holly to bring her a good breakfast, and while the girl was away she dressed in a plain bodice and skirt of brown cloth, slipped on brown shoes with silver buckles, tied a white apron edged with blue and lavender embroidered flowers around her waist.

Holly returned with a tray laden with toast and tea, and a beef pie and smoked fish. Agatha sat at a small ornate table, set her napkin on her lap, and began eating. Holly moved about the room, arranging and rearranging as her mistress dined.

"Oh, I almost forgot, my lady. A boy brought this a short time ago." Holly dipped her hand in her pocket and brought out a letter.

Agatha took it from her and stared at the familiar bold handwriting. It was from Lucy. She broke it open at once and began reading.

"Good news, mistress?" Holly asked, filled with curiosity.

She nodded at the maid as she folded the letter. "Yes, the very best; my friend has accepted my invitation to come and stay with us. I think you will like her, Holly. She is very funny, and loves to eat."

"Cook's bound to like her, then."

"Indeed, I am quite sure."

Holly finished with her work, took the tray away, and Agatha smiled. In a matter of days Lucy would be here! They would have so much to discuss. She would have to show Lucy the garden, and the roses . . . the roses. Drummond.

No, today she would think no ill thoughts, nor unhappy ones. Today was hers exclusively. She would not go looking for him. She would do what she wished to do.

She stood at the threshold of her rooms and stared thoughtfully down the hallway. By heart she knew the layout of the wing in which she stood. Directly below were the salons where they entertained company, the dining room, the library, and the study, as well as the kitchen and storerooms. On this second floor were her compartments, those belonging to Drummond, and suites for numerous guests. Above, on the third floor, the wing housed the servants.

The first floor of the other wing contained the ballroom and suites used for entertaining. The third floor of that wing was used for servants' quarters, as well as storage. Which left the second floor of that wing.

She had never been in it. The day Drummond had shown her the immense house he had taken her through each room on every floor—except that floor. She had asked what lay beyond that door, and he'd replied curtly that those were deserted rooms.

Why, and by whom? she asked herself. Why was that wing not open?

She intended to answer those questions, and to satisfy her curiosity. Though, curiosity wasn't the only prod, she admitted. Perhaps something in these rooms could provide a clue to his mysterious disappearances, to his change in mood . . . to the sadness in his eyes. Perhaps she could simply learn to understand him more than she did at present.

Or perhaps not. Still, she had to look.

She walked to the stairs, pausing when she heard Merton's voice drift up from below. He was reading a lecture to one of the maids for having neglected to dust a table in the library. She held her breath, waiting for him to leave. She didn't want him to witness her entrance into the other wing.

But was she not the mistress of this house? Was she not free to roam it at will? In theory, yes. In reality she was still a prisoner, required to have someone with her at all times when she was outside. How apparent it was, she thought, that he did not yet trust her.

She marched toward the door to the second wing and tried the handle. It was locked, just as Richard had said. She stared in amazement at it, never having anticipated this difficulty.

Still, it piqued her curiosity all the more. Why was the wing locked? Who had done it? More importantly, who kept the keys?

No doubt Merton would have a set, and the housekeeper, too.

And Drummond.

Of course. She smiled to herself.

Looking to see that she was still alone on the floor, she quickly walked back to Drummond's rooms and paused outside the door. Her heart hammered. What if someone should discover her? She took a deep breath, walked in, and looked around.

The furniture was maple, heavy and masculine. A wide bed stood in the center of the bedroom, with a tall chest, the handles of polished brass, on each side. A mirror and shaving stand were in the dressing room, as was another chest. Opposite the bed was a low chest on which sat a number of books. The carpeting was oriental in design, and the walls were whitewashed. Heavy beams showed overhead. Above the fireplace hung crossed Spanish swords.

It was almost a Spartan room, she thought. There was so little of him in it, so little comfort.

She tapped a foot. Now, where would he keep a

set of keys? Surely not with him! She did not recall ever seeing such a thing on him, nor hearing the jangle of keys when he moved. If not with him, then, perhaps he kept them in a chest.

She searched through all the chests, pulling out the drawers, peering under cravats and fobs and discarded buckles and part of a spur. Finally, in a drawer in one of the chests by the bed she found a carved box. Lifting the lid, she found a ring of keys. The keys were tarnished, as though they had not been used in some time. She slipped the ring into her apron pocket, closed the drawer, and had just stepped away when Thomas opened the door and walked in.

"My lady," he said, bowing low, "what an unexpected pleasure."

His expression was clearly one of surprise, mingled with what she hoped was humor, and she blushed a little at the irony in his words even as her thoughts raced frantically. She had to tell him something, had to explain why she was in her husband's rooms, for she knew he was suspicious. Then she remembered precisely who she was—she was the viscountess. She owed no servant an explanation.

She raised her head haughtily, or in a way which she fervently hoped was haughty, and eyes straight ahead, breezed past him without a word or so much as a nod. She dared not risk a single look at him, lest she immediately lose every ounce of the aristocratic hauteur which she had just summoned.

She continued down the corridor, heading directly toward the staircase. When she reached it, she paused and risked a glance backward. Thomas stood in the doorway, watching her, and she fancied she saw a slight frown on his face.

Let him wonder, she told herself, and smiling, went downstairs. She would linger for a while in the library until she knew Thomas had left the second floor and that mysteriously locked door.

Her wait lasted well over an hour before Thomas came downstairs once more. She was impatient, all prepared for her adventure, and she was not pleased by this delay. He lingered in the front hall for a few minutes talking with Merton and disappeared finally in the direction of the kitchen.

Time to go. She ran upstairs to the locked door, and paused to look around. No one was in sight. She deftly inserted one of the keys. Failure. She tried a second; it wasn't the right one. Finally, upon trial of the third key, and with a slight protest from its hinges, the door opened. She slipped through it, then leaned against the once-more-closed door. So far she was safe.

She did not let herself think of what would happen if someone should discover her. Her nervousness was stuff and nonsense, she thought. What could be done? After all, she was the mistress of Falcon's Hall. She had every right to go into each room.

Then why was this wing locked, a small, stern voice inside her asked, but she ignored it. She shrugged and stared down the length of a long corridor. In all ways it seemed to match the other corridor. There were the same number of doors, set in the same positions. She moved forward, tried the first door, and found it unlocked.

The room beyond was a bedroom, or had been, she corrected herself, for it had been many years since anyone had occupied it. Faded curtains still hung at the window; a coverlet was neatly folded at the foot of the bed. All the furnishings seemed to be there. But a thick layer of dust covered everything.

The second room she explored was in the same condition as the first: deserted and decaying, as was the third room, and the fourth, and the fifth . . indeed as were all the rooms she entered.

Why, she wondered, had these rooms been deserted? The furnishings were luxurious, and it was a shame, she thought, staring at the brass candlesticks and porcelain vases, that everything had become so neglected. Somewhere in this deserted wing there must be a clue. Somewhere.

At the end of the hall she found closed double doors, the first time the layout had deviated from that of the other wing. The doors had once been locked, but the lock was now broken. She touched the painted paneling on the door and paused. For the first time since she had come into this wing she was aware of the great silence. None of the usual sounds of the house could be heard. It was almost as though she were alone and about to step into another world.

Perhaps she would. Perhaps behind this door she would find the answer; the answer to Drummond's disappearances, the answer to his brooding nature.

Mayhap. But whatever lay beyond this door, she knew it would be important.

She swallowed, brushed away a curl that had slipped over one eye, and raising her head, pushed open the door and stepped into the room.

PART IV:

THE SEPARATION

SEVENTEEN

SHE WALKED IN AND GAZED at the immense room she had just entered. Heavy drapes hung at the windows, obscuring most of the light, though enough sunlight managed to creep in through gaps to lift the room from total darkness to gloom.

The room was by far the largest of any she'd yet seen in the house—barring the ballroom and entertaining salons—and was square in shape, with only the one door. Like the others it showed much neglect.

The sense of impending discovery increased within her as she moved away from the door. Dustcovers had kept the furniture from ruin, unlike in the other rooms. She lifted one cover to find a dainty settee, its back carved with a medieval pattern. She dropped the sheet, and sneezed as a cloud of dust billowed upward. The carpet was moldering and as she walked more dust rose.

Bookshelves on one side of the room caught her attention, and she went to them, discovering row upon row of dusty volumes. She frowned, confused. Another library? It didn't make sense to have closed this one without removing the books to the library downstairs.

Something crunched underfoot and she glanced down. Pieces of glass. Again she frowned. That made no sense, either. What were they doing here? She had seen no sign of breakage in the other rooms.

She went to the windows, pushed aside a curtain to look outside. From here she had a clear view of the rose garden and the woods beyond the estate. She let the curtain fall, and moved away.

She stared, hands on hips, at the room. Everywhere she looked she saw cobwebs and dust, and the air in the room was still, too still. It made her uneasy.

She had not yet explored one part of the room—the end opposite the door. She moved toward a marble fireplace, and above it she saw an oval portrait. When she was only a few feet away she looked up at the painting and at that moment the feeling that there was something she *must* find, disappeared. Somehow she was certain that this portrait held the answer to her questions.

Its subject was a young woman who possessed abundant dark hair and eyes equally dark. Her face was oval, with fair skin, a rosebud mouth, and delicate eyebrows. Barely out of the bloom of childhood, the woman owned the gentlest face Agatha had ever seen. There was, too, in the subject's eyes a great sadness, as if she had been hurt beyond recovery.

Agatha regarded the girl/woman with intent curiosity. Was this some honored ancestor of her husband's? A close relative perhaps? Frowning, she continued to stare up at the painting. If only the portrait could speak, could tell her what she wanted to know. For she was certain that the girl it portrayed, whoever she was, had some share in Drummond's hidden sorrow. Why else would her portrait be enshrined here, in a locked wing to which, clearly, no one came?

Still frowning, she walked toward the door. Before she left, she glanced once more over her shoulder. It seemed as though the girl's gaze followed her.

She left the room, closing the door tightly shut behind her. She was deeply disappointed. She had been so convinced the room would provide some answer, and she had been wrong. All her exploration had done was raise more questions.

She walked down the dim corridor, paused at the main door to make sure no one was about, and then entered the main part of the house once more. She locked the door.

Well, what now? she asked herself.

Who would know the answers to the questions she was asking herself? The servants, most likely. The ones, that was, who had been here for some time.

Merton—he would know.

She found him on the first floor. He looked up from a list he was compiling and stood.

"Yes, my lady?" His tone was somewhat aloof

and she knew she had far to go before she completely won over the trust of this man.

"Merton, I went into the unused wing today." She saw his eyes widen, but otherwise no trace of emotion crossed his face. He said nothing. "At the far end of the hall I found a room."

"Those doors are locked."

"When I came upon them, I found the lock had been broken." She could see this intelligence surprised him, and she went quickly on, wishing to take advantage of the crack in his complacency. "So I saw no harm in entering." She paused, slipped a hand in her apron pocket, and fingered the coldness of the metal ring. "A portrait of a young woman hangs above the fireplace. Who is it?"

His eyes were shuttered, and she could see no expression on his face, only sensed great disapproval. He was not pleased by her curiosity.

"You should not have been wandering through those rooms unattended, your ladyship. Some of the floorboards are rotted, and you could easily have hurt yourself if they had given way."

Though Agatha controlled her expression, maintaining her pose of careless inquiry, his words angered her. He had not answered her question, and had chided her for being where she should not have gone. Too, she did not totally believe his story of rotting floorboards. The halls had seemed quite sturdy to her.

"I would not go there again," he said. He stepped toward the door of the kitchen.

"But the portrait . . ."

"No one of importance," he said, bowed, and disappeared beyond the door.

No one of importance. Such a brazen lie! Surely he could not expect her to believe it. Of course that girl had been important. But who was she? How had she been important? Agatha was determined now to find an answer.

She wandered away, finally entering the green salon and encountering Mrs. Gordon. Now here was someone who would be more than willing to help her, she thought. The woman seemed to like her and had always been friendly with her, even from the day of her abduction.

"Mrs. Gordon," she called.

"Aye, Lady Drummond?" The woman looked around and slowly dropped a curtsy. Her pleasant face creased with a jovial smile.

"I have a question which I hope you might be able to answer." Agatha smiled her nicest smile, and Mrs. Gordon responded. Good, Agatha thought.

"Ask away, my lady. I'll try my best."

"In the closed section of the house there is a portrait," she began, and watched as the good humor evaporated from the housekeeper's face. "It's of a young woman. Who is it?"

Mrs. Gordon shook her head. The older woman was no longer smiling. She picked her words with obvious care. "A girl, that's all, my lady. She don't signify. Well, I'd best be going to the kitchen now, if your ladyship doesn't need me any longer." The housekeeper began edging toward the door.

"Yes, I do need you," she said, with more than a hint of impatience in her voice. "I need you to answer my question and tell me who the girl was. Why is everyone being so mysterious?" Agatha's frown was back, and she feared it was increasing.

Mrs. Gordon seemed to be on the verge of saying something, then apparently thought better of it. "I can't say, my lady. I can't. Please don't press me. It would make me downright unhappy if you did."

Agatha relented, sighing with exasperation. "Very well, Mrs. Gordon. You may go."

Mrs. Gordon left, and Agatha frowned at nothing in particular. She would find some of the other servants, press them, and see what they had to say.

But though she found Holly and asked her, then later Ben and Cook, no one could—or would—tell her the identity of the young woman in the portrait. And she knew they all knew, knew because of the way their eyes slid away from hers so that they did not have to look at her, knew because their voices were low when they answered her.

They were lying, and she *would* know the reason why!

Drummond did not return that night.

Despite her burgeoning anger, she feared some accident had befallen him. This was the first time he had stayed away two nights in a row. Again she had visions of him lying dead in a ditch, shot through the heart by a highwayman, thrown by his horse, murdered by her father's hired men. Her already dampened spirits drowned in horrible imaginings.

She waited until the early hours of morning, then retired, yawning fiercely, to her bed and slept till well past noon. When she at last arose, she splashed water on her face, flew to the window, and stared out.

There, conversing with Ben, was her husband, intact. Not at all dead in a ditch. In fact, he was at present laughing heartily and seemed in very good spirits. He clapped the groom upon the shoulder and they walked off together toward the stable.

A dull anger rose slowly in her, making her grit her teeth. She tore off her clothing, changed into a dark gold skirt and bodice, and left her chambers just as Holly was entering.

"Good day, mis——" began the girl, grinning good-naturedly, but she was talking to empty air for Agatha had already left.

Each footstep was firm, decisive, and her anger increased as she went downstairs. As she reached the halfway mark, the front door opened and she heard Drummond's voice. She paused, a dainty hand on the balustrade. He said something to a man outside, slammed the door, and headed for his study. He glanced casually up the stairs, saw her, and smiled faintly.

"Good day, my dear."

He reached his study, entered, and closed the doors behind him.

Good day, my dear! Was that all he could find to say to her after he'd been gone for two days and nights? Gone so long she'd almost worried herself sick, fearing he was dead? Did he not care for her concern?

No, she told herself firmly. He did not.

He had used her from the very beginning. From the evening he had surprised her in her father's garden to the next day when he had abducted her from her wedding coach, from the forced marriage to this. He had simply manipulated her.

She would tolerate it no longer. She wanted to know—and now!—where he was those nights when he did not come home.

She strode to Drummond's study, took a deep breath, realizing how high her color must be from her anger, and quickly pushed open the doors and stepped inside. Evidently her entrance had surprised him. He had just begun to settle his papers at his desk. He stood once more when he saw her and smiled questioningly.

"Agatha, what is wrong?"

"Please, my lord," she said coldly, "I wish no false pleasantries from you."

"False pleasantries?" he echoed, drawing his dark brows together slightly.

"Why, yes, you do not think I can possibly believe you are sincerely concerned?" She gazed scornfully at him, and tapped her foot.

"I am quite perplexed . . ." he began, then stopped. He pressed his lips together and half turned away.

"Ah, you understand what I mean now," she said, more than a trace of irony in her voice.

Drummond remained silent.

"I do not care to hear you spout more false protestations of concern for my worry." She clasped her hands together and drew in a deep breath. "I want answers. Where have you been? Why were you gone so long? Where do you go on those nights? Where? And why can you not trust me? Why can you not tell me?" She gazed earnestly at him. He was pale, his lips pressed together as if to prevent him from speaking. "My lord, please?"

"I cannot say," he said slowly, the words coming out with evident difficulty.

"Cannot? Or will not?"

"Cannot."

"You have ill-used me, my lord, and I do not like it at all." Her eyes flashed angrily, and she took a step toward him. Involuntarily he stepped back, a look of surprise on his face. "You have taken me from my family and locked me away in this house. I am not permitted to go outside without a guard. Please!" she said, holding up a hand as he made to protest. "You leave without a single word to me, and when you return you do not speak of it, and now you dare claim you cannot tell me the reason. You do not trust me, my lord. That is plain to see."

"Agatha, please——"

"No, my lord, you *will* listen to me. You have come to my bed and wooed me, tried to gain my heart, and I will admit I had begun to soften toward you. Aye, sir, I had, but that is a thing of the past. From now on I resolve to have a hard heart. Go about your nightly business. I will not care."

She started for the doors when she felt the tears forming in her eyes. They are tears of anger, she told herself, not of hurt.

"Agatha, it's business, I swear to you . . ."

She flashed a scornful look at him as she reached the door. "Keep your oaths to yourself."

At that minute the door opened, and Paul Sterling stuck his head in.

"Hello, Agatha! Hello, Richard!" He smiled amiably. The expression slowly faded from his face as he saw hers. "Agatha——"

"Good day, my lord. Good day, Mr. Sterling."

She brushed past him.

"Agatha——"

"No, let her go, Paul."

She slammed the door behind her and paused only to make sure there would be no pursuit.

There was none.

She leaned against its solidness and panted as if from heavy exertion. She wiped a hand across her forehead, felt the dampness. Her cheeks still tingled from her anger. She forced herself to take long calming breaths.

She could hear the men's voices. Knowing it was wrong, yet unable to resist, she pressed her ear to the door.

"She's been asking after you, Richard."

"I know." Her husband's tone was short, abrupt.

"What was all that about? I mean——"

"Paul."

"Very well, my friend."

There was a long pause and she heard someone pacing about the room.

"She came to confront me," Drummond said at last in a tight voice.

"So I gathered."

"She wanted to know where I'd been. Well, dammit, I can't tell her."

"Are you sure?"

"Deadly sure."

And the voice in which he said it sent shivers down her spine.

"Damned female inquisitiveness." Her husband had spoken again.

There was another pause, this one longer than the first. Someone cleared his throat, Paul, she presumed. After a number of minutes had elapsed with no conversation, Drummond spoke again.

"It must be stopped before she learns too much."

She could sense Paul's shock by the long silence before he spoke.

"Richard, I . . ."

She heard footsteps heading toward the door and quickly ran down the hall, ducking into a salon just as the door to the study opened. She waited there, agonizingly long minutes, until she heard the door close again. Then she cautiously poked her head out to stare down the corridor. The study doors were shut. She ran to the stairs and up to her rooms.

Holly was nowhere to be seen, for which Agatha was quite thankful. She did not have need of the girl's brightness nor inquisitive nature now. Indeed, she must think—long and hard. She sat on a chair so that she could look outside.

It must be stopped before she learns too much.

Her husband had said that. About her. His words, and the cold tone he had used, had alarmed her more than she would have thought possible. She shivered, and hugged herself, but the chill would not leave. He was such a dark man, his mind and nature closed to her. He was capable of anything, she realized. Anything.

She knew so little about him, so very little, though not from lack of trying, she thought sadly. The chill increased. Who knew she was here?

Only the servants, and Paul Sterling, all of them most loyal to Richard. The servants could easily have been bought off, bribed to keep their mouths shut. Sterling was her husband's best friend. He would say nothing disloyal about Drummond. Besides, he was the man who had aided Drummond in her abduction. He could hardly speak out.

Anything could happen. Anything.

Even . . . murder.

She shivered and stared out the window. It was a pleasant spring day outside, but inside it was as bleak as the depths of winter.

She had cared for him . . . had begun to—no. She could not say it. But she had thought it, felt it. She had felt the budding of love for him. But now? What could she feel for this man?

She shivered again, realizing she had not had a chance to confront him with the discovery of the young woman's portrait. Another time. If there was to be another time. . . .

Surely, though, he would not harm her. After all, their evenings together had been so tender; he had been so thoughtful, so caring, so generous, so many wonderful things to her.

Or had seemed to be. Perhaps he had been playacting—from the very first—for whatever twisted purpose it served.

She must always, always remind herself that she did not know his mind and now might never know.

And still she did not know where he went.

She closed her eyes and leaned back in the chair, aware of the pounding in her head, and that tears had formed in the corners of her eyes. She wiped them away with one hand and concentrated on thinking.

He had gone away seven times. There was a pattern. Every three days. Every three days he left for the night, then returned the next day. The exception had been the past two days and nights. Yet she was convinced she was correct.

And so that meant for the next two days and nights he would remain at home, and on the third night he would sneak out of the house.

Leave to go . . . someplace.

Leave . . .

She would be waiting. She would be watching. She *would* know where he went. But not even that resolution served to stem the flow of bitter tears from her eyes.

EIGHTEEN

THE HOURS OF THE THIRD day passed so slowly for Agatha that she doubted it would ever be dusk. But at last the light faded from the sky and it was time for dinner. Throughout the meal, Drummond was as polite as ever, giving no hint that there was anything afoot. Agatha was equally polite, if cooler in tone, but immediately after the final course, she pleaded exhaustion and excused herself. Drummond seemed on the point of saying something to her, then changed his mind. She bid him a good night and retired at once to her rooms.

A few minutes later Holly knocked on the door, just as she had anticipated.

"Your ladyship?" she called.

"Come in, Holly."

The girl entered, a look of concern on her face. "I heard you were feeling poorly, so I came to see if you needed anything."

"Thank you, no. I merely wish to read, and then I think I shall go to sleep early. Perhaps in the morning I will feel more myself. Do you think so?"

"Oh, aye, your ladyship," Holly said eagerly. "Do you need help undressing?"

"Yes, thank you." She paused. "I won't need you after this, Holly."

"Thank you!"

She allowed herself to be undressed and then changed into a warm nightgown. She bade the girl farewell and climbed into the bed after the maid left. She waited until she was sure Holly no longer lingered by the door, waiting for her mistress's call. Then she rose from the bed and drew off the nightgown, went to her wardrobe, flung it open, and stared in.

She pulled out a pair of breeches, a shirt, and dark brown coat. She had sneaked into Drummond's room that afternoon and found the breeches, then hidden them in her room. She pulled them on, buttoned the shirt, and shrugged on the coat. She studied herself in the mirror, and nearly laughed at the sight. The shirt and coat were her own, used when she went riding, and so were a perfect fit. But the breeches were far too long for her. She leaned over and carefully rolled them up. When she pulled her riding boots on the rolled cuffs of the breeches would slip down into the boot, and so would not look as unusual.

When her boots were on she surveyed herself again. Not so bad now. She pulled back her hair, and tucked it up. Then she swept her hat onto her head, and stepped back for a look at the entire costume. The deception was uncanny. She stared at her transformed image and swept a mocking bow.

So much for looks: now for practice. She strode across the room, sat, and stretched, testing the comfort and ease of her costume, and was pleased with the results. Her costume would not hamper her as would skirts, and she would be better able to put her plan into effect.

She had devised the plan in the past two days of restlessness. Now she congratulated herself on her own cleverness.

Glancing at the clock, she saw she had been in her rooms a little above an hour. She did not know how much longer she would have to wait. She took out her riding gloves, blew out the candle, and slowly made her way into the sitting room.

And waited.

The night darkened outside, and still she waited. From time to time she closed her eyes so that she would not strain them. Finally when she opened them after a few minutes she saw a flicker of movement below. She leaned forward, squinted into the darkness, rubbed her eyes, and peered once more.

A dark figure was walking at a fast pace toward the stable.

Drummond, no doubt.

She counted to one hundred, and when she thought he must be well away from the house, she opened the door and peered into the gloomy corridor. Two candles burned in sconces, but otherwise there was no light. She quickly moved to those and blew them out. She tiptoed down the stairs, pausing once when she thought she heard Merton's voice coming from the kitchen. The clock in the hall chimed eleven times. She had just slipped through the front doors when she heard a horse's hooves. She waited until the horseman trotted by, then she ran toward the stable. None of the stablehands were there at present, so she did not worry about being seen.

She found Tally's stall and quickly saddled the mare, led her outside, and mounted the horse. It felt strange to be riding astride—it had been many years since the stablehands at her father's estate had taught her how to ride like a boy, many years since her father had found them out and put an end to that.

She patted the mare's neck, then urged the horse into a trot, which stretched into a canter. She didn't want to lose Drummond, for he did have a headstart on her. But there should be sufficient time, she thought, to catch up. Moreover, she did not want to ride too close lest he should discover he was being followed.

When she reached the end of the carriage sweep, she looked left and right. She couldn't see him in the dark, for there was little moon, so she listened intently, hoping she would hear him. In the distance she could barely hear the steady clop-clop of hooves.

But from which direction? What if she assumed he had gone to the right, when he was actually heading in the opposite direction? It was no use speculating, she thought. She had to choose.

To the right, something in her said. She turned

the mare down that stretch of the road. At first she kept Tally at a slow canter, but as the distance between the two horses shortened, she slowed the mare to a trot and then to a walk.

She could see him now, a faint shadow, and she watched as he stopped. She abruptly pulled Tally to a halt, then reached out to pat the mare on her neck. He seemed to be listening to something. Perhaps he had heard the sound of her horse's hooves and thought he was being followed. Or perhaps he thought it was only a trick of sound, the echo of Grey Sir's hooves.

She wished a wind would spring up. That would certainly help disguise the sound of pursuit, but tonight Nature was not proving cooperative.

Drummond began riding again. She waited a moment longer before urging her mare onward.

She could see little of the surrounding countryside, so dark was the night, but ahead she saw a darker shape, which she assumed was forest. She was proven correct when in a matter of minutes she had entered a deep woods where the trees pressed close to the road. Somewhere to her left, some distance away in the thick trees, she heard the mournful call of an owl. It was followed a moment later by a second call.

Prearranged signals? she asked herself. Or truly night birds?

Where could he be going? she wondered as Tally daintily picked her way along the crude path. It was not a smooth trail, and once the mare stumbled, almost falling to her knees. She managed to stagger back to her feet, but not before Agatha, so engrossed in thoughts of Drummond's destination that she was not paying attention, lost her balance and was tossed over the horse's head. She landed with a thud on her back and for a few minutes lay there, stunned, the wind knocked from her.

The mare nuzzled her, then blew softly on her, and Agatha reached up with a shaking hand to stroke the horse's velvet soft muzzle.

"Good girl," she whispered as she slowly got to her knees and paused to catch her breath. "It wasn't your fault." She ran her hands, still trembling from the accident, down the horse's front legs to assure herself that no damage had been done.

The mare's legs were fine; about her own she was not so sure. She got to her feet, swayed for a moment, and caught the horse's bridle so she would not topple to the ground. Luckily nothing was broken, but she was certainly shaken, she ached fiercely, and she knew that in the morning—or more likely in a few hours—she would be sporting a fine set of colorful bruises. Her teeth chattering a little, she pulled herself up into the saddle and urged the mare on. She had lost Drummond, but she did not think she would have any difficulty in locating him. Obviously, he would keep to this path.

But she was wrong.

When they emerged from the woods and she looked down the long stretch of road, she could not see him at all. She knew she had not been on the ground long enough for him to draw all that much of a lead on her, so he must have turned off from the path in the woods.

Sighing, and cursing herself for not being more

alert, she nudged the mare back into the woods. She stopped close to where she had been thrown, and listened.

Off in the distance—this time she thought it came from the left—she heard the whinny of a horse.

Grey Sir?

Perhaps. She would have to assume it was her husband's horse. She rode on a few more feet, looked for some place where she could easily leave the road, and found something she had overlooked while she rode through the woods. There was a dry streambed, and it provided a natural pathway.

He could have used that. Not for the first time that night she wondered what business Drummond could have, so far removed from home.

Excitement growing inside, she directed Tally to the left, and they picked their way carefully through the riverbed. She paused from time to time to listen, but heard no further sounds of the horse, yet she was convinced she was heading in the right direction.

At last the trees began to thin, and she stopped by a giant oak tree, staring at what she saw.

Ahead was a building. She could see a belltower, but it was not this unexpected discovery which surprised her so much. What astonished her more were the horses—more than ten horses were tethered to the right of the building. Two well-equipped carriages, both unmarked, stood beyond them.

She pulled the mare back into the shelter of the woods, afraid that someone might spot her. Nor did she want the mare too near the other horses, lest they betray her arrival. She dismounted, tied the horse's reins to a low branch, and crept away. Reaching the giant oak, she leaned against it and waited.

She frowned and thoughtfully rubbed her hands together. As if in answer to her earlier prayer, a slight breeze had sprung up. Too late for any good use, she thought with some amusement.

Was this where her husband had come? And for what possible reason? The dark building appeared to be a crumbling church. Drummond, she well knew, was not particularly religious. So . . . why?

More and more puzzling.

She peered at the horses, studying them one by one, searching for a familiar one. Finally she saw a light-colored horse, almost white in the gloom. Grey Sir *was* there, which meant his master was also here.

But where? Inside? In the dark?

That was all the more puzzling, she thought as she absently pushed back a strand of hair that had fallen across her eyes.

From somewhere inside the church a light flickered, as if a candle had just been lit. It was joined by a second, then a third.

Then she heard a high laugh—a woman's laugh—and she frowned.

The interior of the ruin was growing lighter by the moment. Yellow light poured out of the windows, and she wondered what was going on.

She had to see inside.

Cautiously she moved forward and found the grass in front of the abbey to be thigh-high. Walking gave the sensation of swimming in a sea of grass, adding to the strangeness of the night's adventure. If she should fall, surely she would drown as though she were in water, excepting that her lungs would fill with the long blades of grass. She shook her head suddenly. 'Twas all nonsense.

Halfway through the grass, she knelt down so that no one passing by a window could glance out and see her. Then she crawled on her hands and knees, glad she still wore her gloves. The grass brushed against her face and tickled her neck and she fought against a sudden unreasoning fear that began gnawing at her.

She must be calm and think slowly, else all would be lost. She took in a deep breath and immediately felt better.

She did not know why she was acting so oddly this night. Perhaps it was the setting, the strangeness of the ruined church, the fact that she had followed her husband to this godforsaken place.

She reached the wall and sat down, her back against it, and rested. And listened.

Now she could hear the deep voices of a number of men, how many she couldn't tell, and above them the voices of women. There were not many of the latter, though. Underneath the talk, she heard the strains of music.

In the ruins of a church? What was going on?

She would get to her knees and crawl over to the window only a few feet away, and she would peer inside and——

No, she wouldn't, because she was afraid.

Afraid she would be caught; afraid that Drummond would discover her; afraid of what she would find inside; afraid that——

But what could he do to her? one part of her

asked? She shivered. She didn't know the answer. But she had heard his voice two nights before in the study with Sterling. She did not doubt that he would not allow her to get in his way.

She must somehow find courage.

Slowly, ever so slowly, she got to her knees and crawled carefully toward the closest window, some seven feet distant. Something scampered across the back of her hand and she hastily bit back a cry.

A field mouse, nothing more, the reasonable part of her asserted. Nothing to fear.

Off in the giant oak tree she heard an owl hoot, and she wondered if it was one of the pair she had heard earlier. Unreasonably, she felt as though the birds were following her.

Silly goose, she told herself. Calm down, or you'll not be able to see a thing.

It was true. She must steady her nerves. She had never been so scared, so unnerved, in her life. She pressed her hands together, found them trembling, and tried to calm herself. It worked a little. Imagine what her father would say if he could see her now! Hoyden might well be one of the kinder words.

Pausing mere inches from the window now, she took in a long deep breath, then slowly exhaled. She did it another, and then a third time.

She was in a precarious position now. If someone should happen to glance out a window, she would probably be spotted. But that wasn't likely to happen, she told herself firmly. Everyone inside seemed to be having much too good a time to come to the window. They were drinking now, for she could hear the clink of goblets, and there was more laughter than before.

Slowly raising herself, she inched toward the window. Still out of line with it, she paused to lick her lips and to take another deep breath.

Carefully she eased up, ever so slowly, straightening so that she could stare inside the candlelit room of the ruined church.

Could stare—and stared in horror at the sight therein.

NINETEEN

THE HORROR.

She looked away for a moment, convinced that it must be some dream, that she could not be seeing what she was seeing. But when she looked back, she knew it was no dream, knew that it was real.

All the men and the women inside wore masks upon their faces. Some wore robes . . . others did not. And upon the latter candlelight gleamed, revealing flesh devoid of any clothing.

She continued to stare, still not believing she saw what lay before her. For the first time she noticed the details of the church's interior. Black candles provided the light. There was a raised dais at one end of the room. Behind it hung a crucifix—inverted.

She licked her lips as she stared at the defiled cross. Who were these people? Why did they do this?

Thick cushions had been scattered about on the floor, and upon most of them reclined the men and women she had heard.

No more than five feet away from the window a man and woman, in masks of black silk, sat, embracing passionately. The man had removed his coat and shirt, and the woman was running her hands through the grizzled hair on his chest. She was clad only in a stained petticoat, her bodice and corset lying abandoned nearby. Her heavy breasts glistened wetly. As Agatha watched, stunned, the man, his thick lips twisted into a leer, reached with a clawlike hand and squeezed the woman's nipple. She yelped, and they collapsed, laughing, upon the pillows, his hand groping under her petticoat.

Beyond them, three men circled a girl who looked to be no older than eighteen. She stood none too steadily and had obviously been drinking. Her arms covered her bare chest. The waist of her skirt had shifted and hung at a rakish angle from her round hips. One of the three, a man slim and well-built, with his breeches off and his shirt hanging loose, beckoned and held out a goblet, tempting the girl. She giggled, shook her head, and playfully pushed his hand away. A second man, seeing his chance, leaped forward and fastened his mouth on her bared breast. She giggled again, grabbed him by the hair, and jerked him away. Breathing heavily, he unbuttoned his breeches, then grabbed her by the shoulders and flung her down on the pillows, and she laughed again as he threw himself upon her. The two other men drew out handkerchiefs and licked their lips as the girl arched her back to welcome the thrusting man.

Another man, still dressed, lay upon a pile of pillows and leered drunkenly as three women, all clad in filmy robes that concealed nothing, stroked his forehead, caressed his face, and kissed him upon the lips. As Agatha watched in shock, they loosened his cravat, pulled it from his neck, and languidly began unfastening his shirt, button by button until his chest was bare. He groaned as the women took turns running their tongues across his chest. He was soon stripped naked by his attendants, and they quickly brought his body to readiness. One by one, with gales of laughter, they straddled the man, who moaned and bucked beneath them.

She blinked, looked away, and stepped back, aghast at the scenes of debauchery.

A gong rang inside, and instantly the laughter, conversation, and pleasure-filled moans died down. A man dressed in a black robe stepped forward and raised a gem-encrusted goblet.

"To the Master of Darkness," he said.

"Here, here," a second man called.

"Aye, to the Dark One," agreed a woman. Her voice was husky from love-making.

All in the room raised their goblets, toasted the Dark One, and then drank deep of the wine. Seconds on the wine were called for, and slim, beautiful boys passed through the merry-makers, carrying trays laden with filled goblets.

She sank down on her heels, well away from the window, and stared unseeing into the grass.

An abandoned church. A crucifix that was inverted. Toasts to the Dark One. What madness was this? What nightmare had she stumbled upon?

And then she remembered Lucy's words when she had visited at Grey's Manor.

She was witnessing the meeting of a hellfire club. There could be no other explanation. While some were nothing more than convenient excuses for aristocrats to meet and drink and wench to all hours, others also professed an interest in the Black Arts. Some, it was whispered throughout the country districts, worshiped the very Devil.

And the evidence here seemed to point to the latter.

But where was Drummond in all of this? She frowned. What was her husband doing here? She knew he was here—she'd seen his horse out front. Had he been one of the masked men . . . with the women? At the idea, her stomach heaved.

But she could not be certain. She had to know. She had to see him.

Cautiously she raised herself so that she could once more look into the window.

A door in the back opened and two men, both in robes, stepped out into the room. One of the men walked toward the table to get some wine, while the other man lingered in the doorway. He was in shadows, but in a moment he stepped out into the light. He wore a white robe, unlike the others, and in that instant Agatha knew.

The man in white was Drummond.

She recognized his stance, his gestures. All of them were too familiar.

He walked to the dais, and all in the room watched. A few eyes turned to him. Somewhere a man belched loudly, and a woman tittered. The man in black joined him.

The man in black held up his hand for silence. "Brothers and sisters in hellfire," he said, slowly smiling. His voice was slurred by liquor. "Very soon—indeed in a very short week—we shall celebrate the Feast of Saint Secoine. On that blessed night, Brother Discord—" here he indicated the white-robed man—"will be a full-fledged brother with us." There were sporadic cheers from the others, and the speaker's smirk widened.

A girl, so young her breasts were barely more than buds, skipped up to Drummond and kissed him upon the mouth. Smiling, he put an arm around her.

"So you found one, eh Brother Discord?" called a stout man in the front. He had his arms around the waists of two scantily clad girls.

"Yes, Father Luxuria, indeed I have." Drummond chuckled, pinched the chin of the girl with him, and several men nearby laughed.

"Do you swear by all that's unholy that her maidenhead's not been pricked?" the man with the two girls pursued.

"I do solemnly swear," Drummond replied.

"Good then. One week, eh?" The man called Father Luxuria winked at the girls, who both giggled. "Not like these little wenches, eh? They never possessed maidenheads!"

This was met with uproarious laughter, the girls laughing as much as the others. Still giggling, they pushed their older companion back onto the pillows and began unbuttoning his shirt, while he amused himself by pinching them and making them squeal.

"Yes," said the first speaker. "We will meet here

as always, and Brother Discord will then bring the virgin to us for the ceremony. And then . . ." He chuckled, a sound that chilled Agatha. "You all know the liturgy. Each one here will have his way with the virgin. You are required to leave your mark upon her." He ran his tongue across his lips so that they glistened. "When you are finished, and she has tasted the Love of Hell, she will be given to the Master as his bride."

There were wild cheers and renewed applause at his statement, and a toast was called for.

Agatha watched Drummond. All during the other man's speech he had remained smiling, an arm still around the girl.

She shuddered to think that he had kissed her, held her, whispered words of love to her. They could not be the same men—this creature here and the lover so tender in her bed. But sadly she knew they were one. She cursed herself that she had been so blind.

In one week he would become the same as the others here, a full-fledged brother in this sacrilegous hellfire club.

Her husband.

The man she loved—*had* loved, she corrected.

In one week these degenerate noblemen would perform some blasphemous ceremony, one involving a virgin—one which Drummond would so generously provide.

Well, she was certainly no longer one, so she need not worry upon that head. Still, she recalled how when they'd first married he had hesitated to come to her. Was it because he had planned to use her in the ceremony? And had his baser nature then overcome him so that he had given in to his desires and made love to her?

She saw now that he had lied to her when he had abducted her. He had said he sought to help her, but he had not; he had wanted only to use her. Better, she thought bitterly, that she should have married the despised Lord Alford.

He had lied . . . lied so many times.

She swallowed suddenly, her throat dry and hurting. Her eyes burned with unshed tears, but she refused to weep for him.

He had callously used her, used her love, and she could do naught but despise him now.

But against the now-forming hate beat the memory of their evenings together, the rose garden he had designed for her, the beautiful presents he had given her.

More lies, she told herself fiercely. Everything in his life was a lie, most of all his time with her.

He was speaking again, but she didn't want to listen, didn't want to hear his deep voice, the voice that had once sent chills of desire down her spine.

He would be the one to bring a virgin. But where would he find one? And, further, by next week?

Next week. The end of April. Lucy would be coming to visit her then.

She clenched her fists together and stared wildly into the darkness. It couldn't be true, it couldn't—but the evidence said otherwise. He had advised her to write to Lucy and invite her to stay at Falcon's Hall. He had been most particular in specifying the last week of April. Now she knew why.

After he had spoiled his own plans by sleeping

with his new bride, he had decided to use poor Lucy. She shuddered. The men planned to use her, then make her the Master's bride. What did this mean? She knew only that if those within the church had planned it, it must be horrible beyond all imagining.

Her mind raced furiously. She must warn Lucy. She would race back to Falcon's Hall, and she would write Lucy a note, and send it by—oh God, whom could she trust?

Which of the servants would take the note to Lucy, would not betray her to Drummond?

Holly would. She trusted Holly, and the girl seemed to truly love her. She would return, send the note with Holly, and if she were lucky, she would manage to catch Lucy in time. She stood and turned.

A dark shape loomed up out of the grass, just scant inches from her, and involuntarily she opened her mouth to cry out. Instantly a hand was clapped across her mouth. Another hand grabbed her arm and jerked her well away from the window.

She had been captured—and she little doubted that it was one of the men from the ruins.

TWENTY

SHE STRUGGLED AGAINST HER CAPTOR'S grip until he shook her, leaned close, and whispered.

"Agatha, for God's sake, settle down!"

Agatha! Who was this?

She turned her head sharply, but could not see the face of the man in the darkness. She tried to talk.

As if sensing her unspoken question, he said, "It's me, you goose. Paul."

Paul Sterling? Her astonishment grew. Of all those she had expected to find her, Paul Sterling was most certainly not one of them. Surely he was not a member of the hellfire club. She could not believe that ugliness of him as well.

He forced her to move, keeping one hand across her mouth in case she tried to cry out. But to her added confusion they weren't heading toward the ruins. He was taking her *away* from the church!

In a moment they reached the giant oak, then continued to where Tally was tethered. She heard the mare shift in the darkness, and the sounds of a second horse. Paul's, no doubt.

"I'm going to remove my hand from your mouth now," he whispered. "On pain of many things, I beg that you do not make a sound. Will you promise, Agatha?"

She nodded against his glove.

"Good."

The hand dropped away.

"Paul, whatever——"

The hand was back, stemming the flow of words that had begun to tumble forth.

"No talking. No sound whatsoever. I want you to get on your horse very quietly. Understand?"

She nodded, and again he removed his hand. He helped her to mount, and then before she could protest he had mounted and grabbed her reins. He urged his horse into a trot, and Tally obediently followed.

She tried to get the reins away, but he would not let go of them. She hardly needed to be led back to Falcon's Hall as though she were a child. She could certainly manage by herself, thank you.

When they had ridden deeply into the woods and were far enough from the ruins so as not to be overheard, she stirred in the saddle and said, "I'll take the reins now, Paul. Thank you."

"No, you won't."

"I'm quite capable of——"

"Of getting yourself into trouble. That's all the more apparent to me tonight."

"I am hardly in trouble."

A cynical harumph was her only answer.

They continued riding in silence. Each time she sought to engage him in conversation, she was answered with a single syllable or silence. At length she gave up.

The air had grown chill in the time she had been at the ruins, and a touch of frost in the air made her breath crackle. Again in the distance she heard the call of an owl.

"We *are* returning to Falcon's Hall, are we not?"

"Yes."

That ended the conversation until they arrived at the house. Ben waited at the stables to take their horses. Surprisingly, he did not seem to think anything was amiss at seeing them out so late.

Paul merely nodded to him, grasped Agatha's arm, and firmly guided her toward the front door.

"I do not need——"

"Yes, you do," he said.

Once inside they went to the study, where he told her to sit down. She obeyed. He poured drinks, handed her one, and stared over the rim of his glass at her.

She sipped the wine slowly, allowing the warming liquor to trickle down her throat. She had not realized how cold she had grown out there in the tall grass by the ruined church.

For the first time since she'd left the house, she remembered how odd her appearance must be in breeches, but she realized that was the least of her worries.

"I suppose you want me to explain what I was doing there," she said finally after they had spent half an hour in silence.

"No. I know what you were doing there."

"What?"

"Spying."

"I was not spying!"

"Really?" Paul raised one eyebrow. "It certainly appeared so to me."

"I had a good reason."

"Um."

"Don't you want to know what it was?"

"No."

That shocked her into silence, and all she could do was stare at him.

"You're a fool for following Richard."

"A fool!" she echoed, then indignantly: "How dare you talk to——"

"Agatha, hush."

She frowned, noted how weary he looked, and quieted.

They remained silent for another hour, and then she decided she could take it no longer. She rose, set down her glass with a sharp bang, and headed for the door.

"I'm going upstairs to bed."

At that moment the door opened, and Drummond walked in. "No, you aren't."

She sat down again. He was dressed in regular riding clothes, and she wondered where his white robe was.

Paul poured wine for Drummond while he regarded his wife. He sipped the wine, then finally stirred and said, "Well, Paul? What's this?"

"I suspected she might follow, but I was delayed tonight. When I arrived, I found she was already gone. I knew at once where she would be. True enough, I found her at the ruin, lurking in the grass and spying on you."

"I wasn't lurking!"

Drummond's frown deepened into an ugly scowl, and he tossed down a second glass of wine, then poured a third. For a few minutes more he swirled the contents of his glass, staring deep into the ruby liquid, then he turned to her.

"I had hoped you would remain innocent of this matter," he said in a low voice whose very calmness frightened her. It wasn't what she had expected. His eyes were flat, and she could read nothing in them.

She did not try to speak.

"Things must move quickly now, Agatha."

She caught the look passed between the two men, and knew it meant ill for her. Panicking, she rushed toward the door, but Drummond proved too quick on his feet and grabbed her by the wrists before she could dart through.

"Oh, no, you're not leaving."

She defiantly raised her head. "You cannot keep me here."

"We shall see."

He looked across at his friend. "I shall return in a few minutes, Paul."

Sterling nodded. Drummond pushed her out of the study, forcing her toward the stairs. As they reached the steps, she went limp. He smiled tightly, and without breaking stride, picked her up in his arms.

"You are going to your rooms, my dear. Nowhere else, and no trick of yours shall prevent me from taking you there."

She lay in his arms with her eyes tightly shut, pretending she didn't hear him, but she did. Perhaps if he could be lulled into thinking she'd fainted, she might be able to take him by surprise. Yet, somehow, she did not think he would be surprised.

They reached the door of her suite without incident. "Believe me," he said in a pained voice, "I do not want this."

Merton appeared behind his master at that moment and silently handed him a ring of keys as Drummond set her on her feet. He backed away and closed the door, and she heard the rasp of the lock.

She tried the door.

It was locked.

She pressed her ear to the door, and heard nothing. "Let me out, my lord," she called. Still she heard nothing. "Please, I shall do nothing. I will tell no one."

Silence met her words.

She heard footsteps retreating down the hall, and with them went her hopes.

Her back to the door, she slowly slid to the floor. She rested her elbows on her knees, her head in her hands, and closed her eyes.

Well, what was she to do now?

She was a prisoner of her husband. And her best friend was to be sacrificed to a group of devil-worshiping aristocrats.

There was a movement across the room and she stiffened, then relaxed as Bruno padded toward her. Yawning, he lay down, his head resting on her legs. She slowly stroked his fur. What now, she asked herself? What could she do locked in her room? There wasn't—ah, but there was something she could do. She stood and knocked on the door again.

"My lord?"

Again she rapped on the door, this time much more loudly.

"My lord? Richard?" Surely someone would hear her. She was making enough noise to wake the dead.

"Yes, my lady?"

Merton.

"I need Holly to help me, Merton. Please."

"Very well, your ladyship. One moment while I send for the girl."

She breathed deeply and gazed down at the dog, who looked adoringly up at her. She would write her note to Lucy and give it now to Holly.

In a few moments the door was being unlocked.

"Please stand well away from the door, my lady," Merton advised.

She did so, and Holly came in, a most puzzled expression on her face.

"Call when you are ready to leave, Holly," the butler said. "Do you understand?"

She nodded, then her eyes widened as she saw what her mistress wore.

"Why, madame . . ." she began.

The door closed behind Merton. And was locked.

"Come, Holly, I need to change."

Holly still looked at her with a most incredulous look on her face. It was obvious that the girl had been asleep when Merton had sent for her, and that she had hastily dressed. Now, she ran a hand through her tousled hair, stifled a yawn, and went to the wardrobe.

Agatha sat at her secretary and pulled out paper and pen. She dipped the quill into the inkwell and began writing. When she finished the brief letter, she scanned the lines, then sprinkled it with sand. While she waited for the ink to dry, she stared at the door. At last she blew away the fine grains, folded the letter into thirds, sealed it, and set it aside.

As Holly pulled her mistress's boots off, Agatha recalled what she had said to her friend. It had been succinct, and to the point; convincingly so, she hoped.

"Do not come to visit me, Lucy. I fear your life is in danger. Stay where you are, and do not trust what my husband says."

"What's going on, my lady?" Holly whispered as she pulled her mistress's nightgown over her head.

"I fear I have displeased my husband," she said sadly. She crossed to the desk, took the sealed letter, and then beckoned to Holly to follow her. She sat on the bed and whispered, "Please, hold out your hand."

The girl obeyed, though obviously confused by Agatha's words and actions.

"Take this letter to Lucy Wilmot in Reading at once. It is most important that she receive this letter as quickly as possible. It is, indeed, a matter of life and death. You are the only one I can trust, Holly."

The girl's eyes widened, and she stared at the letter in her hand. It quivered slightly.

"Do you understand?"

Holly started to shake her head, then finally nodded it.

"No one," Agatha said, leaning close to her maid, "*no one* must know of this, nor of your errand. You will take it upon the morrow?"

"As soon as I may, mistress," the girl whispered.

"Good girl." Agatha leaned back against her pillows. "You have much relieved my mind. Now you must leave, before anyone suspects you of lingering."

"Very well, my lady. Is there anything else you require?"

"No." She smiled at Holly, noting that the girl looked unusually serious. Good. At least Holly recognized the importance of her mission.

She watched as the girl slipped the note into the pocket of her apron, then walked to the door and knocked once.

"Mr. Merton, I'm ready to leave."

She stared at Agatha once more.

"I will see you tomorrow, Holly."

"Very good, my lady."

Holly slipped through the open door; then it was locked again.

She smiled to herself, reached back to plump up the pillows, and stared into the fire Holly had laid.

Lucy would be safe. All was well—except that she was locked away. Still, she would think on that tomorrow. Closing her eyes, she thought of the portrait in the other wing.

She still did not know the woman's identity. Had she been another victim? Agatha supposed there could be little doubt now. Indeed, she was convinced that the woman had been Drummond's first wife, and that he had somehow managed to rid himself of her. Perhaps she had had a large fortune that he stood to inherit.

Agatha took a fierce joy in the knowledge that she had at least in some measure spoiled his plans. She would save someone, even if she could not save the poor girl in the portrait, nor herself.

But with his failure to produce Lucy as the others' victim, would they not search for another? Yes, but it would take time to find one, would make them wait before they celebrated the unholy ceremony.

And time was something she desperately needed now, time to escape from her husband and Falcon's Hall, time to reach the authorities and tell them everything so that Drummond and his wicked friends would never hurt another young woman.

She leaned over and blew out the candle, and settled under the covers. Bruno padded over and settled on the floor by her bed.

She smiled grimly. She would soon put an end to Drummond's evil reign.

And yet the thought, which should have lifted her spirits, only served to make her more unhappy.

TWENTY-ONE

AGATHA WAS NOT LOCKED IN her rooms the following day, but although she was allowed free access throughout the house, she always saw Merton or Thomas hovering close to her.

They were waiting for her to run, she thought wryly, but she wouldn't. At least not yet.

She was particularly happy because she had not seen Holly after the girl had helped her to dress. By now the maid should be reaching Lucy's home to give her the letter. She managed to contain the triumphant smile threatening to curve her lips.

She did not see Drummond anywhere in the house, and when she inquired after him Merton stiffly informed her the master was out.

No doubt he was at the ruined church, making more diabolical plans.

Plans which she would soon thwart.

Her many hours alone she spent in the rose

garden. The roses would be blooming within weeks, and it saddened her to think she might not see them. For who could say where she would be at that time?

She tried hard not to think of Drummond's motive in designing the garden. He had done it for her, he had claimed. It was to bribe her, she now knew.

Late in the afternoon she had her mare saddled and went for a ride around the estate with a groom escorting her. She smiled as she kicked Tally into a gallop, and saw the panic on the boy's face. She laughed aloud. No doubt he feared what his lord would have to say if she should get away from him!

Within a few minutes she reined in the mare, slowing her to a canter, then a trot, and at length the groom, out of breath and red in the face, caught up with her.

The evening passed in more quiet ways. Drummond was still not in evidence, and she did not see Holly, either. But then that was to be expected. The girl might not yet have returned from her errand, or might have been set at other duties.

She read for a while, then retired to her room to sleep. Before she blew out the candle, she tried the door. Locked. She chewed on her lip angrily, and returned to bed because she could do nothing.

When she woke in the morning, she tried the door. It was unlocked.

So—only at night would it be locked. Night was when Drummond went away; night was when she could not be watched as easily.

When she entered the dining room, she found

Drummond seated there, and managed to conceal her surprise at seeing him. He said nothing, merely nodded his head in acknowledgment.

She stared at him from under her eyelashes. She did not think he looked well. There were dark smudges under his eyes, lines on his face that had not been there before, and the scar on his forehead stood out even more vividly than usual.

He looks like he should feel, she told herself jubilantly, as she accepted a piece of buttered toast from Merton. She bit savagely into the bread, and when she glanced back at Drummond she caught his eyes on her, dark eyes filled with sadness. His look surprised her, and made her feel almost sorry for him—something she very much wished not to feel.

She swallowed hoarsely, the toast scratching on its way down, and she reached for her glass.

"You appear most triumphant, madame," he said, setting his fork down.

"I am." Though strangely, today she did not feel particularly triumphant. Still, he could not know that, nor would she admit as much to him. Not after what she had suffered at his hands.

"Indeed?" He raised one brow. "Why is that?"

She allowed a slightly smug expression to cross her face as she met his gaze. "I think you will soon see, my lord. I don't believe all your plans will go quite as you had thought."

He seemed surprised. "Have I not thought out each step most carefully?" he offered in a grave voice. "What details could I have neglected, Agatha?"

Her smile widened. She languidly took a drink,

then set the glass down. She looked pointedly at the butler.

"You are excused, Merton," he said. "We shall finish the meal alone."

"Very good, my lord."

The butler withdrew.

"Now you may speak freely, my dear."

She frowned. Even now he persisted in the endearment. Why? She swallowed again, aware of a pain in her chest. No doubt it would soon go away if she chose to ignore it.

"Very well, my lord, I shall." She paused, then forced herself to smile widely. "Your ceremony is ruined," she announced triumphantly.

"Oh?" He went to the sideboard to pour himself another glass of wine. He turned to face her and sipped the wine. "How so?"

"You will have no victim for your unholy ritual."

"Why?"

"I wrote a letter to Lucy, warning her not to come because you would harm her. I had Holly take it to her. She will stay away, and be safe! What will your grand friends think of you in a few days, my lord, when you cannot produce a virgin?"

"I do not know." His voice was flat, and she frowned, for she had not expected such a calm reaction. "Perhaps, though, you should examine this."

He walked toward her, withdrew something from the pocket of his dove-grey coat, tossed it into her lap, bowed low, and left the room.

Agatha glanced down. Her smile froze and she felt a sickness sweep over her. With trembling hands she picked the object up and stared at it. What he'd tossed to her was the letter to Lucy.

The following three days passed in a blur of pain for Agatha after Drummond had returned the letter to her. She wandered about the house like a lost soul, and waited, for that was all she could do. She was aware of a vague headache, and the recurring pain in her chest, but chose to ignore them. She did not take her meals belowstairs, preferring to eat in her rooms, although for the most part she simply pushed her food around on the plate and left it uneaten.

Holly had returned to her job, and it was all Agatha could do to keep from looking with accusatory eyes at the girl. She supposed it was probably not all Holly's fault, for Drummond was a formidable force. Perhaps he had anticipated Agatha's letter and had simply waited until Holly was preparing to leave.

Still, Agatha thought unfairly, the girl could have been more clever about hiding the letter. Holly's eyes would not meet hers, and when she spoke it was in subdued tones. Agatha could not be sorry for that.

It was as though, she thought, the entire house had grown subdued. Even the ordinary day-to-day noises seemed softer, and the voices more hushed. She saw little of the servants, for they kept to their chores, and of Paul Sterling she saw nothing at all. Even he had deserted her, she thought, feeling most sorry for herself.

On the twenty-ninth of April, Agatha rose late, a pain pounding in her head. She suffered herself to be dressed by Holly, then fitfully declared her outfit to be an abomination and tore it off, leaving the silk crumpled on the floor. Holly stared down at the ripped bodice, burst into tears, and fled. Agatha, immediately sorry for her outburst, sank down on the floor in a miserable huddle, and cursed herself and the day she had first seen Drummond. Tears flowed freely down her cheeks, and finally when her head ached so severely she sa white flashes in front of her eyes, she retired to her bed.

She slept some, though she was disturbed by uneasy dreams. In them, masked men wearing robes circled her, taunted her, tried to grab her hair and clothes with pincerlike fingers. She managed to rip away one of the masks, and the face underneath was Drummond's. She tore off a second mask. Drummond again. A third time, and a fourth, it was he, endlessly, until she fell into a deep slumber.

She awoke feeling feverish and disheveled, not at all pleased with the world, and particularly not with herself, although she could not have said why.

The room was darkened, and she wondered if she had slept the day away. She raised herself up on one elbow and saw that the heavy curtains at the window had been pulled shut to keep it dark. Someone had entered the room while she slept and had closed the drapes. She frowned. It must have been Holly.

A flash of color caught her eye, and she stared at the boudoir table next to the bed. On it was a single red rosebud in a crystal vase. Drummond.

With a bitter cry she knocked the vase off the table, away from her. It crashed to the floor, water trickling across the carpeting. The unopened bud lay bruised.

She turned and buried her face in the pillows, and wept for what she had lost; what he had caused her to lose; the love that had almost been hers.

The door crashed open and a cheerful voice called out.

"Hello, Agatha! Hello!"

It was Lucy.

My God, what a sight she must be. She leaped from her bed, dashed at the still-falling tears, and paused to stare at herself in the mirror. She looked like a madwoman! Her hair spilled in long curls across her breast and down her back, and her nightgown was untied at the neck and threatening to slip off one shoulder. Her eyes were reddened and wild, and her face as pale as the white gown she wore.

Well, there was no time to repair the ravages. She sniffed, took a deep breath, and headed for the sitting room just as Lucy came marching into the bedroom.

Lucy was dressed in a traveling outfit of cherry pink and it contrasted well with her glossy black curls and bright eyes. She looked the very model of health, unlike Agatha.

"Agatha, you look terrible!" Lucy cried, rushing to her friend and gripping her hands. She stared hard at her. "They said belowstairs you were ill, but I had not thought to find you so affected."

" 'Tis nothing," Agatha said in a voice made

hoarse from weeping. She swallowed, forcing herself to smile. "You look positively radiant, as usual."

"Sheer flattery. Here, you must return to bed at once before you take a chill." She propelled Agatha back to the bed, and pulled the covers up once she'd obediently crawled in.

"Really, I am quite all right," Agatha protested weakly as she struggled to a sitting position.

"Now, there's no need to act a part!"

"But, Lucy, I am not. I——"

"No, no, you must listen to me, and allow me to act as your nursemaid." Lucy paused and a slightly sly expression came onto her plump face. She winked. "You are perhaps in the family——"

"Oh no! No, not at all!" Agatha said, blushing as she realized what Lucy meant.

"Oh." Lucy sounded disappointed. "Still," said her friend, sagely shaking her head, "stranger things have happened by far."

"Indeed, such an event would be passing strange," Agatha said, a sad wistfulness to her voice.

Lucy, watching her, said nothing.

"Come, you must sit and rest for surely you are tired from your travel."

"Only a bit," Lucy admitted. "There is time enough to rest later, I'm sure. Oh, Agatha, I am so happy to see you again! And to think I cried when I learned of your disappearance. I thought surely you were dead."

"No."

"You must tell me again everything that has happened since the day of your wedding, for you must know that to read it all in a letter is extraordinarily unsatisfying. I was obliged to write down all the questions that came into my head."

Agatha tried to laugh with her friend.

"When will I meet your husband?"

"He was not downstairs when you arrived?"

Lucy angled her head, looked at her. "No, I was met by Merton. And Holly was kind enough to show me to my rooms—imagine, I am to be across the corridor from you. We shall be talking to all hours!"

"Yes." To all hours . . . until poor Lucy was taken to the ruins. She had to talk with Lucy, had to warn her. Perhaps it was not too late for her to escape. "Lucy, there is something of a serious nature which I must discuss with you."

Lucy's face lost its cheerfulness as she saw the shadows in Agatha's eyes. "What is amiss, my dear?"

"Something terrible—"

"Ah, there you are, my dear."

She looked up, stricken, to see Drummond standing in the door. He gazed across at Lucy.

"You must be Miss Wilmot."

"Indeed, I am, my lord."

Lucy stood and swept a curtsy to him, while he kissed her hand.

"Please call me Richard. I hope we can become friends, Miss Wilmot."

"Certainly—but you must call me Lucy." She grinned up at him, and he smiled in return, although it was an expression tinged with sadness. Lucy glanced from husband to wife, and back again, and made a mental note.

"I came to see if you were well enough to come down to dinner, Agatha. Paul will be joining us."

"Dinner!" said Lucy. "I vow I'm famished. First, though, I'd best change from these dusty clothes, and rest a bit. I shall see you both downstairs. And then, dear friend, we shall be able to talk more afterward."

She kissed Agatha's cheek, smiled at Drummond, and left the room. Across the hall they heard a door closing most decidedly.

He stared at her. "She is quite the cheering spirit."

"Yes."

"Agatha, please, I——" He stopped as he caught sight of the broken vase and rose.

She wondered what he had been about to say. Had she heard regret in his voice? Surely, she must be mistaken, for was he not callously using her and her friend? But when she looked into his eyes she saw an incredible sadness, a sadness more profound than any she had previously seen in those brown depths, and she almost softened.

Almost.

They stared at one another, as though a great chasm had opened before them and they stood on opposite sides. She could not talk to him, could not ask him all she wished to. She was aware only of an inner coldness, and the throbbing pain in her chest whenever she looked at him. As if from some great distance she wondered that this was the man who had made such delicious love to her, the man who had ignited passionate fires within her, the man to whom she had given her heart.

She thought she saw some echo of her thoughts in his tortured eyes, and could not bear it. She glanced away. She did not want to see him waver, did not want him to be kind to her now, before this terrible ceremony. It would be too cruel.

"Agatha," he said, his voice hoarse.

"Excuse me, my lord," she said suddenly, and rose from the bed, "but I must dress for dinner." On her way to the dressing room she brushed past him. His hand shot out, closed upon her wrist.

"Agatha."

She stared coldly down at his viselike grip. The fingers loosened; she was free. She backed away, then turned and walked into the dressing room and prepared to close the door. She told herself not to look, told herself it was surely a sign of weakness. But she could not help herself.

He was still standing in the middle of her bedroom. He had picked up the rose and it lay, the stem broken, in his hand. When he saw her watching him, he dropped the bud, turned so sharply on his heel that he ground the rose under his boot, and left.

She stared numbly at the shards of glass and the scattered rose petals, then turned away. As she began to pull her clothes from the wardrobe, tears came into her eyes.

When she knocked on Lucy's door, there was no response. Obviously Lucy was already downstairs. She found her friend in the green salon being entertained by Paul, who was regaling her with stories of his travels abroad.

Paul rose when she entered and bowed in her direction, maintaining a reserved smile for her. Lucy was quick to note it, but said nothing.

Drummond was not present, and Agatha scarcely

had time to wonder where he might be when Merton entered and announced dinner was ready.

"I think you will find the meal quite sumptuous," Paul said, escorting Lucy into the dining room. "Drummond's cook is, I vow, the best in all of England."

"I think I shall be enjoying my visit very much," Lucy said, a dimple appearing in her cheek. She stopped as she caught sight of the numerous dishes on the sideboard. "Oh my, I shall certainly be most wicked tonight and overindulge. You do not think I shall grow fat as a pig, do you?" she asked Agatha.

Paul, gallant as always, replied, "You will always be as slim as a nymph, Miss Wilmot."

Lucy's color heightened and she glanced down at her plate, then sneaked a look at Paul. He was still gazing at her.

It could have been amusing for Agatha to see Paul gaze with ill-concealed admiration at Lucy, had her friend not been here under such unhappy circumstances, and did she not think Paul was Drummond's accomplice in this horrible affair. Lucy, obviously quite flattered, could not help but flirt. Once, she would have encouraged the *tendre*, but not now. She regretted she would soon be destroying the last of Lucy's happiness.

Suddenly aware that someone was addressing her, Agatha looked up absently.

"Is that not so, Agatha?" Lucy asked.

She glanced up, to see that Richard was at that moment joining them. "Er, what? I am sorry, Lucy, but I was not attending."

"You have been most bedeviled tonight," Lucy said with concern. "Is there aught amiss?"

Agatha glanced at her husband, who met her gaze, and at Paul, who reddened slightly and looked down. "No, there is nothing amiss."

Lucy said nothing, only continued to eat her slice of roast beef. The meal went on in silence, until at last Agatha, unable to maintain her part in the farce, set her wineglass down sharply.

"If you will excuse me, I am still not feeling well. I would like to rest now."

Both men rose as she left the table.

"Perhaps later I shall come downstairs. I am sorry." She smiled at Lucy, nodded to Drummond and Paul, and left the dining room.

In her rooms she paced the hours away, occasionally sitting in a chair to rest, although she could not sit still for long. The minutes ticked away, and still Lucy did not appear. Perhaps, she thought anxiously, perhaps she should not have left Lucy alone with Drummond and Paul.

No. Her friend would be safe enough with them . . . for now.

Finally when the hour drew close to midnight she lay down on the bed, hoping Lucy would still come.

She fell asleep, waiting.

PART V:

THE SACRIFICE

TWENTY-TWO

Walpurgis Night, 1709

"YOU DID NOT COME TO talk with me last night," she accused Lucy next morning.

"We talked overlong in the salon, and when I finally left for bed 'twas well after two. I did not wish to disturb you," Lucy explained.

"But it was important!"

"Now, now, do not tax yourself, Agatha. Can you not talk with me now?"

Agatha nodded, brushing aside a curl that fell across her cheek. She and Lucy had breakfasted alone, the men being nowhere to be seen, and now she had drawn her friend into the salon. She took a deep breath, and began to pace around the room until Lucy finally bade her sit, saying she was becoming quite nervous watching her. Agatha sat in a chair, favoring Lucy with a mournful look.

"Dear me, is this terrible news?"

Agatha nodded mutely.

"T-They plan to . . ."

"Now, my dear, who is they?" Lucy asked briskly.

"Drummond. The others."

"I see." She grew thoughtful for a moment, then said, "What do they plan to do?"

The words came tumbling out. "They need a virgin for their evil purposes, and they are going to use you carnally."

"They are going to do *what* to me?" Lucy asked, a most incredulous look on her face. She lifted her eyebrows in a perplexed motion, and Agatha knew her friend plainly did not believe her.

She took a deep breath and continued. "Tonight they will sacrifice you to their Master of Darkness. The Devil. It is Walpurgis Night, and they have planned an unholy ceremony. Drummond is to become one of them at it. I overheard them myself, Lucy." At the look of disbelief on her friend's face, she described the events of the terrifying night, shaking at the memory.

"Why me?" Lucy asked at the end of Agatha's recitation.

"B-because," Agatha said. "He planned to use me, but instead his passion overtook him. I am no longer pure. They could not use me."

"Oh."

"Do you see?"

"They want a virgin for their ceremony."

"Yes."

"Well, I think they shall have to find someone else then," Lucy said blandly.

"W-What?"

"Come, Agatha, what do you think I said?"

"You—you are not a virgin?"

Lucy blushed and smiled a secret smile and shook her head. "There was a boy, long ago. We were very young—not over seventeen, I'm sure—and we were very foolish and thought we loved one another." She sighed. "Ah, well. That was many years ago. My aunt found out, and had him sent away, and that was that."

"Lucy! You are not a virgin?"

"I am not." Her voice was filled with some amusement. "Do you think we should tell them?"

"Why yes, we should!" Agatha's voice grew excited and she leaped to her feet. "We must tell them at once; we . . ." She paused. "They would not believe us, would they?"

Lucy shook her head, her black curls shaking with the effort. "No, they would think it a story we'd concocted to save me from such a terrible fate."

"You still do not believe me," Agatha accused. "You are amused by my story."

"Really, Agatha, you must agree it is a most incredible tale. I arrive one day and the very next you are filling my ears with the most lurid accounts of ruined abbeys and men in masks and wicked ceremonies and undressed ladies. My, wouldn't my aunt be shocked." Her dark eyes twinkled with amusement.

"Lucy, this is hardly a laughing matter."

"I am not laughing, my dear. I am simply considering . . . the matter."

Agatha's eyes filled with tears. "Lucy, I want to save you."

Lucy reached out and touched her hand gently.

"I know, my dear, but you must allow me some time to consider it fully."

"You have no time left! Tonight is the ceremony."

Lucy lapsed into silence for a few minutes, watching as Bruno raised his head to scratch behind his ear.

"You say your husband is involved?"

She nodded bitterly. "He is the one who will take you to the abbey to be their . . . sacrifice."

"I really am at a loss for words," Lucy said. "I would not have thought—I mean, he seemed the perfect gentleman when I talked with him last night." She glanced sharply at her friend. "Pray, tell me, what of Mr. Sterling? Is he also a member of this hellfire club?"

"As far as I know, he is not. But," she said as she saw the relief on her friend's face, "he knows of it. Indeed, he is the one who brought me back from the ruins a week ago."

"Well, good enough!"

"But——"

Lucy's raised hand forestalled her. "No, no, I tell you I am not quite as fidget-brained as I act, Agatha. I will allow nothing to happen to you—or to me. So, please do not worry yourself sick."

Agatha shook her head sadly. "I fear there is nothing either one of us can do. Nothing."

When night arrived, Merton and Thomas escorted Agatha to her rooms.

"No, please, do not lock me in," she pleaded, gazing earnestly at the two servants.

"I am sorry, my lady," Thomas said sadly. "We have my master's orders to lock you in."

"But you don't understand. Miss Wilmot—my friend—her life is in grave danger. Please don't lock the door tonight, Thomas."

She thought she saw a glimmer of sympathy in his eyes, but he shook his head. Merton remained as impassive as ever. Thomas started to close the door. She stopped him, one hand against the wood.

"A woman will die tonight," she said.

"No, my lady, you are mistaken."

Firmly he pulled the door shut, and she heard the rasp as it was locked. She whirled away from the door, angrily pacing about the sitting room, then returned to the door and spoke loudly.

"Lucy! Lucy? Can you hear me?"

Lucy had not returned to her rooms; would not now, Agatha realized. Hours before they had dined together—the four of them, for Paul, the ever faithful watchdog, had stayed again—and when the last dish had been swept away, he had invited Lucy to walk through the gardens with him. Agatha had signaled Lucy, trying to prevent her from leaving, but Lucy, pleased by Sterling's attentions, had laughed and said she would be safe enough. They had departed, and the Viscount and Viscountess of Drummond had remained to stare at one another across the table.

"Will you promise me that you will remain inside tonight?" he had asked after a time.

She raised her head and stared at him defiantly. "You know full well I cannot, sir." She knew there was no sense in lying to him and saying she would stay inside. She knew he would not believe her.

"Agatha, please, do not be foolish." He sighed.

"If you will not obey, I shall be forced to have you locked in your rooms once more."

Her lips tightened, but she said nothing.

"I do not want to lock you up."

She would have liked to have believed him, but so much had happened in the past week that she could not. The pain in her chest tightened, and she looked away. When she spoke, her voice was bitter.

"You have a strange way of showing your regret, my lord—or should I perhaps call you Brother Discord? Will that not be your formal name upon the completion of tonight's ceremony?"

The chair crashed backward as he got to his feet. His clenched knuckles showed white, and his lips were pressed thinly together. It was evident he was having difficulty in keeping his temper. What she saw on his face then frightened her—his very scar seemed to show his white-hot fury.

"Merton." His voice was flat.

"Yes, my lord." The butler stepped toward the table.

"We are finished with dinner. It is time to escort her ladyship to her rooms."

"Very well, sir."

She had started to protest, but there had been no use in it. Merton, joined by Thomas in the hall, had firmly escorted her to her rooms.

Now she was alone.

Now Lucy was with Paul in the garden, and soon—so very soon . . .

She had, she reasoned, done all she could possibly do under the circumstances. She had tried to warn Lucy with the letter. She had warned her when she arrived. Surely, she told herself, that was enough. But she knew it wasn't. There had to be more. Something *she* could do now.

Yet what could she do? After all, she was imprisoned in her rooms for the night, and no doubt they had already taken Lucy away.

She walked away from the door and across the sitting room, knelt on the windowseat and stared out into the darkening evening. Pushing the window open, she inhaled deeply of the fresh spring air, felt the slight breeze cooling her warm skin.

What could she do?

The breeze shifted, and she turned her face to catch it.

And stared.

The window.

A frown transformed her face as an idea began to coalesce in her mind. She couldn't do it. It was sheer folly. She would be killed or hurt, and what good then would she be to Lucy or herself?

Yet . . . if it worked . . . She smiled slowly.

The door might be locked, but the window was not.

Shivering with excitement, she forced her hands to lie quiet in her lap. She couldn't do anything now, for it was too early, not dark enough.

The remaining hours passed slowly; once she tried to read, but found herself unable to sit still for long. Instead, she paced through the room, reviewing every aspect of her plan.

At length she heard the clock downstairs chiming nine. Now was the time to act. She opened the wardrobe, pulled out a coat and shirt, then searched through the chest by the bed where she had hidden a second pair of breeches after the first had been removed by Drummond. Quickly dressing, she pulled on her boots, tied her hair back, and went to the window.

The servants would never expect her to escape by this route, so they wouldn't be watching here. Still, she must be careful.

She stared thoughtfully at the tree outside the window, then stepped up onto the windowseat. She eased herself through the window and crawled along the narrow ledge. A gnarled vine grew along the side of the house and she grabbed it for support. Unable to support her weight, it ripped away, and she lost her balance. Terrified, she grabbed at the air, certain she was about to fall two stories to her death. Then, she crashed against the tree and was tangled in its branches just long enough to catch a hold and pull herself to a more secure perch. She took a deep breath, wiped away the sweat running down her face. Her hands trembled from fright, but she forced herself to be calm. She stared down and thought she saw another branch, about five feet below the one she sat on. She eased herself along, lay down, and rolled over so that she was hanging by her hands, and rested her feet on the lower branch. Taking a deep breath, she dropped her hold and grabbed the trunk, then crouched down till she was sitting on the second branch. She repeated the process till she was able to drop from the lowest branch to the ground.

The bushes below broke her fall. When she realized she would fall no farther, she carefully rolled out of the shrubbery and got to her feet, albeit somewhat unsteadily. Her hands and neck were covered with scratches, and there was a gaping rip in her shirt and breeches, but otherwise she was all right. She smiled to herself, pleased she had made it so far.

She listened to see if anyone, alerted by the noise of her fall, came to the windows. No one did, and she slipped away from the bushes and tree. Carefully making her way around the house, well away from the stables, she paused when she reached the terrace. She crossed it and peered into the study.

It was empty.

She slipped through the unlocked French windows and took down the pistols displayed over the mantel. She had one terrible moment when she heard Paul's voice outside the study. The doorknob began to turn, and she felt as though she'd stopped breathing. She watched the door slowly start to open, then it stopped as Merton called to Paul. He answered, pulled the door shut, and she was safe. Breathing with relief, she checked the weapons, found them unloaded. Drummond kept ammunition in his desk, she knew. She searched through it, pulling each drawer open until she found it. She loaded the pistols and placed them in the pockets of her coat, then left the study, heading toward the stables.

She paused in the stableyard when she heard a man's voice coming from inside. No one answered him, so she assumed he was by himself. It was Ben, no doubt, probably talking to the horses while he cleaned tack.

Somehow she would have to work around him,

for she knew she certainly couldn't trust him to saddle her mare. How, though?

She crept closer, then stopped when one of the horses whickered and footsteps sounded across the floor, not more than ten feet from her.

"What's the matter, Tally? Restless tonight? Haven't been ridden much lately, have you? Poor girl. Well, tomorrow maybe you'll go for a little exercise." He laughed and made clicking noises to the mare.

She glanced inside the building. Directly ahead was the tack area, well-lit by a lantern suspended from the ceiling. The light gleamed on the rows of bits, stirrups, and spurs hanging on the wall opposite her. A stool had been placed in one corner and a jumble of bridles lay in front, with a bucket and brush and rags alongside. She had been correct. The groom had been cleaning tack.

She edged slightly to the left so that she could see farther into the stable. The first stall on the left was empty, as was the one opposite it, on her right. The second stall across from her, though, was occupied by her own horse and it was there that Ben leaned against a post, stroking the mare's neck and talking to her. The horse noisily blew on him and he laughed.

Perhaps she could somehow decoy him, lure him away and then quickly saddle Tally before he returned. Short of setting fire to the stable—and she wasn't about to do that—she didn't know what she could do. Too, there wasn't enough time for that. Perhaps she could order him to saddle Tally, threaten to shoot him if he didn't. And if he somehow managed to take her pistols away? She shook her head. That wouldn't work, either.

No, she needed to take a more direct approach to this problem.

She would have to knock him out. Somehow.

She glanced around for something large—though not so big that it would kill—to use to hit him over the head. There were rakes, used in cleaning the stable, but they didn't look sturdy enough for her purpose, and she suspected they'd simply give Ben a headache, and nothing more.

Outside in the stableyard, with the aid of light coming through one small window, she quietly searched through the shadows until she found what she wanted in a pile of discarded wood and scraps of metal. She selected a piece of planking—long enough for her to use as a club, and not so thick that she'd hurt him. Reassuring herself that she really wouldn't hit him that hard, she gripped the board tightly and walked toward the door of the stable.

Ben was no longer in front of Tally's stall. He had moved away to check on a young mare in the next stall. His back was still turned toward her

It was now or never.

She ran toward him. Tally, seeing her mistress, whickered in greeting. Ben turned to see what was disturbing the mare and caught the full brunt of her club on the side of his head. It hit with a sickly thud, and his eyes rolled up in his head and he collapsed. Numbly she dropped the plank and stared in horror. Hot bile rose in her throat, burning her mouth.

She had killed him. She knew it. She knelt by

his side and put a hand on his chest. It rose and fell slowly, and she waited, watching him. No, he wasn't dead after all, thank God.

He was knocked out, though, and she'd best hurry before he came around. She didn't know if he'd recognized her in that brief moment he'd been turning, but she couldn't take the risk he had, and she feared that if he woke up anytime soon, he might try to warn Drummond.

She led the mare out of the stall, tied her to a ring, and proceeded to get her tack. Within minutes she was up in the saddle and riding out of the stableyard.

She didn't know when the ceremony would begin, so she rode quickly, keeping the mare to a fast canter. Perhaps it was already too late for Lucy. No, she thought, she could not believe that. Above her the moon spread yellow light on the landscape. The wind moaned high in the branches of the trees making the night more desolate, and once again she heard the call of owls.

The horse's hooves echoed along the road and she stared steadfastly ahead. So far her plan had run smoothly, without a single problem. Hunching down, her eyes tearing slightly from the wind, she thought of what else she must do. She had to continue, couldn't turn back now. She was so close.

Soon, very soon, she would be at the abbey, and she would pull the pistols out and she would . . .

She would kill him. Because there was no other alternative. She was terrified, but determined to save her friend. She did not let herself think of what would happen if she failed.

Yes, she would kill Drummond. Kill him for

what he did to his poor first wife, what he had done to her, what he planned for Lucy. Then, for some reason she wouldn't name, she saw again, in her mind, the shattered vase, the crushed rose.

TWENTY-THREE

WHEN AGATHA ARRIVED IN THE woods near the ruins, she heard the sounds of merry-making and knew the ceremony had already begun. Cursing herself for being so slow, she hitched Tally to a tree and ran, bent over so as not to be seen, through the grass until she reached the wall. She edged along it until she could peer inside.

Tonight the room was a little different from when she'd last seen it. Flower garlands decorated the walls, and one, of deep purple flowers, had been draped across the arms of the reversed crucifix. Even from where she was she could smell the heavy perfume of the flowers. The pervasive sweet fragrance turned her stomach, and she put a hand to her mouth to keep from retching. Beneath the cross a black cloth, edged in red embroidery, covered the altar. The pattern was a most hellish one, and it sickened her to see the images of demons and damned humans cavorting there. Dozens more of the black candles burned than had a sennight before, and the thick cushions had been pushed aside to give the brothers and sisters of the hellfire club more room in which to move.

Tonight, for the Feast of Saint Secoine, the black and red robes had been discarded. Instead, the monks and nuns were dressed in their finest, most sumptuous clothing—the room was aglitter with diamonds and rubies and pearls—and their plain loos had been traded for masks adroitly fashioned into the faces of animals.

By the altar waited a Badger, dressed in canary breeches and coat, and numerous chains and fobs hanging from his striped waistcoat. Nearby a petite Fox and a Cat, both with full breasts threatening to spill out their décolletage at any second, vied for the attention of a Horse, attired in green velvet breeches with bows on the outside of the leg. His once immaculate cravat was askew, his shirt half-unbuttoned, and he was endeavoring to dip his hands into the two bodices. Toward the second door a Dog in wine satin, her sleeves trimmed with ermine, conversed with a Bull, whose thick thighs strained at the lavender velvet of his breeches.

Wine flowed freely, and the talk was loud and raucous, the laughter abrupt, as if all present merely wished to pass the minutes until it was time for that which they anxiously awaited.

Even from where she crouched outside in the darkness Agatha could tangibly feel the current of tension in the room.

She studied the men and women and their masks,

and wondered where Drummond was. What would his mask be? Was there, she asked herself, any two-faced animal? No, 'twas only man who could claim that dubious privilege.

Her knees ached slightly, and she rubbed them and prepared to creep to another window to see if she could spot Drummond. She had just stepped forward when a hand clamped down on her collar. Not again! She should have known Paul Sterling would be watching and waiting for her. Fool, she told herself bitterly. She never seemed to learn from her experiences.

He pulled her around to face him. With dismay she realized it wasn't Paul.

Her captor wore the mask of a grinning dog, and she could see the glint of his eyes in the candlelight. His lips twisted into a smile and he laughed softly.

"Well, what do we have here?"

She raised her head as best she could, and stared him in the eye. "Unhand me, sir." She thought to brazen it out, for at present she was hardly in a position to try to grab her pistols.

He laughed again, a sound she little liked. For answer, he twisted her arm behind her back and marched her toward the front door of the abbey. He kicked it open, then pushed her inside. She stumbled across the threshold and into the crowd, colliding with a plump Dove, who slapped her. Those nearby drew back to see better, and a sound of astonishment swept through them.

"Look, Brothers and Sisters of Satan, what our net has caught tonight." Again he laughed, and she realized he was quite drunk.

She thought the voice sounded familiar, but could not place it. It wasn't Drummond's, and surely it wasn't Sterling's.

"What's that fellow want?" lisped a Boar to her left. He stared at her through a quizzing glass and shuddered.

"What is your name, boy?" demanded the Dove, who'd since recovered from her shock.

The Grinning Dog laughed again, reached up, and knocked Agatha's hat off so that her hair came tumbling down and started. There was a moment of silence as the monks and nuns realized she was a woman, then everyone seemed to start talking at once. The man in the dog mask raised one hand for quiet. Slowly they quieted.

"Father Avaritia, whatever are we to do?" asked one Cat in a quavering tone, addressing the Grinning Dog.

He drew back his lips in a feral smile. "I think that——"

But he got no further for Agatha, unable to quell her curiosity, half twisted around and ripped the mask from the man's face. It fell, unnoticed, to the floor as she stared, too shocked to take her eyes away.

Lord Alford.

She blinked, unable to believe what she saw. He twisted his lips, sneering at her.

"So you've discovered my identity, my dear. Still, it will do you little good now." Before she could duck, he raised his hand and backhanded her in a most casual manner. She reeled from the blow, and two other men leaped forward, grasping her by the elbows. There could be no escape for her now. Her cheek still stung from the blow, and yet she could not draw her eyes away from Alford.

Alford . . . a member of the hellfire club. And Drummond, her husband, as well. Had the Devil somehow linked her with these demon worshipers?

"It is too bad, my dear," he said languidly, "that you have discovered our club, for you must die now. I admit, I am puzzled to find you lurking under our windows. Now," he said in a thoughtful voice, "what can have brought you here?"

She would not tell him, though she was surprised that Drummond had not yet stepped forward to claim her. Still, he could hardly do that when he'd abducted her out from under Alford's very nose!

She tried to put all the confidence she could muster in her voice as she spoke. "You'd best not kill me, my lord." She lifted her chin in a defiant manner.

"Oh, and pray, why not?"

She plunged in. "My husband will come after me—or my father—to save me!"

"You are married? How charming, to be sure. So, that is where you flew that day? You had a secret lover, did you?"

She remained silent; let him think what he would.

He watched her thoughtfully. "Or, you say, your father will come after you?"

"Yes."

He laughed again, a harsh sound that made her shiver. She realized how hushed the room had grown, and as she stared around at the masked men and women, she wondered when Drummond would appear so he might further betray her. Chewing her lower lip, she waited anxiously.

Presently the man in the jackal mask stepped forward, slowly removing the mask as he did so.

It was her father.

Agatha stared speechlessly at him. In his face and eyes she saw no love nor sympathy, only a cruel hatred. In that moment the pain in her chest burst, and she staggered back, putting her hands up as if they could protect her from this terrible knowledge.

One by one the men and women unmasked. The former she recognized from the party where her engagement had been announced. The women, she assumed, were daughters and wives and mistresses. Ruthen was there, too, smiling slyly at her.

Nowhere did she see Drummond, and that confused her all the more. Perhaps he was due to arrive later . . . with the sacrifice. Or perhaps, she thought with a savage smile, he was having trouble with the intended victim.

As she stared at her father, she realized with a sinking heart that no one could protect—or save—her now. No one, that is, but herself. Somehow she must trick Alford. That would be her only opportunity to escape. She knew they would soon kill her.

Alford started toward her. She closed her eyes and sagged forward in a feigned faint. He managed to catch her before she hit the floor. Picking her up roughly, he walked toward the altar. She kept her eyes open just a slit so that she could watch from below her eyelashes.

No one had moved since she had supposedly

fainted. Good. That would help all the more. The unmasked company intently watched him with his burden.

He dropped her onto the desecrated altar, and Agatha made sure one of her hands flopped down near her coat pocket. She fluttered her eyes, blinked, and opened them wide to stare up into Alford's grinning face. She allowed herself to look frightened—that would lull him.

It seemed to work, for he appeared to relax. "You really should have married me," he said, his voice mocking, "for you would not have come to this, my dear Agatha. Now—" and here his grin spread wider—"you shall become a bride for our Master."

His hands brushed across the front of her shirt and she stiffened. Idly his fingers played with the buttons, began opening the shirt.

Now! something inside her shouted.

She brought her leg up and around, driving it into his stomach. He grunted in pain, and holding his paunch, leaped back away from the altar. He shouted, jerked his head toward her. Two other men jumped toward her, but she rolled to her knees, then pulled the two pistols from her coat pockets as she got to her feet. They stopped dead when they saw the weapons in her hands.

Aiming the pistols at Alford and the two men, she jumped down from the altar, and with her back to the wall and the desecrated crucifix, she ran toward the door.

It swung open.

"Brother Discord," Alford shouted, "grab her before she leaves!"

"Agatha, my God!"

She saw Drummond, a shocked look on his face, standing there. She had little time to register his surprise, could only act quickly, and did so. She glanced back toward the room, saw Alford starting toward her, then darted toward the door. Drummond tried to block her, Alford snatched at her arm, and her finger twitched. One of the pistols fired, and she watched as Drummond staggered backward when the ball hit him, watched as a crimson blossom opened across his coat.

TWENTY-FOUR

HE GASPED IN PAIN, HIS hand clasping the wound, and lunged at Agatha. She did not try to move out of the way. She was watching the scarlet stain spread across the material, watching the blood drip through the fingers of his hand. He hit her other hand, knocking the second pistol to the floor. It landed with a clatter, and she at last raised her eyes to meet his and saw the grimace of pain go across his face.

"Bravo, Brother Discord," Alford said, strolling over to the couple when the pistols were no longer a threat, "for capturing our intruder."

"What's this?" The viscount forced a smile to his pale lips. He did not deign to look at Agatha. "You caught her spying?"

"Outside. She was creeping through the grass like a little field mouse."

Squire Grey pushed his way through the crowd,

ignored Agatha, and looked at Drummond, his heavy brows pulled together in a frown.

"Where's the bride?"

"She'll soon be here," Drummond replied. He shifted his fingers, grimaced, and she saw they were stained with his blood.

The blood she had caused to spill.

She could not take her eyes from his wound. All the fight seemed to have gone out of her after she shot him. She hadn't meant to—yes, she had. She'd fully intended to come here and kill him; to punish him for what he had done. But now that she had wounded him, she felt sick. She had never seen him suffer this way before, had never seen him so pale. She did not know how bad it was; she only knew he was in pain, because of her.

"Come now, friends," said the squire, turning to the others, who were still too shocked by the events to talk. "Drink more wine. We shall begin our feast shortly."

He started to step away, and Alford reached for her. "Father," he said to the squire, "what shall we do with our field mouse here?"

The squire did not pause to look back. "Crush it."

"Father!" Agatha cried. Still he did not look back. "Father, you can't do this—you can't let them hurt me. I'm your daughter!"

He said nothing, but reached for a glass of wine and drained it in one swallow. He looked at two burly men. "Take her to the altar now. I want this over with quickly. Before the bride arrives."

They shouldered their way through the gossiping crowd and had almost reached her when Drummond suddenly reached out, grabbed her by the hand, and said, "Run, dammit, Agatha, run outside! It's your only chance."

Stunned, she looked up at him. "W-What?"

"You heard me. Go on." With his free hand he pushed her toward the door.

She stumbled away, still shocked by his words. A man who had worn the mask of a ram, lunged at her as she brushed by him. He managed to grab the material of her coat and started to pull her back. She twisted away, the sleeve ripping.

"Get her!" Alford shouted.

She thought she would get out safely, but just as she reached the door, someone grabbed her roughly from behind and held on, no matter how much she turned and twisted and fought. Her arms were hauled up high behind her back, and she cried out in pain.

"You damned hussy," her father growled. "You'll pay for all the trouble you've caused me these two months." He shook her until her head snapped back and forth, and tears came to her eyes.

"Agatha, run!" She heard Drummond's voice again, and she tried to twist away from her father. He slammed his fist into her jaw, and she sagged against him.

The man with the ram's mask backed away from the door pointing. "There are horsemen out there," he said.

Silence fell over the assembly, then someone said, "Soldiers! There are soldiers outside!"

"Leave," the squire said, nodding toward the back door.

Three men leaned their shoulders against the

altar, and slowly shoved the great stone against the door to block it from being opened. Just as they finished, someone began pounding on the door from outside.

"Her Royal Highness's Dragoons! Let us in!"

Shutters had been closed on the windows and barred from inside.

The revelers, obviously agitated, began filing toward the other door. A woman who had worn a cat mask put the back of her hand to her forehead and swooned. No one bent to help her. Instead, her companions simply walked around or over her.

"You betrayed us," Alford said, staring at Drummond as if seeing him for the first time. "You didn't bring the bride; you never planned to. Instead you brought *them*." He jerked his head savagely toward the door.

Drummond, though obviously in great pain, managed to draw himself up and to stare at Alford with intense hatred. "I vowed two years ago that I would see you in hell, Alford. That I would get my revenge."

"What revenge?" Alford sneered.

"Do you recall Jenny? A dark-haired petite girl, of tender years?"

Agatha, still in the clutches of her father, saw the color drain from Alford's face. The squire shook her roughly, and growled low.

"Come, Alford, don't listen to the traitor. Kill him, and let's be done. We haven't got time to jabber."

"I see you do recall her," Drummond said softly. "I am pleased she remains in your memory. I received this—" he pointed to the white scar on his forehead— "in the engagement that night. I would have given my arm—or my life—to have saved her. But I was too late. Too late to prevent her from being butchered."

"S-She . . .?"

"My sister."

Agatha lifted her head at this. His sister? Butchered two years ago? What had happened? How had Alford been involved?

The room was less crowded than a few minutes ago. Outside, it sounded as though the troops were using a log to batter the door down. She heard poundings, too, on the window shutters.

Drummond wiped his bloody hand on his breeches, leaned over as he was seized with dizziness.

"Once again you are too late, Drummond," Alford said softly.

At that moment she realized what he was doing: Alford kept her husband's attention, while Ruthen circled behind the viscount, hoping to take him unaware. She opened her mouth to shout a warning, but her father, anticipating her, slapped his hand across her mouth and nose, shutting off her air. Drummond was not so easily fooled; he lunged for Alford, who managed to sidestep the viscount. Leaping forward, Ruthen savagely brought the butt-end of a pistol down on Drummond's skull. Groaning, he landed with a thud on the floor, tried valiantly to rise, wobbled, and fell back.

Ruthen giggled, while Alford nudged the fallen viscount with the toe of one boot. Drummond did not stir. He grinned at Agatha.

"Come along, my little one."

"Where?"

"No questions now!"

As the squire roughly pushed her into a room she had not yet seen, she noticed the acrid sting of smoke for the first time. She tried to look back toward Drummond, but all she could see were flames—someone had set the room afire. The room where Drummond lay unconscious!

"No!" She wiggled out of her father's grip, darted back toward Drummond.

Squire Grey tripped her, then, seizing her by the arm, slammed her up against the wall. She moaned from the pain in her back and head.

"Leave him, bitch," he said in a low tone. "He's a dead man."

A dead man.

He pushed her through the dark smoke-filled room, and she shuddered at her stupidity, at the sheer folly of her life. Tonight she had come to kill Drummond, had managed to injure him, only to learn that she had been completely mistaken about him all along. He hadn't joined the hellfire club because he was like the others; he had joined so he might avenge his sister's death. He had tried to save her life—and she had cost him his.

Tears, from grief and the smoke, stung her eyes, slipped unnoticed down her cheeks.

Her husband *was* dead, just as she had planned. She had achieved her goal all too well. The irony was too horrible.

Ruthen and Alford followed close behind them. One of the ceiling timbers, loosened by the flames, swept down, knocking Ruthen off his feet. It landed across his abdomen and he groaned. Weakly he tried to push it off, could not move it.

"Help me," he called to Alford. "Rupert, help me. I'm hurt."

Alford kept walking. "I don't have time for the injured," he said. He turned, and seeing Agatha's horrified expression, he jerked her roughly forward.

She turned her head away, tried not to vomit though the bile rose up in her throat. Then she had no time to think of Ruthen's terrified expression as he realized what his friend was doing, for the floor had disappeared and she was falling. She landed on her knees and hands on soft dirt. For a moment she was too stunned to rise, then Alford jerked her to her feet.

"A tunnel," she said weakly.

"Oh yes, we weren't about to get ourselves cornered without another route of escape." He laughed, and the sound echoed in the tunnel.

She heard the rasp of flint and a yellow light appeared a few feet away. The walls of the tunnel were thick with mold, and she shivered in the chilly dampness. Alford and the squire stood on each side of her, prepared to grab her if she should try to run.

Where would she even go? she wondered bleakly. Her husband was dead, thanks to her foolishness; her friends didn't know where she was, couldn't rescue her in time even if they knew; and her father had been all too willing to sacrifice her to the Devil. It appeared that she had nothing much to live for, and she did not particularly care what happened to her next.

The three maintained a fast pace through the tunnel, their footsteps muffled by the sand underfoot. Occasionally she saw the bright eyes of a rat in the shadows of other tunnels branching out from the main one. Once she heard several of the animals fighting over something, and suppressed a shudder. This must be a network of tunnels, she thought, under the abbey, where no doubt the monks had stored their wine and cheeses and other foods, where they had kept the coffers, where they had hidden when the Norsemen and others had raided.

Where did the tunnels lead? Where were they going? Did it matter? she asked herself, and realized desolately it did not.

She might as well as be in hell for all that it mattered.

The pounding, he realized with some relief, wasn't just in his head. He lifted it slightly, gazed into the dark murkiness, and coughed. Smoke stung his nose, choked him, and he coughed again. Suddenly there was a splintering, and shouting as the door was broken down. He could hear the soldiers climbing over the altar and jumping down into the room.

"Oh my heavens," he heard a woman's voice in the next moment, and Drummond frowned. A woman? Surely not one of the hellfire club? They had all fled. Who then? It sounded remarkably like——

"Now, Lucy," Paul Sterling's voice said, "please be careful. The only reason I let you come is——"

"Yes, yes," she said somewhat impatiently, "we

shall discuss that later, if necessary. Our *friends* need our attention at present."

Paul had brought Lucy? What the devil was going on? And where was Agatha?

That thought spurred him and he forced himself to a sitting position. Dizziness swept over him and he closed his eyes, momentarily swaying as the sickness hit him. He touched the wound in his shoulder, and his fingers came away sticky. At least it no longer seemed to be bleeding. A flesh wound it would seem, no more. Thank God for that minor miracle.

"Paul," he called, his voice hoarse from the smoke. He feared Paul would never hear him over the din the soldiers made as they searched the abbey. "Paul!"

"I hear someone calling!" Lucy said. She coughed once. "All this smoke!"

"Over here!"

"Is that you, Drummond?"

"It certainly isn't the Devil," he said dryly. In stages, he managed to stand.

"Where the blazes are you, Drummond?"

He tried to tell Paul, but found his voice gone faint from dryness and the smoke. Starting forward, he bumped into something solid and decided to stand still. The soldiers had put out the fire, and had broken the shutters on the windows, and the air was now whisking the smoke away. Through the clearing murk, he saw two figures coming toward him.

"Drummond!" Paul clasped his arms, and he groaned. "Good God, man, you're bleeding!"

"Agatha," he said, gritting his teeth.

"Where is she?" Lucy asked. She had stooped to neatly tear off the hem of her petticoat and was calmly wrapping it around Drummond's arm. He stared with bemusement at her. She was nattily attired in a once cream-colored riding habit, be-grimed now with smoke. There was a smudge of ash on her nose.

"We thought you were dead," Paul said. "The captain waited for your signal, and when it didn't come, he decided——"

"What are you two doing here?" he asked, not letting Paul finish.

"Please, before you two swap stories, we really must find Agatha," said Lucy as she finished her ministrations on the viscount's shoulder. She stepped back to stare critically at the makeshift bandage. "That should do for now," she murmured. She then looked up into Drummond's eyes. "Is she not in danger?"

The captain of the company of dragoons came out of the back room and over to them.

"My lord, we've searched the entire abbey and found no one."

Drummond frowned. His head still throbbed and it was difficult to think clearly. Where could Alford and the Greys have gone? There had to be another way out, some place Alford had never mentioned to him. "A secret door then?"

"We'll check, my lord."

Suddenly one of the men shouted for the captain, who bowed and said, "One moment, my lord." He returned within minutes. "They've found a trap door under a false chest. It leads to a tunnel. I've already dispatched ten men to go down and explore."

"Very good, Captain." He winced as a lance of pain shot through him, then looked at Paul. "Unfortunately, they have a good headstart on us. I don't know how long I lay unconscious."

"Where do the tunnels lead?" Lucy asked. Several dark curls tumbled from under her hat over her forehead, and she had wiped her bloody fingers on her shirt. In her worry, she was oblivious of her disarray.

"I-I don't know," he said haltingly. "Alford never talked of an escape route to me—after all, I was still a novice. But the tunnel has to . . . Wait." He frowned, concentrating. Hadn't Alford once mentioned something about—— "Caves!" he shouted.

"What caves?" Paul demanded.

"There are caves along the coast. Alford said the monks had used them when they brought supplies by water. The tunnels must connect with them."

"Then we will go," Lucy said. She turned and headed for the door. Drummond reached out to stop her.

"*We* will go. Paul will return you at once to Falcon's Hall."

She lifted her chin and stared up at him, not at all afraid of him, he thought wryly, though she was much smaller than he.

"Paul most certainly will not return me. I am riding with you."

"No. It's too dangerous for a woman and foolhardy to——"

"Agatha will need me," she averred, and he

could see from the glint in her eyes she suspected she'd won the argument.

He appealed mutely to Paul, who merely shook his head. "You see how successful I was in keeping her at the house," he said with a small shrug.

"Very well, Miss Wilmot, you may come with us. But—you must stay with Paul at all times."

She nodded eagerly.

"Captain Grant."

"Sir?"

"The caves are about a mile south of here. They may already have boats waiting."

"Very good, sir." The captain left the room, calling to his men still mounted outside.

"Thank you, Lucy," he said at last as they followed Grant, "for tending to my wound."

" 'Tis nothing," she replied offhandedly. "When we return to the house, you'll be bandaged better."

Paul frowned as he stared at the wound. "Alford shot you?"

Drummond's lips twitched. "No, Grey did."

"Damn the squire!"

"Not the squire."

"What?"

"Agatha Grey shot me."

He chuckled at their looks of dismay.

TWENTY-FIVE

THEIR FOOTSTEPS ECHOED EERILY IN the tunnel and as they ran, the two men argued about her.

"She's held us back," Squire Grey complained. "Slowed us down, and now the others have escaped, and we've been left behind."

"She's our insurance, I tell you," Alford asserted, between panting, "just in case."

"Just in case, hell," Grey said.

They had zigged and zagged through the network of tunnels, and she was completely lost. Now she could smell a difference in the air. No longer fetid, it moved with slight air currents, touched with the briny odor of the sea.

A sound grew louder in her ears, a deep thundering sound, until at last they reached a spot where the tunnel widened into a cave whose roof vaulted high over their heads. Something dark flapped by them, and Agatha cringed.

Alford laughed, the sound echoing, and hit her shoulder with the flat of his hand. She stumbled forward. "Stupid slut. It's only a bat."

"Shut up," Grey said angrily. "You're too damned loud."

Alford scowled, but shut up.

The torch flickered in a draft, but continued to burn steadily. They walked through the cave, whose floor was thick with mud. It led into a series of smaller ones, some with ceilings so low they were forced to walk hunched over. Agatha had seen no opportunity to escape, for if she pushed Alford and he fell, the torch would be extinguished. What then? She could scarcely run blindly through the caves. In the dark she would soon get lost, perhaps fall over a ledge or into a pit.

Still, would it not be better to simply act than to walk in this dulled stupor?

Too, she knew it wouldn't be long before her father convinced Alford she was too troublesome to take along, and she had little doubt of what that would mean.

Before she could make up her mind, they had entered an immense cavern, its walls a glaring white. The ceiling was blackened from the smoke of many past torches, and across one part of it she could see the faint outlines of paintings. Obscene drawings, like the ones she had seen in the abbey.

They were standing on a ledge overlooking the cavern floor. Next to them squatted a flat rock, its pocked surface dark with rusty stains. She licked her lips, knowing what had caused the stains. Beyond the crude altar were rough steps hewn from the cave's wall. They led to the sand some hundred feet below.

Alford pushed her toward the altar and the steps.

"No!" Her shout echoed, and he backhanded her.

"Shut up!"

Toward the mouth of the cavern a light bobbed, flickered, disappeared.

"Help!" she called. "Help me!"

"Douse the torch," Grey said. "We'll make it down the steps in the dark."

"No——"

"Don't disobey me, boy. I've listened to your foolishness too long already."

Alford sourly obeyed, and they were plunged at once into complete darkness. For a moment she could neither see nor hear anything, could only feel the weight of the dark pressing down on her, smothering her, forcing the air from her lungs.

Grey's hand tightened around her arm, and she started, yet was glad of the contact.

"Move ahead," he whispered to Alford.

She could hear Alford's hesitant steps as he headed toward the stairs. Her father's fingers still tightly gripped her arm.

She had to do something, now, while they were in the dark where she could catch them unaware. Jerking her arm away from the squire, she slammed into Alford and ran past him. He yelled, and his hands brushed her as his arms flailed. Her father shouted, tried to seize her, and crashed into someone. Her left foot was suddenly over space, and she jumped back, her heart pounding. She had almost fallen over the edge, fallen a hundred feet to her death.

She could hear Alford fumbling with the torch, trying to light it, while her father cursed them both alternately.

She edged along until she found the steps, then making sure she was along the wall, she went down them as quickly as possible. Fifty, sixty, seventy . . . she tried counting them, but the numbers jumbled in her head. When her feet touched the sandy floor, her knees almost buckled from relief. She managed to stand and, her breathing almost a sob, she started to run toward what she thought was the front of the cavern. She thought she saw faint light from the mouth, ran for it, and then slammed into something large and solid. She cried out, thinking what she'd run into was Alford, and for the briefest second light flickered and she was looking up into the pale face of Drummond, her husband, whom she knew to be dead.

The light went out; and Agatha felt herself falling. She slid into oblivion.

Drummond heard the men as he lit his torch, quickly tossed it far away, and leaped to one side. As he had suspected, someone fired a pistol at the spot where the light had been.

Raising his pistol, he cocked it, then aimed where he had seen the burst of orange. He fired. The ball slammed into a wall with a shattering echo, but apparently it was close, because one of the men shouted. Drummond aimed his second pistol and fired. Someone screamed, and he smiled savagely.

Good. A hit.

At that moment Captain Grant led his soldiers into the cavern. Dozens of torches were lit, brightening the cavern, dispelling the shadows. Drummond took out a third and fourth pistol and faced the steps. A few feet from the bottom stood Squire Grey, his face ashen, and Alford, one hand clasped to his side.

Overhead on the ledge the soldiers who'd been tracking the trio through the tunnels, appeared and began making their way down the steps.

As they walked past him, Grey and Alford stared at Drummond harshly.

"You've made enemies," Captain Grant said, strolling back to where Drummond waited.

Drummond, who had stooped to pick up the still unconscious Agatha, straightened and nodded. "They have always been my enemies," he said softly.

"Now I think they hate you even more. But perhaps the Queen will sentence them harshly."

"For murder," Drummond said, staring down at Agatha. "They will hang for rape, torture, and murder."

Grant deemed it best not to pursue that. "Is there anything else you need, my lord?"

"No, Captain. I thank you for your help in this matter."

"Rather," said the man, faintly smiling, "I should thank you." He paused, then said, "Of the others in the hellfire club . . .?"

"I will list them, then personally deliver the list to the Queen myself."

"Ah. Very good."

He bowed, called his soldiers together, and left the cavern with the prisoners.

One torch, planted in the sand, remained to light the cavern. Drummond stared down at Agatha for some minutes, not even aware of the pain in his shoulder, then heard soft footsteps behind him.

"Is she dead?" Lucy asked. Paul was a scant step behind her. Both wore anxious expressions, and pressed close to see.

"No, just in a faint."

"No," said Agatha, stirring. "No, I am not." She opened her eyes and stared hard up at him, as if she could not believe what she saw. Then she noticed the others. "Lucy! Paul! What are you doing here?"

"We came to ensure that you did not injure yourself," Lucy said, "and then we learn you have shot your poor husband."

Agatha had the grace to blush. "I-I——"

"It was an accident," Drummond said dryly.

"Oh." Lucy did not look completely convinced by this explanation, however.

"Perhaps," Paul suggested, "we should all go home and take care of Drummond's wound before he dies from lack of blood."

"A very fine idea," Drummond said stiffly, and his eyes met Agatha's.

She finished cleaning his wound thoroughly, bound it with clean strips of linen Holly had fetched for her, and now, her work complete, she handed him a glass of mulled wine. There were lines of fatigue and pain about his mouth, and his scar no longer showed out as starkly for his face was pale.

He stared into the dark depths of the wine without speaking.

The return ride to Falcon's Hall had been made in silence, the quartet now feeling the effects of their late-night adventure. When they arrived at the house, Lucy had wanted to stay and talk with them, but Paul had persuaded her she should rest—and leave the viscount and viscountess alone.

Now as she looked at Drummond, Agatha found all the words she wanted to say to him catching in her throat. She glanced at his bandaged arm, swallowed.

"You will want to know how I came to be involved in that group." It was a statement.

She nodded, waited, her hands clenched together.

"It was two years ago that Queen Anne became distressed to learn of the numerous hellfire clubs, as they termed themselves, coming to prominence in the country. The membership rolls were drawn entirely from the nobility, and because they were nobles, they assumed they had leave to do whatever they wished.

"I had heard of such groups, of course, but had not been overly concerned as they did not touch my life. That changed when on a spring afternoon two years ago my sister, Jenny, was on her way home from a visit to the rectory. A group of them, led by Alford, waylaid her and took her to the abbey, where they made her participate in their ungodly ceremony. She was brutally used by them, then . . . stabbed and left to die.

"I tracked her down too late, coming upon them in the darkness as they were leaving. I could hear her screams from inside. Alford and I fought. I received this." He touched the scar. "He escaped. I managed to find her, but she was already dying. Even as I held her, she whispered who had attacked her. Then she died. She was but fifteen years old. It so broke my mother's heart that her health failed and she died the following year." Agatha closed her eyes momentarily. "Her Majesty, upon learning of my sister's death, requested I appear before her, and in that royal audience, she commanded me to be her agent and to root out the worst of the groups." He paused to sip the wine. "I have worked since that time to gain the confidence of the members, and finally was to be inducted into the club itself as a full member. Yet, in all the meetings I attended nothing worse than drinking and wenching and vulgar blasphemy occurred. Still, I knew they planned a ceremony—a ceremony where they would torture another girl. And so I bided my time."

Her eyes filled with tears at his sorrow. Certainly she had not helped him at all, she thought with great bitterness.

"Finally, at the beginning of the year, Alford, in his role as Father Avaritia, announced that a ceremony would be held on Walpurgis Night, April thirtieth. At that time I would become a full member of the club. For their evil purposes they would need a virgin. I was determined that no girl would die again.

"But there was a complication. I met the daughter of one of the members and saw that she was in grave danger too. I could not allow her to be hurt—especially as she was to marry the head of the hellfire club. So I abducted her."

She stared at him, unable to speak.

"Actually, I intercepted her when she was between the frying pan and the fire, for her father was also a member of the club." He shook his head with self-mocking humor, then continued. "That is why I did not allow you to wander from the house, Agatha. I could not chance your father or Alford learning of our marriage. Then a week ago you followed me to the abbey and——"

"And nearly ruined everything," she said softly.

"Yes. I had to keep you away, and so I locked you in your room. I did not realize you would climb out the window."

"You never intended to hurt Lucy at all."

He shook his head. "I asked you to write to her, for I thought if she came at this time she might help divert your attention from me. And if something happened to me, you would have a friend here."

She looked down at her hands, the knuckles white. She had misunderstood everything from the beginning. She had been so foolish. Yet, yet he could have confided in her. She looked up at him.

"Why did you not tell me this? Why did you not trust me?"

"I could not take that risk. You still might not have believed me; you might have told your father." He held up a hand to silence her. "At the time I could not be sure how close you were to your father, despite his brutish behavior. Though it was perhaps wrong of me, I kept my own confidence. I wanted to tell you, to reassure you, Agatha, but I could not. Then you turned away from me completely, and I thought you hated me."

She stared at the fire for a few minutes, then stirred. "Why did my father and Alford join the group?"

"Evil men are always drawn to a far greater evil, and it was in the hellfire group that your father could enjoy—without censure—the unlimited freedom of his brutish nature."

"And Alford?"

"Alford was a man completely without morals. He killed my sister," he said, his voice pained. "I know that as a fact."

"Her death is avenged now?"

"Yes. He will stand trial for her death. As will your father." He paused. "It will be hard for you, Agatha. The daughter of a murderer."

"No one need know," she said. "I no longer live in his house."

"As to that," he said somewhat stiffly, "if you would prefer, I could arrange for a house in London so you could live away from me. Or if you wish to remain in the countryside, I——"

"No," she said, rising to her feet. "No, I wish to stay with you."

He blinked, obviously surprised.

"I wish to stay with you, my lord," she repeated. She came to him, knelt, took his hands gently in hers, and gazed intently up at him. "I beg your forgiveness, my lord."

"Why?" he demanded.

"I have so wronged you. I thought so poorly of you, and all you ever desired was my safety. I am selfish and foolish, and I am sorry for the trouble I have caused." Her hands tightened slightly on his. "Perhaps you would wish me to live apart from you, after the pain I have caused."

"No."

Trembling, she reached up, touched the scar. "I love you, my lord. I have never been able to say that to you, but I will now."

A smile touched his lips. "Love? Love a man so dour as me? You are so full of life—can you really want my dark moods, my melancholy disposition?"

"Yes."

He bent down, oblivious to his injured shoulder, and kissed her hungrily. "Agatha, I love you. I have loved you since the moment I first saw you. I have suffered with that feeling, thinking you despised me." He raised her to her feet and bade her sit on his lap. She did so, wrapping her arms around his neck and smiling at him, then tenderly taking his face between her hands.

"Will you forgive me, my lord?"

"Yes. If you will forgive me."

She nodded.

"I think, Agatha, that we have much to learn of one another. We need to spend many more hours in one another's company. Do you not agree?"

"Yes, my lord."

As he raised her chin to kiss her again, he said sternly, "But there is one promise you must make first, Agatha!"

Her eyes flicked fearfully. "Yes, my lord?"

"Please stop calling me 'my lord'!"

She laughed until he bent his head and silenced her with a long, gentle kiss.

When she at last drew away, she was smiling. "I think," she said, her voice soft, "that we are both tired, and that it is time for us to go to bed, Richard."

He smiled, and she helped him to his feet. They walked, arm in arm, up the stairs to sleep, to love, to start a new life together.

About the Author

Kathleen Maxwell, a graduate of the University of New Mexico, was raised in the desert mountain region of the Southwest. She moved East two years ago and now resides with her husband (also a writer), two Oriental shorthair cats, and her beloved library of history books. She continues her love affair with the past, creating historical romances in her white clapboard Victorian home in rural New Jersey.